I0536557

Angelcide
The Spiritscape Chronicles
Book One

By Doug Romig

Copyright 2014 Doug Romig
All Rights Reserved

Dedication

To Seth and Eli
for being the best sons ever

About the Author

DOUG ROMIG lives in Knoxville, Tennessee where he enjoys the writing, hiking and spending time with his sons. Upcoming mystery titles from Doug include *The Spiritscape Chronicles Book Two: New Fallen, Shrink: An Abby Chilton Novel,* and *Interpol.*

Follow Doug's blog at http://dougromig.blogspot.com, see what's happening on Twitter @DougRomigWriter, follow on his Facebook page at http://facebook.com/DougRomigWriter or just send him an email at dougromig68@gmail.com.

Table of Contents

Prologue

Casadore was cornered. There was no way out. This was impossible. In all the battles he had fought there had never been anything like this. Everything he tried ended in failure. It was almost like his adversary was toying with him like a cat playing with a mouse. It was time to try a new tactic.

"You cannot win!" shouted Casadore. "Stop now before I'm forced to do something you will regret." It was just bravado. He already knew there was no real hope. His wounds were severe and his strength was fading fast.

The sound of cold laughter rang through the air. The voice that spoke was dripping with cruelty. "You have no idea what you are dealing with. I know everything about you. All your strengths. All your weaknesses. Goodbye, Casadore. Thank you for the exercise. You will be tasty."

Casadore felt fear down to his core. This was a new experience for the warrior. He had never known fear in all the battles he had fought. Those terrorizing words of this new enemy flooded him with that very crippling emotion. Cutting through his fear in an instant, something within him screamed that there was something wrong. What was it? Wait. How did his adversary know his name? How did this foe know so much about him? That was impossible, too.

The attack was swift, efficient, brutal and fatal. Casadore never even had the chance to defend himself. A scream leaped unbidden from his very soul. The pain was excruciating as he called out for help. "Ezekiel!" Casadore died with the name on his lips that was only heard by two others.

The laughter of his attacker rang out knowing that Ezekiel wouldn't be able to save him. Fading into the shadows the attacker spoke. "I think I need to find this Ezekiel. Perhaps he will be more of a challenge than this pitiful excuse for an angel. Not even that much fun. But he was tasty."

"I'd better find this Ezekiel. I hope he is more fun than that creepy dude in the shadows," thought the only other who had heard the cry and arrived just in time to see Casadore die.

Chapter 1

The path was quiet with the only sound being the multitude of unseen bugs in the high grass. Zeke glanced around. He could have sworn someone had called his name. Listening carefully and looking around with hazel eyes that saw so much more than normal sight, all Zeke could see was the natural Earthscape around. As beautiful as the scenery was this was no vacation. He was hunting. Ezekiel was not like the angels that humans pictured in paintings and picture books. He had no halo or feathery wings. He was one of the most bad-ass angels in the four realms and was feared by many for good reason.

Humans who met him when he chose to look human had varied reactions. Some people found him intimidating and terrifying. Some men and women found him so appealing that they fell in love with him on the spot. He honestly preferred it when they were afraid. It was impossible to hide how attractive he was no matter how ugly he chose to look. Women who were attracted to the bad boys were driven nuts by the bad angel. They really had no idea how bad he could be. He kicked ass and sent demons to Hell with no mercy, pity, or second thought. Zeke was not one of the sweet, touchy-feely, angels who took care of humans in need. That was for the nice angels. He was definitely not a nice angel.

The sound ahead more than caught his attention. It enthralled him. The giggles could mean so many things but Zeke could tell by the hushed tones that this was a romantic encounter. Two lovers on a hike. *"Wonderful,"* thought a sarcastic Zeke. *"I'm hunting a soul eating, life sucking, grotesque demon and there are humans getting lucky in my way."* Even with his hiking boots and walking stick his light step could lead to embarrassment for the lovers in nature so he began to whistle a haunting tune. It would have seemed familiar to anyone who heard it even though they would never be able to place it. Those notes would stay with anyone who heard them for the rest of their lives even though they would never be able to duplicate it. Zeke smiled a very mischievous grin thinking about all the heavy metal songs he had inspired even though they never got it quite right. AC/DC got close a couple times though.

In a low, rich baritone Zeke's voice rang out. "Don't mind me. Just passing by." The female giggle rang out and a man's "shhhh" followed. *"Humans,"* the angel sighed to himself. *"If they only knew what real intimacy was like."*

Zeke had long since given up trying to look unattractive to blend in. It never worked anyway. Seeing him anyone would say he looked good but not angelic by any means. The hazel eyes and coal black hair were the focal point of his six foot, two frame. He looked like someone who knew his way around the gym but was not so muscle-bound as to be disproportionate to a normal person. It was his real spirit-form that would have really blown their minds. Describing an angel to a human is totally impossible. It was outside any frame of reference. Imagine peace yet power, light and lightening, calm and a storm all rolled into one. Angels were not what everyone thinks with the wings, harps and halos. Zeke had played a harp a few times but only to scare the Hell into demons. It was one of his favorite tricks to make them run. It was so much more fun when they ran. He was not a messenger or an angel of service. Ezekiel was a warrior. Tracking down demons on Earth and sending them back to Hell was his passion. He was far from omnipotent and omniscient. But he did operate on a level that made nuclear weapons seem like potato guns.

Zeke worked for the most powerful of the archangels. Michael was his mentor, his friend, and his defender. Some of the "nice" angels found Zeke's methods too aggressive for their taste. Zeke was often compared to the rogue cop who would shoot first, shoot later, shoot some more, and then not bother asking any questions. In his defense, Michael pointed out that Zeke had never shot a demon. The twisted humor was one of the reason Michael and Zeke got along so well. That and the fact that Zeke would take the jobs no other angels would dare and do it with such brutal efficiency that no one could challenge his results. That led him to the current assignment. There was a demon trying to feed on human souls somewhere nearby and the smile on his face told any who saw that Zeke was ready to kick some serious demon ass.

The Appalachian Trail was where the trail began. The angel could see a faint trace left by some kind of demon. It was nothing as dramatic as withered flowers or worms crawling up from the ground where the demon had passed. That was what human movie makers thought it looked like. It was just an ethereal blue haze in the air and traces of blue on things that the demon had touched. He knelt down to examine a rotten log that his angel-sight allowed him to see demon essence pervading it. Looking up he saw an older man, who was obviously a seasoned hiker, approaching with his grandson who could not have been more than twelve. The discussion between the two transcended the generations as the commonality of nature brought them closer together. They both looked at Zeke as they approached and looked at what he was examining. Since they could not see the blue of the demon he called their attention to an orange speckled mushroom growing on the log. Zeke smiled an easy smile as he rose and ambled on while he listened to the discussion about the dangers of poisonous mushrooms far beyond the range of normal hearing. He looked into their future and saw the grandson sharing the same information and the source of that trivia with his son twenty-three years down the line. Sometimes he helped humans a little bit.

The Appalachian Trail continued beyond the road but the trail Zeke was following did not. The beauty of the Smoky Mountains was amazing to the tourists at the overlook where North Carolina and Tennessee meet. If they only knew what was lurking among them – trying to hide – they would not be enjoying their day. It was his job to take care of the things they could not see so they could go on in blissful ignorance. Zeke began looking around at the people who were milling about trying to track down his prey. A large bus was idling nearby with a large group taking pictures and sharing their "oo's" and "ah's" at the view. Zeke walked up and began a conversation with a couple who were taking pictures.

"Would you like a shot of the two of you? The background is breathtaking," said the angel, as he examined them for demonic traces.

"Why, yes that would be..." the woman's voice caught in her throat as she looked into the intense eyes that belonged to the baritone voice. "Ummmm..." she tried to speak as her hormones skyrocketed through the stratosphere.

"Not again," thought Zeke as he found the perfect spot with an evergreen in foreground and the misty mountains in distance. With a thought from the angel the breeze picked up and the mist lightened a bit just prior to the snap of the shutter only to die away and darken the distance as the click echoed through the air.

"Thanks," said the man snatching the camera back from Zeke. He had not missed the affect the angel had on his wife. He was very anxious to put some distance between the two.

"Did you feel that breeze?" came the question from the woman who was still gazing at Zeke. "I hope it didn't blow my hair in my face. Can I see?" As her husband handed the camera back she turned quickly to try and get a snapshot of her photographer only to find him gone. As the couple strolled away the woman gasped. "That is an amazing shot! It caught my hair just right! And look at the mountains! They look better in the pic than they do right now." She looked around for Zeke again, calling out, "Thank you." To herself she thought, *"Thank you so much. Mmmmmm."*

The hunter had slipped away but still had no trouble hearing her thanks or her thoughts. *"I will never understand that,"* he laughed to himself. As he continued his search, he found that everyone who was admiring the view really was human. That meant he was looking for a demon who was hiding somewhere between the realms. This would be tricky to track. *"Excellent. That makes it much more fun."* He loved his job. It made some of the other angels uncomfortable that he loved it as much as he did. That was their problem – not his.

He looked at every person around and finally found the one who had the touch. A young man was boarding the bus who had a bluish glow that had nothing to do with a Vegas three-man entertainment group. As the bus driver called for all to board Zeke's name was naturally on the list as he took a seat next to an older woman. The natural conversation began like they were old friends as the angel eyed the young man three seats in front of him. To say that they were old friends was not far from the truth as Zeke looked into her past and saw all the wonders she had seen. He also saw the mistakes, errors, and little white lies told for darker reasons. Still, he liked her. The hunter liked most humans but did not really have time for them. As she spoke of her deceased husband and her grandchildren Zeke looked in on them. Her husband was not the saint she remembered and the angel knew that he was not playing a harp as she thought. Looking across the country he could see her entire family and especially her third granddaughter who was about to get in trouble thanks to a demon whispering in her ear. The young man wasn't going anywhere and this could be fun.

"Rachel sounds like she is a character. When was the last time you talked to her?" Zeke asked as be prepared to divide his consciousness into two.

"Oh my boy, she is too busy to talk to this old woman," came the expected reply.

"You may not have signal anyway," was Zeke's leading response as he continued talking while his spirit crossed the miles in less than a blink of an eye.

"Of course not! No one has signal along these roads. Take a look." Her eyes widened in surprise as she flipped her phone open. "Well! Full signal! Maybe I should give her a call."

Zeke smiled at the woman with the body he had created while his spirit was right beside Rachel. As her phone rang, Rachel went to ignore it but Zeke moved her finger to accept the call. As the two humans spoke, a demon screamed first in frustration and then in pain as an angel showed all the mercy of cheetah attacking a helpless gazelle. The conversation only lasted a couple of minutes. That was enough time for the danger to pass and a demon to be tossed unceremoniously into Hell as a grandmother and granddaughter shared the joy of the Smokies in a place where no one had a phone that worked.

Returning to the body, the angel decided to share some humorous stories with those on the bus. *"A joke could be just the thing to distract young Jerod over there,"* he thought to himself. As Zeke began to entertain the people around him, he sensed it. He found his target.

4

Chapter 2

Zeke continued his storytelling on the outside. Never losing a step he went on to another joke about a pastor skipping church and the trouble that ensued. The spiritual level was another story entirely.

People love to think they can multitask. Listening to music while walking and reading is mildly impressive. Angels have no concept of single-tasking. Zeke again divided his spirit leaving part in his body telling jokes while the other was someplace far different. His spirit had slipped from Earth into the Spiritscape. Here light and dark, solid and insubstantial, stillness and movement were all the same. Distance was not the same here as it was on Earth. Moving beyond what others saw was simply something that an angel did. Like looking forward and back in time and across the distances, this was simply part of angelic existence.

Angels are not easily seen by mortals unless they want to be seen. When an angel does not want to be seen by demons they are well versed in remaining in the blind spots of the demon senses. Zeke's spiritual form would normally be spectacular to behold if he was not moving stealthily toward his prey. The creature was not close to the young man in a geographical sense; but it was right on top of them in its ethereal essence. The blue tinted beast was not especially terrifying by demonic standards. It was still worse than any humans had conjured through their computer-generated creations. It had the body that was covered in something between fur and feathers. The eyes of the devil were blue, glowing slits that saw much more than mortal eyes. It seemed to have changing limbs coming out of its body at odd angles. One limb would be absorbed and another would be forming for whatever purpose the demon needed. This was what he had been tracking and it was manipulating the young man.

The creature was well known to Zeke. It went by many names but Zeke knew the real name was Atheodoro. This beast had heard his joke through the ears of Jerod. The young man unknowingly had one foot on the Earth and another hanging over the over the open jaws of a demon, hungering for his spiritual essence. As Atheo clawed at the spirit of the young man, trying to get him to not listen to another "lame joke," Zeke silently approached the demon.

With a blast of power, the angel appeared. "Hello there. What are you up to today?" asked the far too friendly hunter with a not very subtle undertone of menace. His appearance in his true warrior form would be enough to scare any non-angelic creature in any of the realms. The golden flames that burst from the humanoid body created a light and heat that was searing to demons. His arms and legs were flowing and expanding around the devil. There were even extra appendages that looked like wings of spirit and flame expanding behind the warrior. It was the golden eyes of Zeke that were the worst for any who crossed him. The power of an angel and the coldness of a hunter combined in an unexpected fusion of frost and flame.

This particular devil was more cowardly than most and was a mass of trembling and terror. As shock and surprised diminished to allow the demon to speak, it wheezed, "You! What are you doing here? And there?" hissed the Hadian with sudden realization.

"Why do you ask a question to which you already know the answer, Atheodoro?" There was a cringe and flinch at the sound of its full name. A smile crossed Zeke's lips as he relished the reaction.

"Do you really need to do that? You know it's cruel." spat the demented devil.

"I'm afraid so," taunted the angel. "I don't drink, smoke, get high or have one night stands. Tormenting you demons is the only vice I have left."

"Can't you just call me Atheo?" screeched the hoarse voice with both begging and malice mixed in an unearthly blending.

"Atheo? Really?" The demon shuddered even at that name. "That's not very creative. I think I'll stick with Atheodoro. Feel free to call me Ezekiel. I don't mind." The subtle undertone was gone and true menace was heard with a crystal clarity.

The sound of the partial name of an angel can make a demon shiver with pain and rage. The sound of the full name creates a suffering that is beyond anything apart from Hell itself. The pain of the name spoken by an angel as powerful as Zeke takes that torment to levels that defy human perception. The agonizing experience brought out the hate that is a hellion's guiding emotion. The hatred that flows from the devil is a venom that poisons no one but the tortured hater. That hatred harms and tortures the already damned soul even further with every lash of the evil.

Enjoying himself, Zeke looked at him with a power that glowed brighter than the sun. "Are you sure you want to be doing this today? Do you remember what happened last time we met?" Fear replaced hate on the fiendish face as the memory came back clearly. They had met time and time again throughout the eternity that is their existence. Atheo never came out on top. Quite the contrary. But last time was especially difficult. Angels and demons can be injured. They can be hobbled for a time. But last time when Zeke caught Atheo in a maternity ward hovering near an infant the response was quick, efficient and brutal. Zeke passed right through the diabolic delivery boy who had been sent to bother the babies. The power of an angel passing through a person is what gives the warm, fuzzy feelings of power, pleasure, and peace. That same warm, fuzzy feeling when inside a satanic spawn feels more like unbearable, searing flames and the quills of a porcupine shooting from the core and bursting through the entire being. Zeke had passed through the demon and then caused an explosion of angelic fire that incinerated all but the most basic essence of the demon. Theo had been incapacitated for eight decades in earthly time.

"You're not supposed to be here," said both beings at the same time.

"I can go anywhere I want. See? No bindings?" proclaimed the angelic being.

"Shouldn't you be bound to your problem?" Atheo looked at the angel with a twisted version of an insignificant smile dawning in its essence. "Wait! You don't know! Do you?" inquired the incubus.

The angel was taken aback momentarily. He had expected begging and pleading that would lead to an instant attack. Ezekiel was not one to listen to a demon whine. But this was something new. Atheodoro was not known for great intellect or creativity. This being was a bottom feeder who preyed upon the weak. "Know what?" asked Zeke cautiously.

A hellish hilarity erupted from the demon. A malevolent leer split his face. "You'll see soon enough," came the haughty reply.

The angel knew that he had to act even though this creature seemed to know something. With one swift movement of his spirit, he severed Atheodoro's grasp on the human and, with it, part of his spirit. Four more movements from the hunter and there was nothing left but pieces of Atheo all of them crying out in pain. The scream of pain beyond the hearing of the human ears told that Atheodoro was both surprised and terrified at the sudden assault. With a movement of his hand, something resembling a blue tinged rip in in the ether appeared. Zeke took the pieces of the demon and tossed them through the jagged hole into the depth of Hell. The cold, empty feeling that had been plaguing young Jerod for over a week was quickly and cleanly removed. Returning his full spirit to his body, Zeke merely smiled a little brighter as he told another story with the young man entranced in the humor.

Spiritual battles can be fought quickly and efficiently in the hands of a warrior of Ezekiel's caliber. Many medieval paintings picture robed, winged angels wielding swords over tortured demons. Zeke was amused that humans needed to see the battle through terms they understood. Through the ages there had been other paintings that showed different angels battling the hordes of Hell. There was one painting that Zeke had guided in 1943. Zeke had been on the trail of a demon working on Nazis but had stopped when he spotted an artist. The hunter took a rare break to guide the painting of a spiritual battle. Since the painter was in Spain, he had used the inspiration of a bullfight for his battle. The angel held a rapier behind his wing as the devil sprang toward him, claws tearing the air. The hidden sword was more accurate even though Ezekiel never used one. Sadly, that painting was never seen by anyone. As the last stroke of the artist's brush was lifted from the canvas a Nazi bullet caught the Spaniard and the painting was burned. Zeke did take the opportunity to escort the artist to his new canvas as they laughed aloud about the painting they both painted that day. After his work was done with the artist, Zeke made sure the demon who had guided the bullet was soon thrown into a pit that had depths beyond even that artist's vivid imagination.

Perhaps it was time to inspire another artist. Playing the role of muse was a fun way to attract demons to annihilate. Perhaps he would take a modern artist and help her see a sculpture of metal and machine guns. Welds and wields all at the same time. He pondered the possibility of a spiritual Uzi on an unsuspecting demon. That would be interesting and totally inefficient. With a touch he could devastate an unholy creature with the power of an angel. But a holy Uzi? *"I'm more of the sniper type,"* thought Zeke smiling.

"What did Atheo mean? I wonder what I don't know," thought the warrior. "This trip is going to be fun."

"You're right, Zeke. This will be fun!" said a voice from nowhere.

Chapter 3

Someone was watching him!

Zeke experienced a new sensation: surprise! Being watched was not unusual in any of the realms. He was something to be carefully studied for so many reason. What was bothering is he could not tell who was doing the watching. That was also new.

"Relax. It's all right," laughed a voice. "Don't panic and please don't attack."

Zeke looked around the Earthscape and the Spiritscape and still saw nothing. The voice was surprisingly lighthearted and friendly considering what it was doing. Playing games with an angel is not a wise move. It can be a painful experience for a demon. Angels don't typically play games like this. Nothing else has a concept of playing with angels. Playing games with Ezekiel was a really bad idea. It tended to piss him off.

"Well, that's not totally true Zeke. I know about playing with angels and I think you would be great at Battleship," said the voice that somehow knew his thoughts. "Would you mind slipping all the way into the Spiritscape? I really can't see you that well when you are only looking at this side."

Zeke stepped outside of the time and into the ethereal realm resplendent in his full angelic form. "Who are you?" came Zeke's question that also conveyed menace. This was something unknown and anything unknown was a rarity for the hunter. He knew of the angels, the demons and humans that were somewhere between the two. This didn't feel like any of those. This was something different.

"Impressive wingspan. Very shiny. Wait. Those aren't wings. What the hell is that? Or should I say what the heaven is that? Is that just you all stretchy? Too cool. Look at those blazing eyes! Do the girl angels find that sexy? You have got to tell me what you use to make your hair look like that! I mean, seriously! That is an amazing glow. Even with conditioner mine is just so listless," teased the voice.

Zeke finally found his words. "You sure talk a lot for something unseen. This is annoying. Why can't I see you?" Zeke was searching with all ten of his senses but was still finding nothing. He hadn't thought this was possible.

"Strange concept, isn't it? You look forward and back in time. You can read people on some massively cool levels. You see demons who don't see you sneaking up on them. Dude, you really have to teach me how you do that. But I'm an enigma to you. I don't know about you but I'm having a blast with this!"

Zeke expanded his presence to fill the spiritual space around him to try to find this joker. Every nook and cranny of this part of the Spiritscape was being filled up.

The voice spoke up. "You seem to be gaining weight. Too much angel food cake?"

"I have a great sense of humor..." began the hunter.

"For an angel!" interrupted the voice. Zeke could hear the smile.

"...but this isn't funny. Who are you?"

"Relax Zeke. I couldn't hurt you if I wanted to. Which I don't. That move on the demon was very cool. I think you cut off his... I want to call that an arm. Was that an arm? And then you did an impression of a blender on what was left. And did you rip open Hell to toss the pieces in? That is so bad ass. What was I talking about? Oh yeah. I'm really here to help with that problem." The childlike sound in the voice had taken on a very earthly quality. He had never heard this voice anywhere during any time. "Please don't disappear on me. I am stuck in this area. I don't get to jump around."

The good natured poltergeist made Zeke more curious than concerned. "Are you reading my thoughts? Isn't that my job?"

The mirth in the voice was almost palpable. "Now you're getting into the spirit." Laughter seemed to be all around Zeke as the voice amused itself. "I said 'getting into the spirit' to an angel. That is funny!" Giggles made conversation impossible until the voice regained its composure. "Don't worry. I couldn't do your job. You are just too good at it. And no I am not reading your thoughts. I'm reading your whole being. There's a difference."

Zeke lost patience for this total nonsense. None of this was possible. If this was a demon it was about to regret this subterfuge. Using just a taste of angelic power he sent it out to get this creature's attention. Laughter burst through the ether.

"No fair tickling!" laughed the voice.

"Enough of this." Zeke was not angry. He merely needed answers to so many questions that were beyond his experience. Real power burst from the bad-ass angel sending golden fire and a splash of colors that went beyond the visible creating tones no human eye could capture. The shades of visible spectrum combined with the invisible light made a display that was blinding in its beauty.

"Oooos" and "Ahhhhhs" were interspersed with hysterical laughter that escalated. "Stop! Stop! I can't stand to be tickled! I'll show you who I am!" came the breathless plead. "Please, no more!"

It appeared right in front of him. Zeke could not believe what he saw. He had expected any number of things. He was prepared for another angel testing him for some unknown reason. He would not have been surprised to even see Michael or another archangel with some strange mission that had to be brought to light like this. Zeke was even prepared for a demon with power that could defy the angelic heat he had sent out. What he saw left him astounded as his divine glow faded to a level that was barely visible.

The spirit was simple. No wings. No fangs. No halo. No barbed tail. It was just a simple spirit...of a human.

"Hi Zeke. I'm Anthony but my friends call me Tone. Nice to meet you! Now about that problem..." said the man who smiled with his whole being.

Chapter 4

"A speechless angel. Just the effect I was going for!" smirked Tone.

The never before seen look of shock on Zeke's face was the source of amusement for this seemingly human soul wandering around the Spiritscape. Zeke began to take in the being before him. Saying there is a look to something in a spiritual sense just does not apply. An angel does not see in this realm with just their eyes. They can see the splendor of the spiritual but that does not capture the true essence of the ethereal. It is sight, sound, smell, taste, touch, plus the feel of the essence, the aura of soul, a mental print, raw love or hate, and warmth or cold to the core of the soul.

All of Zeke's senses were trying to make sense of the insensible. As his entire being raced for an explanation Zeke began to narrow down the possibilities. The look of the being before him was insubstantial. It had no distinctive features and seemed like a blurred version of a human. With the absence of ice this did not look like a demon but there was no glow of an angel. The sound was like something on earth but never heard in the spiritual sphere. The heavenly sounds were of joy and happiness and the hellish were of agony and hate. This had a happy sound; but still had the sound of some hidden pain. Smell works differently for an angel than a human in the scent deprived spiritual world. The smell of this soul was one of peace and still there was a scent of conflict about it which were smells that cannot coexist. The taste in the air was one of chili dogs which made no sense since there was no food here. How could this creature create that taste? He reached out to touch this creature and he passed through it as if it were not there. Now he knew how humans felt when he did that to them. It was so annoying he made a mental note to do it to humans that pissed him off.

As Zeke moved around this creature the creature moved opposite him. They were like two predators sizing each other up. The angel's other sense began to explore this creature. The sense of feel to Zeke was not touch but the way the core of the creature made him feel or react. A demon made him feel the uncontrollable urge to attack. The feel of an angel made him powerful. A human substance made him want to defend it. Moving in closer to the moving creature Zeke could tell it had the feel of a human; however, he did not have the need to be defended as much as to do the defending. The aura of this soul was totally unique. There was something absolutely human about him; but there was something extra. It was almost like supercharging his soul that made him more human, but with an extra boost. The mental print of this spirit was something entirely unexplainable.

The hunter moved farther away to gain perspective on this enigma before him. The closest thing that Zeke could comprehend is that it had the mind of an angel, the twisted humor of a minor devil, and the innocence of a human. He did sense love radiating from this soul; but it was not a perfect love like would be found in most angels. Yet there was no hate showing at all. When the warmth of this somewhat salacious soul came through it was similar to the love in that it felt warm; but it was not warm enough to be an angel but maybe a newly saved soul that had gotten away from one of the angelic guides.

That was what had to be happening here. This had to be a soul that had somehow gotten out of heaven and lost in the Spiritscape between Earth, Heaven and Hell. A demon would not have laughed at his assault and it could not fool Zeke by looking like this. This was a human; but how was this possible?

"Zeke, you're gonna sprain your halo thinking that hard. I can see sparks and a little smoke! Just talk to me. Ask me what you want to know. You're thinking, 'What the hell is he?' aren't you?"

The ability to communicate finally came back to the misunderstanding messenger. "That's pretty close to my exact thought. You swear like a demon."

Laughter erupted again from this spirit. "You don't know me so forgive me for laughing at you when I tell you that you better get used to it. I'm on your side but I'm a rebel, dammit! I can tell you never met anyone like me, have you? I have a hunch we have a lot in common, demon hunter."

"I have never encountered anything like you in the Spiritscape. On Earth there are a few people similar to you. Assuming that you are a human soul, how did you get out of heaven? Are you lost?" inquired the angel.

"That is so cute you think I'm one of you. Never been to heaven. What is it like? I always imagine it like a beautiful nature scene with a bitchin' soundtrack. I don't suppose that Hendrix made it up there did he? I would love to hear what he could do with Amazing Grace," came the unorthodox reply.

Changing his glow in a way that was the equivalent of shaking his head in sadness, Zeke continued. "That means that you must have somehow escaped from Hell. I will need to find out how and take you back."

"Never been to Hell either. Is it really hot there like Hollywood makes it look? I have this image right out of Dante's *Inferno* in my mind. Fire and brimstone! Wait. What the hell is brimstone anyway? That's sulfur on fire, right?" Mirth escaped into the ether. "I said, 'what the hell is brimstone?' That was funny and I wasn't even trying!"

Zeke could sense truth and lies without even trying. He knew this was true even though it was impossible. "All right, Anthony. So what are you?"

"Please Zeke. Call me Tone."

Zeke smiled his angelic smile. "You said your friends call you Tone, Anthony."

Mock shock spread through Tone. "Burn! That hurt! Not as much as putting out a campfire with your ass. But it still hurt, Ezekiel!"

The spiritual equivalent of a sigh shown in Zeke's aura. "Anthony, there doesn't seem to be anything I can do to make you talk to me. So let me try this again. WHAT... ARE... YOU?" said Zeke very slowly and condescendingly as an adult would say trying to get through to a mischievous child.

"Have you ever wondered what would happen if a human on earth could leave his body and enter into your spiritual space? Voilà!" said Tone taking what looked vaguely like a bow.

This time the laughter came from the angel. "That can't happen. Humans are as spiritually bound to their bodies. Talking a stroll in the Spiritscape is not possible until they die. So you are telling me you died and no one noticed you and so you are wandering around in limbo? Give me a break, kid."

"Uh oh! Let me check." The enigmatic entity paused as if contemplating. "The bod is still warm and the heart is still beating. It seemed like it had missed me a little but I don't think it really knew I was gone. I'd say I'm still alive. It seems like I am one of a kind, eh Zekey-boy?"

Truth again. Zeke did not know what to make of this. Michael would need to be consulted right away. Just as he began to reach out to call Michael, Tone interjected. "Do we really need to call the manager? I don't even know what I am. All I know is I can leave my body and I want to

11

help you solve a murder. That's the problem the demon was hinting about. If you call an archangel he may not let me help."

As he paused in mid-thought Zeke asked, "What murder? I don't really get involved in worldly murder investigations. My world is one of hunting demons and taking out the trash. Are you asking me to reach out to a murderer or a victim?"

Tone seemed to be shaking his head. "Zeke, this is a Spiritscape murder case. An angel has died and you will need my help to find out what happened."

A human in the spiritual space Ezekiel could believe was remotely possible. A human who could leave his body was incomprehensible since it was spiritually bound to the body. The murder of an angel? Some things were just "not". This was one of the "not" things. Angels were eternal. They did not cease to be.

"You are thinking I'm bat-shit crazy, aren't you?" asked Tone, trying for shock to get Zeke's attention. It worked.

The angel grew and glowed again. "Whoever and whatever you are, you have no idea what you're talking about! Angels do not die. Demons don't even cease to be. We may need to heal; but even I can't kill a demon and I am very good at hunting and hurting them."

"Hey amigo! Don't shoot the messenger! All I know is I heard it happen while I was in my body. I can kind of eaves drop even when I'm on earth. It was a scream like something out of my worst nightmare. I jumped over just in time to see an angel fading away calling your name. It was like it was being squashed inside a trash compactor. If I could wet myself here I would have. In fact, I think my body did have an accident on the other side." A shift in the glimmer of Tone showed his genuine fear and revulsion. "I know you don't believe me so let me show you. Follow me."

With those words, Tone began moving through the spiritual plane at the pace of a snail by angelic standards. Movement in the Spiritscape was more than walking. Angels flew at blinding speeds to human eyes. Tone was swimming through the ethereal essence by forcing his spirit forward and up and down and left and right. Movement was an act of will and not an action of limbs. "I wish you could give me a piggy back ride. Don't think for a second I don't know you can fly circles around me."

Even in his disbelief the spiritual hunter knew he had to follow to find out what was happening. He moved along with him wishing he could push him and even trying from time to time to boost him on his way. *Now I know how parents feel when their babies start to walk,"* thought Zeke.

"Want to know a secret?" asked Anthony.

"I have a feeling you will tell me no matter what I say," came the humorous reply from the hunter.

"Hey! You're getting to know me!" laughed Tone. "I have never really moved around here before. I just leave my body and find myself watching things here. You are the first critter that has ever seen me! Not even sure how I let you see me. I just kind of decided to do it and here I am. Be honest. How do I look? There aren't any mirrors here."

"How long have you been watching us 'critters'?" queried the warrior ignoring the inquiry.

"Let me pull a Zeke and answer your question with a question. Why don't you ever answer my questions?"

The attitude of Anthony was one that Zeke had never met. He had almost a demonic style to his sassy sense of humor. As much as he tried not to, he liked Anthony. In some ways he was a kindred spirit. "You look like a human soul. Mostly. There is something not quite normal about the way I perceive you. Now, how long have you been watching?"

"'Not normal' about sums me up. Well, when I was eight I knew I was not like other people. There was just something different about me. Then I started hearing things that no one else could hear. My dad thought I was a few beers short of a case and my mom just said I was just 'special.'" An audible sigh escaped from Anthony. "Then one day it felt like I tripped and fell and then I was watching a demon and an angel in a prize fight over some guy who was really blurry. The angel totally kicked the little devil's ass and then reached out and helped the guy get unblurry. That was the first time I saw someone move from Earth to the Spiritscape."

The angel was intrigued. "You could see the human? How did you know what it was?"

"Well, like I said, I can't see clearly into the physical here; but I can see a little when an angel is looking out or in. It looked like he was in some kind of hospital bed and had some woman by him crying," admitted Tone.

Zeke searched the shared memories that he had of all the angels and narrowed down the incident based on the tale being told and essence around the storytelling. "How old were you when you saw that?"

"Ezekiel! Are you trying to find out how old I am? Dude, just ask! I'm thirty-six. Been doing this since I was 12. You really don't need to be subtle. I told you I can read you like a really cool sci-fi novel. Are we there yet?"

Zeke actually laughed at that. "You are the one leading the way. Why don't you just phase out and reappear there? I can find you if you let me."

Tone seemed to contemplate that as he moved. "It doesn't really work like that for me. For twenty-four years I've been taking short vacations here and have yet to see the same place twice. I just show up. We are going in the right direction; but can you please tell me how much farther? If I know we are going to be traveling a lot longer we can start singing 'ninety-nine bottle of beer on the wall'."

The anxious angel wanted to throttle the annoying human but chose to condescend instead. "Anthony, this may be hard for you but try to focus. You know we are going in the right direction but I don't even know where you were or if this is even real." The last words showed a trace of temper seeping through Zeke's strained patience.

"Oh yeah. So, ninety-nine bottle of beer on the wall. Ninety-nine bottles of beer. Take one down. Pass it around. Ninety-eight bottle of beer on the wall."

"Before you continue with that – for lack of a better word – singing, how did you find me if what you do is so random?" asked a smiling, yet curious Zeke.

Tone stopped moving. "I'm not totally sure. It just knew where the angel was pointing when he called your name. It is very strange. That has never happened before."

"It is called imprinting. It happens once in a while during Spiritscape battles when we are injured," said Zeke. "One of us leaves an imprint on a nearby item so we can make sure another angel knows who caused the pain. We tend to take care of our enemies. To be honest, it is usually me who does the punishing. But I still don't know about you. No human has ever been the source of an imprint."

Tone glowed. "Told you I'm special." The ether was once again filled with the off-key singing of Tone as they moved on.

By the time Tone had reach sixty-two bottle of beer he stopped in mid-song. "Take one down... We're heeeeere! I only have six senses. What are you detecting, Sherlock Angel?"

Zeke could sense something had happened here. The Spiritscape has scars from every battle that ever happened in it. This one had an open wound. Could Anthony be right? Zeke spread out and reach out with everything he had and quickly retreated back to his normal spirit. The place was cold. There was an evil that was unlike anything else he had ever encountered. Demons have a basic feel. Even the vilest demon has the same root as the least of them. They did not bother Zeke at all. He relished frying them. This was not like that at all. He sent a breath of power into the space around them in an attempted to remove the astral angst that permeated the place. Every bit of energy he sent out was devoured by whatever was here.

"Anthony, go home now! There is something wrong here. We are not safe. RUN!" yelled the guardian as he sent out a call to all angels.

"Holy shi-!" shouted Tone and blinked out just as a legion of angels appeared surrounding Zeke and this dark void. Michael was at his side and all were made aware of the situation in a thought. A thousand angels filled the void around them and sought to subdue this unknown and invisible evil. In a flash it was gone as though it had never existed leaving behind the felled form of an angel that was quickly fading into nothing.

"Casadore!" screamed Ezekiel, moving toward the lifeless husk. The body of an angel was shrinking and fading. In no time at all it was no more.

Chapter 5

The absence of the angel was a total sensory void ten times over. Then all the angels erupted at once! Angels do not need voices to talk. They share their thoughts as easily as human converse. Every angel had thoughts and concerns that created a thousand voices talking, debating and arguing at once.

At the center of this cacophony of concern were Ezekiel and Michael. Ezekiel had regained his composure following his outburst at the death of one of their own. Michael took charge. "Let's find out what happened. Ezekiel, bring us up to speed."

In no time Zeke shared his experiences with Anthony and the confusion surrounding him. "Can he really be what he claims?" asked one of the many minds who all had the same thought.

Michael asked the next question that all had pondered but had feared to ask. "What really concerns me is not Anthony. If Ezekiel is not concerned about him then that is good enough for me for now. What is more troubling is what happened to Casadore. How did he just cease to be? Everything is eternal here."

Rapid fire questions, theories and brainstorming happened simultaneously. The angels blended together so the sum was greater than the individual parts. This legion of angels came to many conclusions as fast as they could think. These two entities were truly puzzles to be solved.

The biggest threat was the being that could destroy the indestructible. Not even the most powerful devils had been able to do that in many tries. This was not a demon that any of the angels had ever encountered. Was this a new or hidden demon that had stayed out of their way? That thought was rejected as every one of the devils was accounted for in battles throughout time, space and astral areas. Demons seemed the least likely. A newly fallen angel was considered and reconsidered. All were accounted for with only one exception and that one was dead. Not many could not hide or disappear in the way this creature had.

Anthony was also troubling because of many things. Many angels believed he was capable of deceiving an angel therefore he had some disturbing power. Others feared he was telling the truth and he could leave his body which was even more of a conundrum. No angel in history had met a living human soul that could leave its living body on its own. What other powers did Anthony have? Did he even know what he could do? Was he watching them right now?

"Well yeah! You think I'd miss this? How the hell do you keep all your voices straight? It confuses the shit outta me!" came the disembodied voice.

Every angel but Ezekiel was in instant attack mode, spreading out and filling the area with power, ready for action. "I'd like to say he didn't do that on purpose but I'm sure he did. I don't think I will ever get used to that," said Zeke to lighten the mood. "Anthony, are you going to let us see you?"

Laughter rang out that left Tone unable to speak coherently. "STOP....TICKLING....ME!" came the voice that sounded as though it were near hysterics. With a thought from Michael all power was drawn back in. "Thank you! I know you mean that to be an attack but it just gives me the giggles," jested the voice of Tone.

"Anthony, we need to talk to you," came the commanding voice of Michael. "There is something happening and we need some answers immediately."

"Mike, I like you; but you should really try asking nicely. I'm really not the order taking type. And no you cannot have fries with that! Besides, I'm shy. I don't want all of you staring at me. I feel naked without my body!"

15

Zeke and Michael shared a look and thought. An instant later they were alone with the voice while the legion was off on a quest for answers to these queries. Zeke spoke up, "Is that better, Anthony? Michael and I would like to have a spirit to spirit with you."

As Tone appeared in front of the warriors he corrected, "Don't you mean a spirit to spirit to spirit with me?"

Zeke knew Michael from the eternity they had spent together but he had never seen Michael at a loss. They shared thoughts and experiences, but this was something beyond their combined wisdom. Zeke knew that Michael was trying everything he could to read this human. It wasn't that Michael didn't trust Zeke and his abilities; it was that Michael worked on a more powerful level than the hunter and could push harder and farther.

"So you want to help us?" asked the archangel whose mind was racing for explanations. He moved around this fuzzy spirit, trying to touch him and reaching out with all fourteen of his senses.

"Well, boss. You know everything that Zekey knows. Let me help you see something," said Tone. "I can't stand Zeke. He is so not shiny! I don't want my eyes to have that luster that makes the babes swoon!" The sarcasm was thick in the ether. "Now since you can tell when a human is lying, what part of that was false?"

Michael and Ezekiel knew the lies from the truth. "So you are either telling the truth about who and what you are or you don't really like my eyes," said Zeke dryly.

"I want to meet you in the physical world where you will not have the power position. This is not a negotiating position that is tenable. You know that my angels are searching the world for you right now," declared the voice of the angelic commander.

"Mike, I knew that the moment you sent out the order. I'm going to let you in on a little secret. They won't find me. My body is really working fine without me. I told Zeke I'm special!" taunted Tone. "And why would I give you an advantage? I know it pisses you off but I don't play by your rules. It is up to you if you want my help or not. But ask yourselves this: would you have found your missing amigo without me? I have nothing to gain other than the good will of every angel out there by helping you. But if you want to get me an Aston Martin Vanquish for helping, I'm cool with that."

The thoughts between the two angels were quick and laser precise. They needed this human to help them in an area that was beyond their nearly limitless experience. Zeke spoke up, "Anthony, we want your help. But you must trust us as we are going to trust you. We want to meet you in your world. What's the harm? If you can read us you know we are not capable to lying to you."

There was a nervous laugh from Tone. "Guys, since I don't know how I do what I do, I don't know what meeting you will do to me on earth. What if I meet an angel and shaking your hand drains my mojo? Make you a deal. I will meet you, Zeke, when this is all over. Deal?"

The two looked at one another and realized that further debate was useless. "Deal!" said both angels in perfect accord.

"Cool. Now help me out here. What was that evil void shit that had all of you hyped up like you were running with the bulls in Spain? I couldn't see a thing!"

"So you do have limits?" asked Michael. "I am glad to hear that you are somewhat human."

The smirk came through the entire soul of Anthony. "You have no idea how human I am, dude. Come on! Doesn't the attitude give it away? I'm a rock star! Well, among my peers I am! It really makes your wings itch knowing there is someone like me out there you can't intimidate into dropping a load in his tighty whities, doesn't it?"

Michael shared a thought with Zeke. "Well if you don't know why he likes me then obviously you have no sense of humor, Mike. Now if you don't mind we have some work to do. Go wax your halo or something while we protect and serve. Hey! Can we call ourselves the Spiritscape's finest? I want a badge!"

Zeke spoke up. "He can tell what were are thinking to each other, Michael. He is like a little boy who has already peeked at his Christmas presents around us."

"I never!" exclaimed the human. Both angels looked at him with the same knowing look. "OK. I always. But can you blame me? They shouldn't keep secrets. It's rude."

Michael spoke up. "Keep me posted and let me know what you discover. I'm only..."

"A thought away. Yes. We know. Now run along, Mikey. And yes he will tell you all my secrets when he coaxes them out of me. Just to get you started, I prefer boxer briefs," said the sarcastic soul.

Michael disappeared leaving the angel and human alone for the first time since the discovery. They looked at one another for what seemed to be an eternity until Ezekiel broke the silence. "You like provoking Michael. You know he is one of my best friends and the most powerful angel you will ever meet. He really bothers you doesn't he? Why is that?" Zeke knew the answer he had already asked but wanted to hear the words from the human.

"He's a self-righteous jerk who thinks he's better than me because he's an archangel. Please!"

With a smile, Zeke taunted. "He is better than you in many ways. But I have learned something about you. On earth you are not a politician. You have no clue how to win friends and influence people. And you are a little too brutally honest."

A rare look of surprise arose on the spiritual form of Tone. "Why Zeke! You are a sneaky bastard, aren't you? I didn't see that coming. Keep digging. You'll figure it out. Now let's get to work. Tell me what you saw."

As Zeke explained the phenomenon to the curious creature, he painted a picture of the senses. "It was not something that touched my senses as you know them. This was not like any demon I have ever fought. They are pure hate that is steadily flowing. I felt hatred bursting out like a geyser. Very pin point and gushing. But it was cold. It was not as cold as a fallen angel, but a more intense cold. It is like being out on a day that is freezing but the wind chill makes it feel colder than a day that is colder but no wind. It was both warmer and colder than those demons I have fought billions of times. Can't you just read all this in my essence like you do when you can tell what I'm thinking?"

"Well sort of but not totally. I can only read what I have in context. You have more senses than I do. It is like me trying to describe a sunset to someone who has never had eyes. So this thing – let's call it Bubba – was like a demon but not?"

"Bubba?" asked the amused angel.

"I was in second grade. He was in sixth grade. There was a playground, underwear and an atomic wedgie that made my undies into a thong. He's my personification of evil."

"OK. Bubba it is," continued the amused angel. "This is hard to explain in ways you understand but he was here. The mind was one of the most powerful I have ever sensed. There was a complexity that was almost angelic in its method but without the completion that we have."

"Not confident, are we?" joked Tone.

"Anthony, I am perfectly confident. I'm sure that is a strange concept for you; but it is the way I am. All I am doing is telling you what I can do. I'm just trying to put this Bubba into context for you. It seems you still have a lot to learn about angels."

17

"Well, I have learned a couple things. First, you don't have any idea what an ego is even though you have a big one. Second, you don't really have wings," said Tone right before wings appeared on Zeke. "OK. I learned you have wings that you keep hidden from sweet, innocent humans who only want to get to know you better. But that ego thing is dead on."

"True. I hid them from you, too. They are not real. You have been seeing my natural form." With those words the angel's wings faded from sight.

"I also know that some angels are smart asses who give almost as good as they get," pouted the human.

Ignoring the comment about his ego, the angel continued. "Back to Bubba. It was something that seemed like it absorbed the power I sent at it. Or at least it was not even affected by it. Now I need to ask you something. What did you see?" came a very serious and sober question.

Zeke was learning how to read the various ways this new found ally shared his information. Like a master poker player looking for tells in his opponent, he had started to see the different shimmers in the soul of Anthony. The angel detected this human was about to say something and stopped as his glow showed a joke was stopped before it was shared. He prepared to speak a second time and stopped with the essence of an insult being stifled as well. Each time he shone with a slightly different glow.

A third try and words came out in a different tone than Tone had yet used. "All I saw was the body of the angel shrinking and fading. There was nothing around it. 'Deep into that darkness peering, long I stood there, wondering, fearing, doubting, dreaming dreams no mortal ever dared to dream before.'"

"Are you wishing you would nevermore see anything like that? We, at least, have that in common," agreed the holy battler. "Where do you think we should begin out investigation?"

Tone instantly regained his nonsensical nature. "I would say, 'The game is afoot!' but we don't really deal in body parts here."

"Holmes?" asked the angel.

"Henry the fourth," replied the human.

"Very nice!" Discovering Anthony was a fan of Shakespeare was another clue to this strange man. "No body parts and no body. But can you focus on the place where Casadore diminished. I sense nothing there other than a residue of his warmth. Can you find anything? You sense things differently." The encouragement of the angel gave the tone of Anthony a new shade.

"Stand back and watch your eyes!" exclaimed Tone.

Nothing happened. It looked to Zeke as if Anthony was motionless. As he considered this he realized that he had never seen this human when he wasn't moving in some way. As soon as he had become visible to the angel he had been always in motion. He was kind of twitchy in fact. Seeing him staying still was first odd, then it became eerie, and finally a little bit concerning.

"Anthony?" called out Ezekiel trying not to sound worried.

"I'm here. You said to focus so I'm focusing." There was strain in Tone's voice as he asked, "What does it look like? Am I getting brighter?"

"No. You are just still and fixed. No changes."

"Damn! I was hoping for a supernova kind of thing when I focused. Guess what I can see?!" challenged Tone.

"What is it?" asked the anxious angel.

"Not a damn thing. It just looks like everything else around here. Sorry. You are the one with the super senses. I'm just the one who sees weird things once in a while." There was genuine disappointment in his voice. "I told you I don't know what I can do."

18

"Hmm. I wonder. I want you to keep focusing while I try something." As Tone continued to focus on the empty space left by the void and the dearly departed, Zeke expanded his power toward him.

"Wow! Too cool! That really tickles but this is like opening my eyes for the first time and the first thing I see is a rainbow! There is something like a vapor trail leading toward..."

Ezekiel heard a primal scream. It was had a horrific sound that even chilled the warrior of a billion battles. That pain and anguish was something that he had not even heard from the depths of hell. Then he realized the scream was his own.

Chapter 6

Ezekiel, the angel whose victory count was only rivaled by Michael, floated in a state that angels called "the phase". He was only half present in the Spiritscape. The part of Zeke that was his personality was floating in pieces around his spirit form. It was as if something had taken out his essence and shattered it into shards and dust floating around him and slowly spreading out. The angel could see himself beginning to dissipate. His mind tried to call out to any angel anywhere in any time but he was too splintered reach out.

In the epic battle between the legions of Heaven and hoards of Hell, there had been many wounded like this. There was a difference for him. There was no one to gather him together. He had helped heal many of those who had been phased; but he knew they were never the same. *Would anyone know what happened? Is this what happened to Casadore?*

"ZEKE!" came a cry from a voice that sounded familiar. He could not concentrate and remember what had just happened. All he remembered was Anthony beginning to see something and then unfathomable pain. There was something moving around him but he was too phased to tell what it was.

"Talk to me, buddy! What happened? What is all this stuff floating around you?" asked the voice that was getting stronger by the second. "It looks like angel crap! Well angel food cake crap. Zeke? Come on. That was funny." There was genuine concern in the voice. "Zeke? I can't read you."

Ezekiel felt something pushing and pulling him. He began to think again. "There you are! What is this stuff? Just think. I can hear you."

"What happened?" thought the angel. "That 'stuff' is me. Who are you?"

"Dude, you better be joking. I'm trying to stuff your angel guts back in to you. I have no idea what I'm doing. Can you call Michael?" asked Tone.

His thoughts were beginning to make sense to him. Anthony was here. What had attacked? "How are you doing that? Even I can't put angel essence back together by myself. Please don't make it worse."

"Zeke, your parts are numbered. Sort of. Everything has only one place it fits right. Just hold on. I really need a dust pan here. The bigger pieces are easy. How is that?" asked the human. "Can you see me?"

At that moment, the spiritual sight returned and Ezekiel saw something that confused him. His memory had gaps in it but he was pretty sure he knew how Anthony's spirit had appeared. This was not it.

"Who are you? You sound like Anthony but you don't look right?" pondered the injured angel. "My memory must be fractured worse than I thought."

"No, my friend. Your memory is fine. I'm different. What did you do to me?" asked Tone with some genuine confusion and curiosity. "I'm not complaining. Hell, this is awesome!"

The human soul was no longer a wraith that had little substance. There was a strong spirit in its place that looked like a cross between an angel, a demon and a human. Tone had definitely toned up. His head looked somewhat human but it had a very generic look to it. It was almost like a doll face but with a smirk. It was the body that was the real shock. Zeke had seen human souls in Heaven enough times to know that they operate differently than angels with a different kind of power. This thing was shimmering and shifting and changing colors constantly. It was like the visions of the drug addicts who saw so many colors blending.

"OK. I'm definitely broken," came the thoughts of the heavenly combatant.

"Well if you are seeing something that looks like a really strange acid trip then you're fine. I feel funky. Not sure what happened there but... hold on... how's that?" queried the earthly assistant.

Zeke could feel the sense of heat once again. It was as if there were pieces of him being plugged back in one at time. Beyond a doubt the feel around him was the unique feel of Anthony. It was a little stronger but there was no mistaking it. Yet this could not be the same soul who had been a thorn in his side.

"I was trying for pain in your ass to be honest. You're coming through loud and clear now. Just let your mind wander while I... where the hell does this go? Must be there... play all the kings horses and all the kings men. It's a good thing I can read your essence because you have way too many pieces." Tone began whistling a tune about being happy. "Talk to me, big boy!"

His voice did not have the same rich baritone he had used when masquerading as human. "How do I sound?" came a shaky sounding spirit.

"Like a Shih Tzu in a blender. Hold on. Magic dust do your thing!" Tone, moving faster than Zeke had ever seen him, separating the tiny shards and dust into groups, and taking one group and putting it back inside the angel.

"It is strange seeing you putting things inside of me," joked the voice that had been healed to its normal sound.

There was a momentary pause as Tone examined the pieces to Zeke's spirit. "I'd better save this one for last," he said more to himself than the angel. "But let's work on this first." He began to put several pieces together from one group of pieces. The final product looked like the warped, unnatural offspring of a squid and a Rubik's Cube. Reaching into the angel he twisted it into a spot that could have held no other part. With an almost painful flash Zeke could once again sense the mental print of Tone as he worked.

As he continued to work and add pieces Tone sang to no one in particular. "The halo bone's connected to the ass bone. The ass bone's connected to the aura bone. The aura bone's connected to the nose bone. The nose bone's connected to the... where the hell does this go?"

Each time a piece was added back a little more of the hunter angel became clear. Finally all his senses were restored but something was still not right. *"So this is what they meant when they said they were never the same again,"* thought a despondent Zeke.

"Just hold your horses. I hate seeing you with a tarnished halo. I saved the best for last. Watch this magic!" Anthony took the last remaining spec and placed it at the very core of the bruised and beaten fighter. His senses were all linked once again in perfect symmetry with what seemed to be a slight improvement. There was some kind of enhancement to his power that was indefinable. He would have to get checked out when he saw a healing angel.

When all his sense began flooding back to him he found his memory cleared. His thoughts were razor sharp. He knew what had happened.

"How did you do that to me?" demanded the demon desolator.

"Put you back together? It was easy. You had flap A and slot B that just looked like they went in the right places. Then I..."

"NO!" interrupted Ezekiel. "How did you phase me apart? I have fought seventeen demons at once and none of them even got close. WHAT DID YOU DO?!"

The spirit before him took on the aura of embarrassment. "I was hoping you didn't notice that. I guess it is kind of hard to blame a demon, right?"

Zeke grabbed Anthony and held him in his grasp. "WHAT! DID! YOU! DO?!"

21

"Well... Zeke... old buddy... old pal... I... uhhh... exploded," admitted the sheepish spirit.

There was silence for the longest time. Both stared at each other. The concept of blinking for spirits is laughable; however, neither one blinked. They just took each other in. Zeke was pondering the possibilities of an exploding human who was still in one piece, albeit different, in front of him. Tone spoke up first.

"Can I ask a favor?"

In a leery voice Zeke replied, "That depends on the favor?"

"Well when you boosted me I think you opened a part of me that I didn't know I had. You did two things to me. First you opened up my seventh sense. I can see trails all over this place. I can see where you and I traveled and where Michael and everyone else trampled all over the place like a herd of wildebeests fighting over the last apple pie in the savannah. Do they like apple pies?" came the wandering musings of Tone.

"Wait! Can you see a trail for Casadore?" asked the angel with real excitement.

The bravado of the Anthony that Zeke was beginning to appreciate was back. "Oh course my obtuse friend. But I can do even better than that. Did you know Bubba leaves a slime trail? It looks a lot like this stuff I played with as a kid that was just like snot. Well, technically, it was snot because I really liked picking my nose."

"How far does the trail go?!" The enthusiasm in this revelation made Ezekiel forget his recent injuries.

"I'll let you know when I can see the end!" said the smiling spirit of mischief.

"You said there were two things. And the favor?" came the response from Zeke.

"Look at your hand. Can you please put me down?" asked a smiling Tone.

Chapter 7

His hand was actually holding onto Anthony. Zeke hadn't even considered that. It was just a reaction to the attack. Yet another impossible thing in this impossible situation. He knew that this human had been insubstantial. What had happened? And why hadn't he noticed?

"Dude? Please? It doesn't hurt; but if you want to hold hands at least buy me dinner first," laughed Tone.

Ezekiel release his acquaintance. "I need some answers." After a pause he added, "I seem to say that a lot about you."

Giggles came from the freed soul, "Yes you do. All I know is when I was focusing you tried to help me. All the sudden I started seeing those trails. It is almost like after images. Hey did you see *Toment 2* with those crazy trails they left behind them in the computer world? Probably not. Well it's nothing like that anyway."

"Anthony! Please try," begged the angel. It was like pulling teeth.

"No teeth pulling is easier!" boasted the man. "Anyway, it was like I suddenly overloaded. How much power did you shoot me up with? I don't do drugs! I'm screwed up enough without them! But that was like a cocaine buzz that doesn't stop. Well, so I have heard!" He seemed to get lost in a memory for a moment. "Then it felt like my body just blew apart and I pulled myself back together better. I can move!" Tone did a very bad impression of a moonwalk. "I can dance!" His version of the chicken dance was even worse than his moonwalking. "I can..."

"I get the picture. Please don't do anything else. I have had enough pain for now," sighed the angel.

"What are you saying? I can't dance?" asked Tone with an attitude that failed miserably at conveying true hurt feelings. "Well, then that gives you another clue. I could be any member of a boy band!"

A smile shone all the way through the eternal angelic essence. "I know all the boys bands. You are not in one."

"You do?! Can you introduce me? Pretty please?! I'll make my bed and eat all my veggies. I love the way they use computers to make themselves sound like they can sing!"

Changing the subject back Zeke said, "How did you manage to get back together so differently? Let's be honest. You look great and have substance."

"Flattery will get you... well... everywhere. I'm shallow!" joked the now seemingly solid spirit. "When I focused and you tried to boost me I could feel the power differently. It tickled, but it felt really good. Do we have cells here? Let's say we do and call them soul cells. Can you make a microscope for me in here?" Looking at his companion, he realized even this angel was beginning to lose patience. He continued, "It felt like my soul cells were supercharged for a second. Then all Heaven broke loose!" He chuckled at his own joke. "When I blew up I held on to the power that you were using. That's what I used to pull myself back together and I just kept a little bit. Does that make me a vampire for angels?"

"No wonder you seem to have a stronger essence about you. You were touched by angelic power and held on to it. That's something else that's new. That must have been what changed your vision of the trails too. So you have some hidden talents other than the ability to try the patience of angels. Don't expect me to ever do that again. I thought we were both following in the same steps as Casadore."

"Don't worry. I won't ask you to. I think my body pooped a little!" joked the smart mouthed soul. "There is something I am wondering though. Can you hit me? Be gentle. It's my first time."

Without hesitation the angel struck out with his spiritual power and gave Anthony more than a love tap. He tried to knock him quite a ways and perhaps knock some respect into him at the same time.

"Hey!" came the voice of the human who was flying backwards from the blow. "That doesn't tickle anymore." Tone was righting himself where he had stopped. "It didn't hurt; but it didn't pass through me either. Was it like hitting a brick wall? Did it hurt you? Tell me I'm tough!"

"You are really something else, Anthony. It felt like hitting anything else. I felt you give just a little; but you didn't break. Since you didn't feel pain when I picked you up you wanted to see if I could hurt you if I hit you. Let me try something else. Don't worry. I'll put you back together just like you did me," taunted the angel.

"Hold on a sec..." began Tone. He was flying through the ether as the force of a more serious blow knocked him in several directions at once. He spun to a stop. "This is payback for all the times I've gotten the last word, isn't it?" asked the dizzy spirit.

Anthony had gone from insubstantial to a substance that couldn't be ruptured. Both beings voiced the same thought at the same time. "This is interesting," they said in unison.

"I'm a comic book hero! Woohoo! I always wanted superpowers. Why couldn't it have been x-ray vision? Oh the things I could do with that!" mused the amused man.

"Please don't go there. We have a job to do. And, as much as I hate to say this, let me carry you," sighed Ezekiel knowing the reaction this would bring.

"Piggyback ride! I get a piggyback ride from an angel! Watch me dance the happy dance!" Tone moved around in a way that would have been painful in his body. In the spirit is was just one more thing that should be "not".

The trail of Bubba moved in two different directions. There was no way for Tone to tell which way was coming or going. As they picked one as a starting point, a rare serious moment came to Tone.

"Strange. I see my original trail. We have a trail leading into this place. Michael and the angels appeared without moving the way we did. It leaves a different mark. Bubba came and left just like us. He is not jumping. He's moving."

"Maybe he can't port from one part of the spiritual world to another. Perhaps he has some of the same limits that you do. But how did he move away so fast? None of us saw him go. You didn't did you?" asked a curios Zeke.

"Nope. I was hiding from all of you but didn't see a damn thing. Pun intended."

As Ezekiel pick up a squirming Anthony he carried him infant style. The protests of the coddled human faded as the scene moved past him at a speed he had never conceived possible. The Spiritscape does not blur at the speed of the angels. It becomes clearer! Tone began to see the details that escaped him when moving at his snail-like speeds. The problem is the speed of the spiritual is faster even when not moving. Without the heightened senses of the angel, Tone could not see the different shades, tones and Spiritscape around him. As he moved in the arms of the angel, the blur that he had always seen was cleared and the breathless beauty and breathtaking horrors of this world became clear for the first time.

Great golden vistas and enormous crimson chasms stretched out far and wide and up and down. There was a blood-red chasm above them that seemed to fall forever with indigo mountain peaks jutting up from the sides. There were vast planet sized rocks with colors that could not exists on earth that seemed to be floating in a sea of mist creating the view of worlds within worlds within worlds.

Even the very verbose Anthony seemed to have lost the ability to add his usual colorful commentary. At last he found the words. "There are so many colors and shades and brightness and darkness and some things that I can't really figure out! Do you see like this all the time?"

Zeke glowed with pleasure. "Yes I do. I hoped you would be able to see more clearly like this. Go ahead and ask it."

"Where is the door?" came an unexpected question.

"Door? There are no doors. The brighter and more golden the Spiritscape, the closer to Heaven. The darker and more indigo, the closer to Hell. Earth is all around. There is no one place for any of them though. You always find new ways to see things. I'm really starting to like you, Anthony," beamed the beatific being.

"What's not to like? Other than the smart ass part I mean. But that is part of my charm!" claimed the human who was still struck by the beauty surrounding him.

Charm would not have been the word choice Ezekiel would have used. As Tone guided him, between asinine observations and questions, they began to get close to an area that was darker than others.

"Stop!" shouted Tone. "There's something wrong. You know how I said there are trails? Angels have one kind that is like whipped cream. Demons have another like crude oil. I have one all my own. And Bubba is just snot. Here is a place where Bubba moved around some and there is an oil slick. I see an oil trail in but no oil trail or port mark out."

"So Bubba kills demons too. This makes things worse," shared Zeke with more than a little dread.

"Just when things couldn't get any weirder. Now Bubba is killing demons, too? I really thought he was working with them." Tone seemed to be genuinely confused. "I wonder what he would do to a human if he got loose on earth."

Ezekiel hadn't considered that eventuality. That could have a very apocalyptic effect on humanity. This creature who could kill angels and demons without difficulty might be worse than the angel of death during the punishments of the past. Perhaps this creature was the demonic version of Samael. All the demons seemed to delight in destruction therefore Zeke had never found one to have more of a blood lust than any other. What if it were some kind of Grim Reaper that was freed to cause chaos? Why would Heaven or Hell release something like this? Having a super weapon was a human concept. Neither angels nor demons needed anything like that. This paradox was becoming more and more confusing. A being that killed both his enemies and his allies was something beyond his experience. Or was it not on either side?

"It is hard to follow your train of thought sometimes, oh great halo-less one," said Tone who had obviously been eavesdropping again. "Who is Sam?"

"Samael is who you would call the Angel of Death. In your terms, think angel assassin. You wouldn't think he has a sense of humor. You'd be right. He is a very good angel. But even you would not want to mess with him." Zeke could see right away that was the wrong thing to say to Anthony.

The sparkle that was a constant state for the man took on a stronger luster. "You've got to introduce me! I'll be good. I promise. Pay no attention to the crossed fingers behind my back!"

"What will it cost me to get you to focus for more than five seconds?" questioned the angel.

"You don't have enough. Anyway, can you tell which one of the bad guys bought the farm or caught the bullet or... what the hell is a good figure of speech for a demon dying?" pondered Tone. "Fading into black? No. Losing his pitchfork? Those suck. I'll think of something."

Ezekiel looked with everything in his arsenal of senses and finally detected a trace of cold. Just as each angel has a distinctive warmth, each demon has his own kind of cold. "S'theno?" It was a statement and a question in one. There was little doubt in the angel's intellect that this was where that demon had died.

"Who or what is a Seth Uno? Tell me he was really bad. I have this thing about people getting what they deserve and demons really deserve all kinds of really bad shit!" Anthony was engaged for the moment.

Zeke pondered trying to explain Hell and how the demons made it home; but that was something he didn't want to deal with just yet. There were so many things that he was not certain this human investigator could comprehend. It wasn't as if he were not intelligent. There are just certain things that are too much even for one as gifted at Anthony. *"Yes, I know you're listening,"* thought the angel.

"Come on! Tell me! Tell me! Tell me!" begged Tone. "I can take it. Look at my big boy body. I'm colorful!"

Trying a different tack, Zeke said, "You work with me and try to focus and I'll take you to edge. But you are not going into Hell, young man! Even you would have a hard time there. I don't care what your new, colorful body can take. You are not ready for that."

"You got it, mighty warrior without a weapon. So about this Sloth Emo guy?" asked the enthusiastic entity.

"S'theno," he corrected. "Well I only fought her a couple of times. She was fairly minor when it comes to demons," began the angel.

"She?" asked Tone. "Bubba beat up a girl? That's just rude! I guess he's not a gentleman. Well then, neither are you!"

"No, I'm not. The gender choice of a spirit doesn't matter to doing my job. That is how S'theno liked to appear. Honestly, none of us have gender. I usually appear male because that is my preference," admitted Ezekiel.

"OK. This one's on you. You can't expect me to stay focused when you say shit like that!" Zeke sighed in his spirit and nodded in acquiescence. Tone continued, "I've got to ask you something personal. When you appear on earth as a guy, are you anatomically correct or are you like a Ken doll? Please explain that one too me."

"You are really asking me if I have a..." as Zeke trailed off amused again by Tone.

"Dick? Yes. Do you?" ask an enthusiastic Anthony.

It was Zeke's turn to smirk. "I appear fully human. The times I appear as female I have all the appropriate parts, too. 34B," said the angel before Tone could ask the question.

"Cool! So, was Sith-Oh-No a hot demon?" Zeke was surprised that Anthony was almost on topic with that question.

"That depends. Do you like women with the body of a lizard, the eyes that paralyze with fear, and pit vipers for hair?" inquired the angel.

"Well, does she have a sense of humor or big boobs?" retorted Tone.

"No and yes. In that order. She could appear quite normal or as a gorgon. She enjoyed playing with men and corrupting them for Hell."

"So madam Medusa was a bitch. No great loss. Got ya! Not the kind of woman you want to meet in a singles bar. Not that I ever go clubbing!" said a defensive Tone. Zeke could see that he was telling the truth as another piece of the puzzle of Anthony slipped into place.

"I do not want to see anything scattered into oblivion. Even S'theno does not deserve that. She deserves worse! Destruction would be better than the punishment I could lay on her." A visible shudder and dimming could be seen as the angel contemplated the powerful desolation he could have inflicted on her.

This gave them so much more to consider. A being who could kill both an angel and a demon without any kind of remorse was almost enough to create fear in the fearless. What had that kind of power? "Any thoughts, Anthony?"

"Several. Most of them are from my worst nightmares and my one experience with tequila, rum and vodka." Tone shuddered. "But right now I'm more concerned with those things. Are those pterosaurs or dragons flying toward us? Can I keep one? What do they eat?"

"They eat you! Disappear now!" commanded Ezekiel as he expanded to his full angelic form. As he reached out, there was no sign of the human.

There were five demons flocking toward the angel. They moved with nearly angelic speed. Within the time of two thoughts they were upon him and surrounded Ezekiel.

"Well look who we have here," came the five voices in a hellish synchronicity. They sounded nothing like the human's imagined. They were far worse than anything fantasy can conjure. Taking the sound of nails on a chalk board, screeching brakes, breaking glass, poorly played violins and bagpipes on an air compressor would not even come close to the sound. The voices alone could tear at the souls of any human unfortunate enough to be near when they spoke. Zeke hoped Anthony was far enough away to be safe.

"Where is S'theno?" asked the monstrous quintet.

The glow of Ezekiel, the warrior of Heaven, blazed brighter than the sun. "Quinquies," called out the angel. The five functioned as one. They fought and fed as one. They flinched at the name as one. "Do you really want to have a bad day? I am busy today. I don't have time for your obnoxiousness."

"Where is S'theno?" demanded the demons again.

"Destroyed. Now move on while I..." commanded Zeke.

"Attack!" cried the fiendish five.

Chapter 8

The Quinquies sprang into action. They had surrounded Ezekiel on equal points as if a five pointed star had guided them. Each one had the same essence as the others; yet vastly different. All had the wings of a raven that were tattered from many battles that had never wholly healed. Each had skin tones of deepest indigo with no hair whatsoever. There were no horns or jagged teeth. Each one was different in size and spiritual build. Their bodies pulsated with a malevolence that sought to overpower the power of the angel. For Zeke, the stench of the putrefaction that clung to them reeked and would have made a lesser being retch from his soul; losing a part of itself in the process. There was a taste about these creature that was palpable from a distance. It sought to fill him with the foul flavor and destroy from within as the assault closed from without.

Five attacks hit at once. There was no mercy. There was no stopping. There was only a fight that lasted for the blink of an eye. Five demons lay around Zeke as his power radiated back in. There were three and a half wings separated from their owners that flapped on their own. Three of the devils had been split; one diagonally across the chest, one across the knees, and one from the top of its head to its crotch as it lay in two equal pieces. Zeke had spared one evisceration so it could converse. It had lost a wing and an arm but it was still able to think.

"Are you listening, Anthony?" thought the guardian.

"Holy shit! That was amazing!" came the disembodied voice.

"Thank you. Could you hear them when they spoke? Are you feeling all right?" came another thought.

"Yes. They sounded like they have mono, strep, croup and severe constipation. I felt my throat get dry just listening to them. Is that how they all talk? I'm fine. They made me feel a little dizzy, but that's all." replied the invisible.

"Who is that?" growled the grotesque.

"No one you need to worry about. I'm your biggest problem right now. I need some answers." The power of Ezekiel surrounded the evil being. "Now the first question I have is, how long do you want to be in a succubus sleep while you heal? I'm thinking a century. Is that long enough, invisible voice?"

"I don't know. They did start it. You were trying to be nice," answered Tone.

"Very true. So Densiel, you don't mind if I use your real name do you?" asked the angel, as the demon quaked in fear, rage and pain. "Now Den, why were you looking for S'theno? How long has it been missing?"

"Go to hell!" snapped the satanic spirit.

"Wrong answer." Zeke turned to one of the injured demons and a wave of holy heat washed over it as it shot away deeper into the dark as if it were being thrown at the speed of light. The four remaining demons cried out in distress as they felt the absence of their comrade. "Now where were we?"

"I'll tear your soul to pieces, devour you and shit you out!" screamed the devil.

"Slow learners are sad," said Ezekiel as another wave of power sent the two equally split pieces of demon into the darkness.

"I blame the educational system in Hell. I'm sure good teachers are hard to find. There must be a quite a few lawyers and politicians though," joked the voice of Anthony.

"Who is that?" wheezed the incubus being interrogated. "I demand you show yourself to me now!"

A scream of pain came from the next felled fiend to fly into the darkness. "We are almost out of demons. Do I get to play with one? You are having all the fun!" came the toying voice of Tone.

"Not until you finish your vegetables like you promised," jested Zeke. The two remaining devils hissed as the laughter of the angel and human brought even more light to bear on them. *"Stay hidden. I don't know what they can do to you. Let's not take any chances,"* thought the angel.

"Densiel. I almost forgot about you. Let's see. When was the last time you were alone without even one of your buddies here?" said the spirit as he started to send out power to the diagonally split spirit.

"STOP! Why do you want to know about S'theno?" The bottom half of the split demon flew far away as though it had been kicked. Zeke looked up just in time to see the form of Anthony winking at him, grimacing as he vanished.

"I ask the questions. Why were you looking for her?" demanded the hunter.

"She has been missing for a while. The last place anyone felt her was here. What did you do to her?" The arrogance of the demon was greater than its intellect.

A radiation of power sent the remaining half of the other devil off into the abyss. "One last question and I will let you go back to Hell. How long since she was last sensed? More than 3 quolls?"

"Much more!" hissed Densiel as it was sent to be with its other teammates.

Tone appeared next to Zeke. "Something tells me that more than three quolls is a bad thing."

"This just keeps getting worse," exclaimed the sanctified spirit.

"Two things. One, what's the hell's a quoll? Two, why is three such a bad thing?" came the quick questions of Tone.

"We don't measure time here the same way as on earth. It is very linear there. Here it is based on thought more than the ticking of a clock. Haven't you ever noticed that not much time has passed when you come here?" asked the angel.

"Yeah. But I just thought it was a *Narnia* kind of thing. This is the most time I've ever spent here."

"A quoll is a measure of effort. Since we are working outside of linear time here we measure things based on the force of will it takes. The stronger the will the faster we move. Only angels move fast enough while standing still to see this world as it is. For a demon the details are hazy but they can still make out enough to be troubling. For a human, as you know, the whole place is blur." Zeke paused to let Tone take in this information.

"So there is something like relativity for you? The faster you move the slower things look?" asked the human.

Zeke was impressed. "That is not far off. When we are moving at angel speed you see things clearly because you are moving with me. But a quoll is more than just speed. It is the effort and power and senses combined to give the will it takes to get the job done. For me a quoll is how long it takes to scan through all my collective memories from beginning to end while using all my senses to examine them. I have known you now for just about three quolls. That's why I asked about three," explained Zeke.

"So you could have gone through everything you know three times in the time we've been hanging out? Cool. So what kind of hard drive you running in there? We talking exabytes?" asked the wondering human.

"I don't work in limitation. I have total recall of everything I have ever experienced and everything any angel that has had contact with me has ever experienced. There are really no limits since I am spirit without the biological constraints of a human. That may be a bit confusing. It's hard to explain," shared Ezekiel.

"Dude that is data overload. And I thought the Internet was bad! You must have quite the mental house to keep all that in. Or it is more of a mansion with a pool, hot tub and boathouse?" queried the impressed human.

"You have no idea," teased the spirit. "But do you see the problem? If S'theno has been missing longer than I have known you..."

"Then she died before Casadore. Oh shit! How many have died?" exclaimed Tone.

"Do you think we could answer just one question before another makes things even more complicated? This is really starting to get on my nerves. Do you even know how that feels?" asked Tone.

"Having something getting on your nerves? For about 3 quolls now, yes," said a smiling Zeke. "But here is the dilemma as I see it. If this thing is killing both angels and demons, what is it? And how is it doing this? And why?"

"And what is the airspeed of an unladen raven?" added the quirky human.

Was it possible for Anthony to take anything seriously? Obviously not. He looked at Anthony and noticed something was off. One of his lower extremities was cooler than the other parts. If it were a body part it would be comparable to a leg. The half of the demon that he had attacked! What had he done?

"It's nothing. Really! I just found out that I am not much use in a fight. That son of a bitch almost froze my leg off when I kicked him!" replied Anthony to the unspoken question. "It's not like it feels like I stuck it into a vat of liquid nitrogen or something. Oh wait! That is how it feels. Am I going to lose it, doc? Give it to me straight! I can take it. Unless I am going to lose it then please lie your ass off to me!"

Zeke was amazed at his audacity. "First, I told you not to touch them. You do realize I have been around longer than you and may know a thing or two. You are lucky that you didn't get ripped to shreds. Demons are still dangerous when injured. Sometimes they are worse when you corner them like a wounded animal."

"That's the best you can do? 'I told you so?'" Tone's taunting words were an attempt to hide his very real fear.

Ignoring him Ezekiel continued. "Second, no you are not going to lose any part of your soul. It doesn't work like that. You have been touched by evil far worse than your childhood nemesis. Demons are not to be taken lightly. They are not the flaming beasts that writers love to portray. The movies love the special effects of the flaming devils but the truth is that it is very cold in Hell. That cold has touched you. You will probably heal but I have no idea how long it will take. No part of any human soul has ever remained unfrozen when touched by a demon."

A smile crossed Tone's face as Zeke prepared for the commentary he foresaw a quoll ago. "So you're saying that Hell has frozen over? We need to hurry up and solve this because Silvia James owes me a date! Is there any way you could make me the last man on earth? There are six more women who would date me then, too."

"Women do not fall prey to your patented style of over the top sarcasm and rudeness? What is wrong with them?" asked the sarcastic angel.

"I don't know. You'd think with my looks, charm and je *ne sais quoi* I'd be beating them off with a stick!" There was something about his words that was wrong. He was truly bothered by this but was not revealing the truth behind his words. "OK. We have more important things to talk about than my lack of luck with the ladies. What the hell is wrong with my leg?"

"That's one way to get him to focus," thought Zeke. "Will you tell me something? Is there any way to keep my thoughts private? It is very disquieting to have you reading me so much."

"Yes there is. Now about my leg?" answered the mischievous man who was obviously not going to explain.

Ezekiel was learning when to press and when to let things go. This felt like one to let go for now. "Let me give it the once over." All of his sense expanded into the injured part of the human. The normal senses did not reveal much other than it had the look, smell, taste, touch and sound of a residual demon touch. It was not all that different than the young man on the bus he had helped. The touch of a demon can be very disturbing for the human on earth. Going farther into his senses he saw the real issue. The love of Anthony was battling the cold of the demon touch. It was losing. The cold was very slowly spreading. He was not warm enough to fight this and it was slowly chilling his soul.

Zeke moved closer to the hurt human. "I don't know if this will work but I want to try." As he reached out to touch the frigid form, he paused. The last time he had touched Anthony with his power it nearly destroyed them both. If something happened this time, would Anthony be strong enough to pull the pieces back together?

"Zeke, stop. It's not worth the risk. You are hiding an alternative from me. What is it?" asked the uncharacteristically sober soul.

Blatantly ignoring him Ezekiel sent the slightest surge toward the squirming Tone. The impact sent both of them flying in opposite directions. Zeke was spinning and spiraling in several direction at once as he was stretched and twisted but not broken. After what seemed like an eternity he regained his control. Moving as fast as angelically possible he reached the still form of Anthony.

Reacting to his presence the grimacing Tone growled, "What the hell?! What part of 'it's not worth the risk' did you not understand, asshole?!"

"You're still with me!" declared the relived reliever.

"No thanks to you, that's for sure. Don't do that!" commanded Tone. "You don't know a damn thing about helping me. Who does?"

With a thought he sent out his plea for help. "I just sent out a call to Arino. Just wait." Zeke added, "I'm sorry. You're very complicated."

"No shit!" said the still irritated Anthony. He paused and added, "Did you call the right number?"

It was odd that Arino did not respond right away. Michael appeared. "What happened to you, Anthony? It seems your new playmates did not like to be played with."

Some of the old Anthony returned. "Just when things couldn't get any worse. Now you decided to grow a sense of humor." Swallowing his pride he said, "Yes I was a bad boy and kicked a demon in the nads. Lesson learned. Demons are not toys. Now if you would be so kind as to get me a holy electric blanket I'd appreciate it."

"'Kicked a demon in the nads'? That was almost funny," said the archangel, obviously hiding his real concern.

"You said 'nads' to make me laugh. Michael almost made a joke. Holy shit! I'm in trouble, aren't I?" said a worried Tone.

"Yes you are. But we will take care of you." Turning to Ezekiel he said, "Zeke, I'll take him to Arino. There are too many injured right now to spare one healer."

There was surprise in Zeke's voice as he asked, "How many?"

In an instant the two shared the knowledge. Nearly two legions were injured in an attack by the hordes. The demons were like sharks on the water who could smell the blood of an angel and had decided now would be a time to attack. The angels who specialized in healing were all occupied with the restoration of those who were needed to continue to the fight.

As Michael reached to pick up Anthony, he stopped. Zeke knew Michael all too well. For Michael to pause meant that he sensed something that Zeke had missed. "Anthony, do not move." There was something in the command that made even Tone afraid.

"Come with me Ezekiel," were the last words Tone heard before Michael and Ezekiel ported away leaving him hurt, alone and scared.

"I'm so screwed," said Tone to no one.

Chapter 9

Tone looked at the blurred Spiritscape around him. "I'm going to die or turn into a demon or just freeze off parts of me that I really like," he said to himself.

Something was beside him. "No you're not," said Zeke. "I'm back."

A visible relief spread across the spirit of Tone. "Dude, what the hell? Don't scare me like that. I didn't know if I had leprosy or BO or what!"

Smiling at his comments Zeke said, "Interesting choice of words. It's both. But if I were you I'd call it SO." Picking Tone up, he began to move at a speed that clarified the spirit world around them.

"Spirit odor? Please don't make me laugh. It hurts when I laugh. Actually, it doesn't but I'm trying to be pissed at you and making me laugh totally ruins that for me." The sense of humor that had given Zeke a firsthand understanding of a love/hate relationship was creeping back into the young man.

After giving him a moment to take in the beauty once again, Zeke told Tone, "Read me, please." As Tone began to read the angel he went into sensory overload. Ezekiel was multitasking on a level that totally overwhelmed him. There was no way to discern all the thoughts and memories that the angel was processing.

"Now that's just rude! How did you figure out how to mess me up?" asked the impressed spirit.

"I didn't," smiled an amused angel. "I'll give you three guesses who did."

"That rat bastard! Mikey! Get your ass over here!" called out Tone who could not hide his real amusement. "Where is he? Afraid to face me since he knew I'd be pissed? Yeah. That's right! Run away and hide!"

Zeke's smile faded but not because of the humans word. "Tone, we need to talk."

A smile brightened the being of Tone. "You finally called me Tone. We are friends! Woohoo!" Pondering the implication of use of the name, the smile died a quick death as he asked, "How bad is it?"

"Well, do you want the good news or the bad news first?" asked Ezekiel. "I'd go with the good if I were you. It will keep you from really worrying about the bad."

Zeke could see Tone was pondering what that could mean as he gazed off into the distance. He really expected him to do the opposite of his suggestion even though he had been honest. Reverse psychology and playing games with people was really not in Zeke's repertoire. He had no problem with humor and joking but he was straightforward when it came to serious issues.

"Give me the good news," said a cautious Tone.

As he contemplated a myriad of other topics to keep Tone from reading him, Zeke stated simply, "You are important to us."

"THAT is the good news?" asked a flabbergasted Anthony. "Couldn't you have said something like, 'Everything is going to be peachy and we have unicorns who fart cotton candy ready for you ride to our mythical healers'?"

"Cotton candy I can find. Unicorns are more difficult and they won't enjoy where we are going. But everything will probably be peachy."

Tone looked excited. "Unicorns? Really? You really know where to find unicorns? You better not be yanking my chain."

"I tell you that you will only 'probably' be peachy and unicorns is your take away from that?" Keeping his mind occupied to block him reading, Ezekiel wondered if he would ever understand how this human thought. It seemed unlikely. There was just something exceptional about this man that made him intriguing and maddening all at the same time. He made a mental note to give this some thought later when there were less urgent matters needing his attention since adding that to the multitasking may make him more readable.

"Tone, you are so important that any other time Arino and at least one more healer would be here helping you. No other human has ever had that. But right now we have a problem with demons attacking. If they leave then we will have angels who will be out of commission for longer than we can afford. You and I have to go to them..." said Zeke leaving something in the ether that hung between them like tension that could be tasted.

The shimmering of his soul told Zeke that Tone was processing all this information at a rate that was impressive by human standards. As his aura took on so many hues, many of them simultaneously, it kept coming back to one that would have shone beautifully to an infrared telescope. Faster than he thought possible for a human Zeke saw Tone reach the conclusion that he had dreaded.

"So the bad news is we have to walk. Right?" asked Tone, knowing there was much more to the news than that.

"Well, I'll have to do the moving. You know it's not walking, right?" said a concerned Zeke.

"Really? I tell you that I know we have to get to the healers on foot and that is your takeaway?" joked Tone trying to take the edge off the situation. "Since this is bad news I'm guessing there is at least one or two problems. Am I going to make it to the healers in time?"

Anthony was truly extraordinary. He had grasped the problem without Zeke having to explain. "That is a concern but we should have enough time. That is not what I'm really worried about. The real issues are..."

"Where we need to go," said an interrupting Anthony. "I'm going to go out on a limb here and guess that the distance thing isn't the real problem, is it?"

"No," said the angel simply as he saw that Tone had amazingly discerned the situation.

Making the sound of a sigh to create the mellow drama he wanted for the moment, the human said, "So how many hoards of hellions will we be wading through to get to Arino?"

Ezekiel decided to try to phrase it in a way that would best convey the dangers they faced. "Have you ever seen the painting *The Fall of the Rebel Angels* by Pieter Bruegel? No? That's probably a good thing then. Imagine the worst battle you can imagine and then add more bad to that."

"*Lord of the Rings* kind of bad battle?" asked Tone who was more curious than careful.

"Worse," said Zeke. "There were several armies fighting those battles. We do not have an army with us to get through to the healers on the far end of the war zone."

Momentarily impressed that an angel liked Tolkien or Peter Jackson, Tone stated, "So much for being important. Mike couldn't even help a little? Where all are the multitudes of angels I've read about? Is that battle really that big that we can't get a few hoard haters to help?"

"That's the other part of the problem. Michael and the others want to help but can't be close to you. Didn't you wonder why Michael made me leave with him?" Tone wanted to reply but Zeke spoke first. "We were not trying to be cruel. We needed to talk privately. Michael and all the other angels are worried about you. They care but we also need your help. The problem is that you are explosive to all the other angels."

"Beg pardon?" said Tone who genuinely did not understand.

When Michael had reached out to carry the injured Tone, he felt power being pulled from him before the touch. The closer he got the more power was being leached away. Had he continued toward the human, the power of an archangel would have mixed with his new found body to cause another explosion that neither being would have enjoyed. Michael speculated that it would have phased him into more pieces than even Arino could repair. No one knew if it would destroy, shatter, or supercharge Tone. It was just too dangerous to risk. Michael wasn't even sure if Arino could help without danger. All this was totally new to the angels.

"Somehow my boosting you has changed you. I can be near you and can touch you without danger as long as I don't try to use my power to boost you again. No one else can touch you or send power into you without it being cataclysmic," explained the angel.

"So right now I'm an untouchable. This totally sucks. Put me down. I'm taking my toys and going home," said Tone preparing to return to his body.

Not even pausing as he moved, Ezekiel said, "Don't do it, Tone. It will be bad if you go back in your body. Worse than it is now."

A look of disbelief shone clearly on the form of the human. "Dude, we are getting ready to wade through a sea of demons to go to a healer who probably can't even touch me or charge me up to heal me. How much worse can it get?"

"Here I can shield you from the demons. They can't tell you are touched by evil. If you go back to your body they will find you before you blink." Ezekiel began glowing, building up his radiance. "They will be able to accelerate the process and take you over with full access to all your memories and all your power. They will take turns using you to pass over onto earth. You will be the bridge they need to free themselves from Hell and make Hell on earth!"

"OK. That would be worse," said Tone. "So I can't even pop into my body for a drink? I could really use a shot of ranch dressing to ease my troubled mind." The man was unbelievable. He had just been told he could end up being the source of Hell on earth with demons using him as a key to escape from the prison of Hell and he wanted ranch dressing.

"Did you know when you get dumb stricken you do not multi-think very well?" said a smiling human. "And now I am up to speed on what you're processing. I do have an evil, manipulating, twisted, cherry cheesecake loving dark side. But you can't say I'm not creative."

"Then tell me how you see the situation, Tone," came the knowing response of the angel who had let him see only what he wanted.

"I am a total and complete doofus for kicking a demon in the balls. Since I was bad and didn't listen I now have the demon version of gangrene moving up my leg to the place where my balls would be if my spirit had them." Looking down and grabbing that area he asked, "How do you tell boy souls from girl souls? Is it the boobs?"

"It is the aura. Please continue." The angel was traveling, talking and trying to keep an attention deficient Tone on target. *"I wonder if he is this bad on earth, too,"* thought Zeke to himself. *"I hope they have him on medication."*

Not satisfied with the answer Tone began to press the issue but thought better as he said, "Now we have to go find this angel doctor who may or may not be able to fix the pain before it makes me into a soprano. We have to wade through a battle all by our lonesome because the other angels are too chicken shit to get close to me. How is that for a summary of how screwed we are?"

"Not bad, but you forgot that the part about every single demon will sense you coming long before we even get close and their lust to drag your soul to Hell and that will make us the focus of the battle as soon as we are in it," said Zeke, as if he were talking about the weather. "There is one thing I want to try. Do your disappearing act for me, please."

Tone popped out of view with the notable exception of his leg. It was a blue, glowing, disembodied limb that appeared to be floating in the ether.

"I hoped I wouldn't say this, but I see your leg. Sorry, Tone, but if I can see it so can they," said the worried hunter.

"Shit! Well, I guess I'm getting what I deserve, but I really don't think I deserve this much," said a dejected Anthony.

"Neither do I," agreed Zeke.

There was silence between the two friends as the seriousness of the situation strengthened their unusual bond. As Anthony considered the situation of being trapped due to his own stupidity, Ezekiel was focusing his nearly unlimited energy for the battle ahead. Both beings knew that this would be something that would beyond their experience. Since he knew he could not go back to his body until this was resolved Tone had to think about job ahead. He had only witnessed a few minor skirmishes between angels and demons during his voyeuristic voyages to the Spiritscape; but had never been in the middle of the battle or a target of the demons. He did not know yet that he would be in even more danger that he ever dreamed in his worst nightmares.

The challenge for Zeke would be altogether different. As part of his mind focused on his attacks to come he also considered the past. He was always in the cold of the battle, fighting and attacking any kind of hellspawn that came near. He had long ago earned the curse from the nether beings that every angel sought and cherished as a title of highest honor: Demonbane. There would be little chance for him to remind the hellions around him of why he held that title. It would be his task to take the hits and keep moving without response. He had never turned from an attack even when wounded in ways that would make many other angels phase apart. His was the strength to persevere and win the conflict. But this time he was forbidden from fighting. His only purpose was to get Anthony to Arino. Nothing else mattered.

Breaking the silence Tone said, "Well at least we still have each other."

With a smile Ezekiel said, "Yet another thing in the loss column."

Both beings laughed. "You love me and you know it. I'm as cute as a bug!" declared Anthony.

With a look that showed that he knew something that Tone did not, Zeke said, "I will remind you about that when we get to Arino. I know it is pointless, but I'm going to warn you anyway: do not look at the demons. You will not like it."

"Isn't there any way you port me there without this? Come on. There's got to be a way." pleaded Tone.

Zeke smiled a grim smile. "Not while you're injured like this. It would make things worse than you can imagine. This is the only way."

As the area began to feel colder Zeke said, "And here we go!"

Tone was surprised to see so many trails going in seemingly random directions. It almost looked like a perverse game of tag had happened. The fluffy trails and oil trails overlapped and mixed and seemed to mingle. There were puddles of oil and piles of whipped cream all around but no angels or demons. Then it was as if they were surrounded by so many beings moving faster than his eyes could see. All were lit by a glow that seemed to be coming from behind him. Quickly Tone saw that the glow was carrying him.

Zeke had shown brightly around Tone many times but he had not let him see his warrior form. It had not been needed. Every situation he had encountered had simply called for him to be in his angelic form. Now he needed every advantage he could muster. The power of an angel in battle was a terror to demons and humans. It was like a million simultaneous lightning strikes with the requisite thunder rolling with a shock wave of power that never stopped. The horror of a hurricane devastating a seaside city was nothing when compared to an angel ready for battle. There were wings of heat reaching out in every direction that seemed to want to destroy all hellions anywhere near them. There was a sense to any demon nearby that they were not going to be able to stand up to the power that was before them. Zeke was pouring everything he had into appearing ready to annihilate any who approached.

The blur of the demons retreating and running made it impossible to see their appearances. Forgetting the warning from his friend, Tone, for all his amazing ability, was still a human with the same inability to look away from a disaster. Like a driver craning his neck to see the horror of wreck in the median, he wanted to see the demons who would be pursuing him. As soon as he saw the first, he regretted his curiosity because he knew he was now hypnotized into looking at the horror around him.

The demons were different than anything he spied during his years of watching. He had seen more than a few; however, he had never seen them in a war zone. Just as Ezekiel had taken on his battle armor so had they. Each one was worse than the daily demons he had seen on occasion. The first demon to sense the human was a shade of green that brought to mind disease. It was not anthropomorphic in the least. It was as if an amoeba had grown and gotten sick. It seemed to be moving in every direction at once trying to reach them and stay clear of the power coming off Zeke. Amorphous appendages tried to snake their way past the defenses of the angel. There was an attack in his mind that would have made any mortal paralyzed with fear and hopelessness. Zeke absorbed the lion's share of the attack so that Tone only felt a level of fear and dread that made him dim to the level a weeping infant. Then all the emotion was suddenly gone as demon was shattered into trillions of pieces.

Before he could express relief, a face loomed ahead of them that was right in the path they needed to travel. There was nothing that could have prepared Tone for the beast before him. It was as if someone had taken the face of a baboon and turned it inside out. There was what could only be described carrion eating leaches all over the face that were devouring it and defecating different flesh in a constant state of decay. Realization hit Tone as he discovered that the face was all there was to the being. Thoughts came unbidden into his head as he struggled to fight them off. *"Why am I doing this? I should just stop fighting. If I jump out of his arms at least Zeke can get away. It can't be that bad."* The psychic attack was a thousand times worse on Zeke who was shielding his charge as much as possible. *"I need to fight them off. If I put Tone down I can protect him better."* And then the thoughts were gone as the face was lying in four pieces around them as they passed.

Another demon came at them from behind and below. It seemed so unfair to Tone that the demons seemed to be coming from everywhere. The stench of the rotting souls enveloped them in a haze that made them both feel ill. As he craned his head to see this new threat, what he saw made no sense. It was just a cloud. Vapors were splitting and reforming in the trail of power that stretched out behind them. The hideous odor was becoming stronger as Zeke's pace began to slow as if trying to move through peanut butter. It was shifting between greens and reds reminding Tone of a chaotic Christmas display. Just as one of the columns of cloud had almost reached Tone it was engulfed by fire that caused it to evaporate and fade away like smoke on a breeze.

Again and again came attack after attack. Each time the attack ended at just the last possible instance. "Are we there yet?" came the question from Tone who wasn't even trying for humor. It was truly all he could muster.

"Almost," came a reply that barely even sounded like Ezekiel. "Do you see that shimmering wall? That is the hospital..."

As his words died around them, they were surrounded. These all seemed to be the same type of demon. They had bodies of sorts. They seemed to be segmented with multiple limbs stretching out in impossible angles. It was the place where their mouths should have been that would be the source of nightmares for years for the human. There were six pincers that worked in a way that gave them a mutant insect look. One set was vertical on each face while the other two sets were at odd angles that made it appear as if they were an offset X. The pincers clicked creating a thunderous feel akin to shock waves in the ether around them. The pressure became more and more intense as more and more of the insect-like demons approached closer and closer from every conceivable angle. Zeke and Tone both felt the compression wave of the unholy clicking that caused them both to fade and shrink. They both felt as if they understood how Casadore must have felt.

The explosion all around them was spectacular in intensity and effect. There was something around them that defied all description. Tone felt like he was in the middle of a supernova that demolished the demons. "MOVE NOW!" came a command inside the blast.

Zeke stepped through a wave of light, energy and heat into a calm amidst the storm. Looking at Tone he said, "I agree. You are as cute as a bug." The angel collapsed at the feet of the most breathtakingly beautiful being Tone had ever seen.

"You must be the notorious Anthony. I'm Arino." Tone passed out.

Chapter 10

When Tone came back to his senses the first thing that he saw was the form of Arino standing over him. "So this is heaven. I like!" came the witty reaction to the beauty before him.

"I have heard about your sense of humor but no one told me you were a flirt," replied the angel giving back as good as she got. This Arino definitely had a female flare to her. "It is so cute when you turn that shade of fuchsia. Sorry if I can't chat but I have my wings full," laughed the healer as she quickly turned and began helping an injured angel.

Tone had seen many angels in his years of spying on the spirit world. He had seen fighters and messengers. He had seen small skirmishes and escorts. He had now seen an angel in full battle dress. He had never seen an angel like this. She was amazing in her stunning shine. Her long flowing hair was black as the dead of night. She had a body that was slight yet seemed to radiate a strength and a grace that made her flow rather than simply move. She never stopped smiling with every bit of her essence. That must have made her have an exceptionally good bedside manner. But it was her eyes that took her from beautiful to devastatingly breathtaking. They were a moving, shifting amber with traces of lightening dancing within them. One look in her eyes and Tone felt captivated and captured. He did not want to get free.

"She's something else, isn't she?" The voice of Ezekiel startled him. Being totally enthralled by the healer he had not even known his friend was nearby. "Even other angels have that reaction to her. You may want to close your mouth. Drool is not attractive."

His hands quickly moved to his mouth before realizing that he could not drool if he wanted to. "Asshole!" snapped an embarrassed Tone. He could not tear his senses off the healing beauty who was moving from angel to angel with a joy that healed the spirits in so many ways. "I thought angels were not burdened by the struggle with gender."

"We don't but some appears naturally like one gender or another. Most don't though." Zeke felt the need to try and explain. "Michael and I come across as male. Arino comes across as female. It is just part of the natural role we play. It has nothing to do with being a healer or warrior. It is just how we are perceived by humans. We honestly look the same to each other. That probably makes no sense to you."

Tone glanced at his friend for the first time. "No it doesn't make a damn bit of... What the hell happened to you?!" Zeke didn't look like himself at all. There seemed to be several bites out of the angel and different shades of his aura showing how much he had been hurt. One of his arms where he had been holding Tone looked like it had been mangled by a Rottweiler on a steroid induced rage! The other arm was hanging limply at his side and it seemed to be useless. Part of his lower back was just gone leaving a slowly healing jagged wound.

"Dude, are you okay? You look like you had a price on your halo and got tackled by the Saints defensive line. You look worse than I feel!" stated a worried Anthony. Then he added with a grin, "Did something bite your ass off? I've heard of getting your ass chewed but not bitten off."

Ezekiel laughed. "Please feel free to make jokes. Laughter really is one of the best medicines out there."

Not letting him get away with avoiding answering the question, Tone asked again, "What the hell happened to you? Is all that my fault?" Zeke hesitated a little too long. "It is, isn't it? What's wrong with you? Why did you keep waiting 'til the last second to do anything? I've seen you do your thing. You are a major demon-ass kicker!" stated Tone. He paused and added, "Do demons have asses?"

After a long pause the angel replied, "Yes they do and yes I am good at kicking them and taking them down several notches. But I didn't attack any of them. My job was to get you through the gauntlet."

"But then who was kicking ass and taking names? I thought it was just you doing your extra arm gizmo with the power blasts doohickeys to make their thing-a-ma-bobs fall apart. Was that too technical?" asked Tone making a joke to cover his shame that his friend had sacrificed so much to keep him safe.

"Really? You thought I caused the angel-blast and I threw my voice telling myself to run?" came the leading questions from Zeke who had a mischievous look about him.

"I thought that was Arino helping us out." There was genuine confusion from Anthony.

There was a smile that radiated from his whole being as the angel said, "You are really going to hate hearing who was helping the whole time."

"Oh no," said Tone with false dread in his voice. "Dammit! That totally ruins several jokes I was going to make at his expense." Sighing with his whole soul he asked, "Where is he?"

"Michael is still fighting. He ported back as soon as we started moving. He was basically hiding in my battle-form wake. There was power that trailed off behind me where he stayed at a low burn until we needed help. He then struck and hid again." Zeke was taking pleasure in telling his friend about his other friend who had saved them. "Trust me. That was one of the most difficult things he has ever done."

"He's an angel. It's his job to save even smart-asses like me," came the reply from a defensive Tone.

A sad smile crept across the angel's essence. "You really don't know him at all, do you? He gladly risked himself for you, my friend. He stayed far too close to you for his safety. If he missed by just a fraction he could have charged you instead of devastating a demon. It would have rebounded on to him and phased him. You can be certain that every demon out there would gladly suffer the burns to take the parts to the far reaches of Earth, Hell and the Spiritscape. That angel-blast right before we made it was his greatest weapon. He had to hold back to save both of us. As injured as I was I could not have held on to you if he had really let go."

"Shit. How am I supposed to hate him now? That was so selfish being selfless like that. I had a whole golden arches routine I was going to use on him. Now I have to... I can't believe I'm saying this... thank him." Tone tried to shudder.

"You're welcome," came a voice from behind him. A smiling Michael was beaming at them. He looked like he had taken a few blows himself.

"You know you make it hard to think of you self-righteous, sanctimonious prick when you do things like that," complained Tone.

The glow from the archangel bathed them in light. "Yes, I know. You are not the first person to make that observation. Now let's get you two back in action." Turning to Ezekiel he said, "You were spectacular! I know it was not easy for you to run but you did what you had to do. You cared for Anthony and kept him safe even when you wanted to do what comes naturally. Are you all right?"

"I'll be up and fighting in no time. How goes the battle?" asked the angel who obviously wanted to fight now that his charge was safe.

"It is over. As soon as you made it into the hospital I called the legions back in and they wrecked vengeance on every one of the demons who had tried to get to the two of you." Seeing he was about to ask he told Zeke, "Yes I did absorb many of the blows. You are welcome, too."

Suddenly there was a fourth member of their conversation. "I hate to interrupt your mutual admiration support group but I need to get to work on each of you," said Arino. Neither of the angels objected to her directness and Tone had lost the power of speech in her presence. "Tone... May I call you Tone?" He nodded with the vague, goofy look of a teenage boy meeting a movie starlet. "I checked your leg while you were out. We need to save you for last. Let me see..."

The healer seemed to be looking deeply at the two angels. Her normal smile and joy stopped cold as she looked even closer at them both. The change in her aura spoke volumes as to her shock and awe at their stamina and resistance to suffering. After a minute examination she finally spoke. "Mike? Zeke? What did you two do? How are you holding yourselves together? You both should have phased apart with those injuries!"

All eyes turned to Tone. "What? Do I have boogers?" asked an uncomfortable Anthony.

"No Tone. You look decent all things considered. Do you even know what you did?" asked Arino as she began to work on the injuries of both Michael and Ezekiel.

A still confused human spirit replied, "Yeah. I nearly got two angels scattered to all parts of the spirit world because I'm an idiot who tried to kick a field goal with half a demon."

The three angels glowed brighter at his self-deprecating humor and new humility. "He is so cute when he's clueless, isn't he?" said a teasing Zeke. There was still work being done on the injuries of the angels.

"Well, when he is not being annoying. To be fair, he's usually clueless," tormented Michael.

"Now boys. Let's not pick on the human. Don't you think he's been through enough?" asked the smiling Arino, already knowing the answer.

"NO!" responded both angels together causing laughter among all the divine beings.

Anthony had reached his limit and was finally able to get a word in. "What the hell are you talking about? I didn't do anything but get your asses handed to you."

Arino took pity on Tone. "Tone, sweetie, you played a part in the battle that you didn't even realize. Yes, Michael and Ezekiel did take many blows to protect you. But haven't you wondered how you were able to heal Zeke when he was phased? It has been the topic of discussion around here." There was a change in her glow as she worked on Zeke's injured appendages.

"I'm gifted?" smirked the human.

Zeke interrupted, "Can we return some of his 'gifts'?"

"Now who's the smart ass?" bantered Tone.

"You!" said all three angels at once. Laughter again filled the space making all who heard it heal even faster. Had Anthony been paying attention he would have seen that the wounds on Zeke's arm were filling in faster than before due to the laughter and the proximity of the healer. The wounds that Michael would not allow Tone to see were also being cured by a combination of the same two factors and his own power working as well. The conversation was to distract the worried human until he suddenly looked at Zeke.

"That is too cool! How are you doing that? And am I helping? You gotta throw me a bone here people." The enthusiasm Tone shared was contagious.

Michael spoke up. "Angels. Not people, Anthony." There was a gentle teasing in his voice as he once again played upon the easily distracted Anthony.

"Aren't we beyond calling me Anthony now, Mikey? We are all friends here. I'm even thinking about asking Arino out for gelato."

"Gelato? Sounds tasty." There was a subtle shift in the aura of Ezekiel as Tone flirted with Arino. The healer was doing all she could to bring healing to the angels spirits while building up the mental state of Tone in preparation for what was to come. "You helped them by bleeding some of your power."

The look on his soul told them that this had not clarified anything for Anthony. "You are confusing me here."

"It wasn't until I got to examine you that I saw it. You are a healer in your own right. It is a rare gift. That's why you were able to pull yourself back together and why you could put all the right pieces in the right places for the most part when you phased Zeke. I fixed the one part that was in the wrong place." Arino let that sink in for a moment. "That is similar to what you were doing as they were fighting and running through the demons. Your fear cause you to unintentionally send out some of your energy into Zeke and some leaked off his wake into Michael. They would have made it here but there would have been bigger pieces missing."

"So I did help! Woohoo for me!" proclaimed a proud Anthony.

Suddenly, Tone stared at the healer with a stunned glow about him. "Why didn't I know that?" Focusing, he exclaimed, "I can't read you!" The outburst caught all the angels off guard. "I can read Zeke like a cheap novel. Mike wears his... well... everything on his halo. You are a total mystery to me! I'm not even getting that sensory overload when they over-think things to mess with my head. How do you do that?"

"I told you he would notice," said Zeke.

"But it did take him a while," added the archangel.

"There was the little thing about my rotting leg here. And she is hot!" defended the human. Turning to the healer he asked, "What's up, Arino? Are girl angels as hard to read as girls?"

Laughter from the healer lightened the mood. "It is part of being a healer. We are different than other angels. We are naturally shielded against mental assaults because what we do can be a little painful. It protects us from accidental soul shocks that can come back on a healer while healing. It's just how we were made. Here is the fun part for me. There is also an opposite part of being me. Healers can read almost anyone. It is how we can heal so well. I read my patients so I can mend them more effectively." The smile on the face of Arino was a twisted mirror of the horror on Tone's.

"And the secret identity of the notorious Tone is..." Arino paused for dramatic effect. There was an apprehension in the ether as Ezekiel and Michael waited in anticipation and Anthony waited in fear. She had a strange sense of humor for an angel. "I have no clue. I can't read him either. That is an impressive trick you have there."

The aura of Tone returned to its normal kaleidoscopic colors. "Don't do that to me! I'm pretty sure my body needs a tranquilizer after all the excitement of my... Do I call this a day?"

"Call it whatever you want. We don't measure time like that here. I had hoped that we would find out who you are on earth. Zeke, I want to see you when this all done and you two meet face to face," said Michael in a very business-like manner.

Tone chimed in with his characteristic flippancy. "Now that's the Mike I know and..."

"I am all done with angels," interrupted Arino, stopping an insult. Tone looked at Michael and Zeke with astonishment. The healing that had occurred while he had been distracted was truly phenomenal. "And now I have a human soul to that needs my tender, loving care." Arino paused again. "This will be fun." Yet there was no trace of mirth about her.

"What is going to be fun here?" inquired Anthony.

Ignoring the question, Arino continued. "I want everyone out of this area now. Zeke, you can stay. Michael, go. Everyone one else," the healer said to those who had been healed or had been healing, "needs to be away from here."

"Are you sure about this, Arino?" asked the archangel.

"Yes, Michael. You are too powerful to be here when I try this. Go to keep us all safe." At the order of the healer, they were suddenly alone.

"A control freak like Mike just leaves? How did you do that? He's like herpes or a bad song that get stuck in your head like 'Who Let the Dogs Out?'." The bad boy of the Spiritscape was trying to be causal about his question.

"Everyone knows what you can do, Tone. No one argues with me anyway. So let me see what I can do." There was a joy to Arino that was part and parcel of her healing. She had healed every angel time and time again in the war that waged for all eternity. Michael and Zeke were frequent visitors to her house of healing, but they rarely need more than a spiritual bandage. She had never healed a human like this since there had never been one in a battle.

Zeke spoke up, "Do you mind telling Tone what you plan to do? He has a right to know, don't you think?"

"Unless it's really going to hurt like a mother in which case don't tell me anything. I'm a wuss," joked Anthony.

Smiling with her eyes, Arino began to explain. "You are such an enigma, Tone. I am going to try to transfer the most miniscule amount of healing power into you to see what happens. This will not be enough to heal anything, but it will tell me how you react to my power. We are going to do a little bit of trial and error before we try anything for real. How does that sound, sweetie?"

"Anything for you, sweetheart," bantered the flirtatious Tone.

Zeke moved away to allow Arino to work. Based on his experiences with Tone, he wanted to be at a safe distance in the event of a catastrophic disaster.

Arino gave Zeke the angel equivalent of a nod through her glow and began her work. Her form went from anthropomorphic angel to an amorphous blob; yet she still had the same shimmer about her that was distinctive. As Tone watched in awe, the smallest tendril of healing power began slowly inching toward him. It was moving toward him in a way that was almost painful in its slowness. It wasn't until it touched his arm that the true pain began.

There was a soul scream as Tone writhed about as sparks of healing energy threatened to pull him apart.

43

Chapter 11

"Stay back!" shouted Arino as Zeke moved to help. The ribbons of energy that normally healed were quickly killing Tone. He was being torn and shredded as if everything about his spirit was rejecting the healing while the healing power tried to work. Deep, dark gashes were beginning to appear on the color-infused form of the human whose screams were deafening.

Slowly but steadily Arino began pulling back the healing power from the pain drenched form of Anthony. She continued to work as more and more energy was being drawn out as poison from a wound. There was pain on the countenance of the healing angel as she continued to pull the energy out of Tone. Her aura began to take on the psychedelic look of her patient as he began to slow his gyrating and writhing. Finally Anthony collapsed in on himself as his spirit curled into a fetal position trying to recover some semblance of order.

Arino looked at Zeke with a confused mixture of pain, power, and puzzlement. "I am overloaded!" said the healer and disappeared, quickly porting away leaving Tone alone with a concerned Zeke. The angel remained nearby but was afraid to touch him. Even though he was not the most caring angel Zeke could not let Tone suffer in solitude. Reaching out very slowly, keeping his power in check, he laid a hand upon the hurting form of his friend. Tone flinched at the touch and quickly looked up at the angel.

"Can we not do that again, please?" came the shaky sound of Tone. He closed himself off as he curled even tighter in on himself. "I don't think that was supposed to happen."

A smile and chuckle escaped from Ezekiel. "Do you ever not have a joke?" He was indomitable in his humor. Even though it was a simple defense mechanism, it was also a barometer for Tone. The worse things seemed to be, the more he joked and made light of the situation to make himself and others feel better about dire straits. Zeke decided that he would begin to worry when Anthony ran out of smart remarks.

"Well if I can't laugh at hellacious, debilitating pain, then what can I laugh at?" came the expected flippancy.

Zeke called out to Arino, asking what to do. There was no reply. He called out to any healer. Silence remained the only answer. Michael appeared and instantly knew what had happened.

"She will be back. The power that she absorbed was more than she could hold in for very long." Michael's explanation did little to clarify the situation.

An injured Anthony looked up at Michael. "Where did she study medicine? You know those med schools in Mexico are not as good as a Johns Hopkins. Please tell me it wasn't online. I think she needs to get her tuition money back."

Michael decided to let the remark pass without saying anything since Arino appeared at that moment. She moved to be at Tone's side. "Are you all right, Tone?" came the sincere question from the healer.

"I know you're hot and all but may I ask a favor?" Tone waited for a moment but did not get a response from Arino. "Please don't help me. It hurts a little too much."

Arino took the criticism with the air of a professional taking a constructive critique. "I promise that I will not try that again. Healing should not have done that. Do you know what happened, Tone?"

"Well you zapped me and I went all exorcist on you. Did I spew that green shit and make my head spin like the girl in that movie? What was her name?" asked Tone.

"Linda Blair," said all three angels.

"Required watching in angel school I take it?" said Tone with humor and curiosity.

"Don't ask." It was Zeke who spoke to his friend.

The spark that was central to the character and characteristics of Tone was beginning to come back. "Let me guess. It involved a VHS, a big bag of pot, playing *The Dark Side of the Moon,* eating Taco Doritos while watching it with the lights off. Are demon possession movies like porn for angels?"

"Closer to horror movies for angels," said Arino. "Did you do any of that on purpose?"

Before he answered the angels knew the truth. "Do what? Have the experience of an electric chair while being sawed in half? Sure. That was my plan all along! You have got to be shitting me! How can I make this as clear as possible? Hell no! Any questions?"

Michael chimed in. "Tone, you took the most miniscule amount of healing energy and turned it inside out on yourself while magnifying it to an unbelievable amount. You nearly overpowered the second most powerful healer in the legions with healing energy."

"I had to leave and release that before I imploded. Nearly four hundred angels were healed where I went thanks to your power boost to me. Now we just need to figure out how and why that happened." Arino began examining Tone again. "You do not seem to be much worse for the wear. Your aura is was shaken but no lasting damaged. You heal quickly. I take it the pain was intense?"

"You could say that. I am in love with you, babe. But if you try that again I will eat chili dogs with extra onions, jalapenos, sauerkraut, and Dijon mustard to give me laser breathe before I let you kiss me." Zeke flinched and Michael looked at the human wondering if there was a way to get Tone to take anything seriously. Zeke and Michael agreed that it was as likely as the demons apologizing for anything.

"May I ask a really silly question?" asked Anthony.

"Of course you can. It is the serious questions that seem to be challenging for you," replied Ezekiel.

"First, nice one. You are becoming quite the smart ass. I'm rubbing off on you." As that sunk in he continued, "Second, have we forgotten about the leg that started all this mess? I can't feel very much down there anymore."

All three angels examined the demon damaged appendage. There was little trace of the natural heat of Tone left to it. The cold was spreading faster now. As the three angels linked their minds and spirits they knew what each needed to do. Michael examined the hate factor of the wound where it was taking the once loving human and beginning to infuse him slowly with a hate that was previously unknown. He found that there was a core of hatred that seemed to be the source of all the hate that was embedded deep within his spiritual leg as if...

At the same time Ezekiel was using his skill in reading the cold of a demon to try and discover why the cold was moving faster now that the healing had failed. There were tendrils of cold that spread out with tentacles that had now reached the bottom extreme of the damaged limb and were now beginning to work their way even faster toward Tone's core. He could see the heat of the spirit of Tone becoming cooler and cooler as the outgrowths of the demonic wound grew ever closer. Following the cold to its source from above and below, he discovered that there was a spot that looked as icy as a demon. In fact it, looked as if...

Arino was using her angelic diagnostics to discern several things at once. She found the initial wound that had caused all the problems in the first place had changed since her attempt to heal Tone. What had once been a spot to be cured was now glowing with an aura that was not one of Tone's normal tones. There was even a strange odor wafting off him now that was totally alien to

45

his normal scent of chili dogs. There was even a sound of screaming that seemed to be coming from Tone even though he was not making any sounds while the angels tried to discover the problem. As all three of these areas became clear Arino realized it looked as if...

"There is a fragment of demon in your leg!" said all three angels at the same time.

"There's a what in my what?" asked an incredulous Anthony.

All three angels were staring at him with the same look of disbelief that he was giving them. This was yet another impossibility with this impossible man. A fragmented demon was as rare as a phased angel. It would have taken something catastrophic to create the fragments in the first place. Demons did not phase into separate parts like angels did. The corruption of their spirits makes them less malleable than angels. Zeke experienced the stretching when he tried to heal Tone. A demon in the same situation would have resisted the stretching and instead fought the battle to maintain its form against the forces trying to pull it apart. Part of the damage in their fall was the inflexibility of the devilish nature that spilled over into the spirit forms. Demons neither bent not changed. They were static in their hatred and evil.

"How did that happen?" came the query from Michael. "There hasn't been a demon fragmentation in over three hundred and sixty-two quolls. The demons you split were still intact, weren't they Zeke?"

"Separate pieces but no fragments. I was careful. I had no idea what fragments would do to him," Zeke said gesturing to the human. "Could he have fragmented Glomoq when he kicked it?"

"I kicked a Glomoq?" said Tone more to himself that anyone in particular.

Arino spoke up. "Well, it looks like we know what nasty effects they have on him. If this weren't so horrible it would be fascinating." Looking at Tone she continued, "I doubt he could have fragmented it but it is possible. He works on a level that is radically different than any of us or any human I have ever seen in Heaven, Hell or Earth."

"I kicked a Glomoq?" repeated Tone to himself trying to say the name in a different way.

"Why did none of us sense this until now? I would think it would have stood out before this." There was concern in Zeke question.

Michael was also curious. "I can understand you not seeing it, Zeke. This is not your specialty. But Arino and I should have discovered this. Even with all his ability to block us we should have sensed a demon shard in our friend here."

Arino looked deeper into the wound getting dangerously close to touching Tone. She examined him more carefully than ever before. "It is almost like it was dormant until I tried to remove it. There is a viral quality to it now that it is not hiding as a demonic touch. I think it is trying to take over to make him into an active bridge between Hell and Earth."

"I kicked a Glomoq?" repeated Tone trying a third way to say the name.

Zeke chimed in, "But how could it have gotten in there and hidden itself so fast? Tone is fast for a human but not that fast."

"I kicked a Glomoq," stated Tone again with subtle resolution to the fact that he would never like the sound of that name.

Arino had been examining the demon infected appendage. "This is not a fragment of Glomoq. Everything is totally wrong about it. It looks like..." she trailed off. "Mike? Is that a piece of who I think it is?"

"How is that possible? She is gone." Michael was as confused as Arino.

"Glomoq. Glomoq. Glomoq. Glomoq," repeated Tone ignoring the conversation happening around him. "Glomoq. Glomoq. Glomoq..."

Ezekiel, knowing their thoughts, asked, "How could Tone have a piece of S'theno in him? She was dead when we got there."

"Glomoq. Glomoq. Glo..." The human stopped and finally began listening to the angels. "Wait! What? Seth Uno? How could I have that bitch inside my leg?"

Michael was looking at Anthony in intimate detail. There was something in Michael's eyes that made Zeke uneasy. He knew Michael well enough to know that he was considering all options available to an archangel. Michael could call on any angel he needed to do whatever the situation required. Zeke did not like the options that Mike was considering. A shared look was all Zeke needed to tell Michael that doing anything to Tone was not an option. Tone was needed wasn't he?

Arino, knowing the silent battle happening around her, spoke to the human. "We don't know, Tone. I know from your conversations with Zeke that you had not met her as far as you know."

"As far as I know? What the hell does that mean? I'm pretty sure I would remember meeting a babe with glowing eyes and a do done by Fantastic Snakes." Tone's sarcasm was understandable.

The silent battle between the two warriors continued as the healer and human debated. "Could you have met her on earth and not known? She has gotten loose before and appears as a beautiful woman to many men."

"If you only knew," laughed Tone. "No. I'm sure I didn't meet her."

The silent battle was over with Michael saying, "Are you sure about this?"

"I'm betting myself on it," came the confident reply of Ezekiel.

"Did I miss something?" queried Tone. "Do I want to know? Based on your glows I'm pretty sure knowing would give me nightmares and daymares and afternoon-mares and tea-time-mares."

Ignoring him, Michael asked, "Do you have any idea how you got that fragment in your leg, Tone?"

"Shit! Now Mike is calling me Tone. I'm so screwed!" Anthony was trying to make light of the situation which was obvious to all. Even the human knew that the archangel was thinking about all kinds of options. "Dude, I don't know how it happened. I can tell you when. It was when I kicked Glomoq. It was right at that moment that I felt it."

Michael was taking on the air of an interrogator. "But Glomoq is not the soul fragment that resides in your leg. S'theno was long dead when you got there and, if you can be believed, you had never met her." Turning to the healer he asked, "What are the options you can bring to the table?"

Arino had been examining the demonic splinter in Tone. She paused before answering to look at the leg one more time. "I can drain it."

"No you can't!" declared Michael. "That is too dangerous."

"Excuse me..." began Tone.

There was a defiance and a smile in the eyes of the healer. "No it is not. I know what to do. The danger will be minimal with help from both of you."

"Really? You are serious?" asked Michael, hoping he had misunderstood.

"Excuse me but..." tried Tone again.

Arino continued. "Of course I am and of course we can. We have done this kind of thing before. It will be harder without being able to touch him but Zeke can help with that. If Zeke can touch Tone, I can use him as a conduit to draw the power of the shard off. If it is too much for me to absorb then I can let some bleed off into you. Between the three of us we can help Tone

47

and keep him from becoming something totally consumed by the shard of evil trying to take over."

"Excuse me but can..." Before Tone could continue Zeke interjected.

"That sounds dangerous but I'm willing to risk it. That is why we are here anyway. Let's heal the human!" There was genuine excitement about this option since it derailed Michael's more radical solution.

Michael was not convinced. "What if he explodes? Have you considered that this shard may be the source of all our problems with touching him? There are so many possibilities." Michael finally said aloud what all three were wondering. "There is one question we must ask before we continue. What if he is the entity killing angels and demons?"

"Excuse me but can someone... wait! What if I'm the bad guy?" Tone looked hurt.

"I'm sorry Tone but look at the facts." Michael began his list. "You have power to keep us from really reading you. For all we know you have been lying to us all along. On earth you could be almost anything. Plus you are the only witness to the murder of Casadore. Ezekiel was almost destroyed by what you both describe as an 'accident'. You also have a fragment of another victim embedded in your leg." He let all that sink in. "All we have to do is let Arino use her healing energy and you will be no more."

Chapter 12

"You really think I'm causing all of this?" asked an incredulous Anthony. "Why the hell would I be helping track myself?" He was nearly shouting. "Mike, you have got to be messing with me. Right?" There was concern, curiosity and more than a little fear in Tone's voice.

Michael's gaze was as riveting as it was intimidating as it fell upon each one of them. The unimaginable power of the archangel could be felt by the human and the two angels. Zeke knew that if he gave the order Arino would act even though she would hate doing it. There was a logic to Michael's argument but it still did not feel right.

"Please do not do this Michael." There was a pleading in Zeke's voice that was a surprise even to himself. The silent debate that had been happening behind the scenes now spilled over so that even Tone could hear as Zeke lowered his defenses.

Michael was concerned about the bond between Anthony and Ezekiel. There was something that was too intense for such a short time. There was no jealousy or envy from the archangel. He knew that the angel's loyalty to Heaven was unassailable. However, when it came to the human it seemed that there was a blind spot on the part of Zeke. A friendship between a human and an angel was not unprecedented. There were many times throughout the ages when an angel had befriended an unknowing human. An angel would be assigned to be the protector of a human during his earthly life and would make occasional appearances to that person. Casadore had even been the spiritual guardian of Joan of Arc. She had only known him as a soldier named Cas during her life who had saved her on several occasions. At her death she saw him in his true form behind the crucifix held before her to comfort her in death. Casadore always loved telling of the joy of escorting her to heaven after her martyrdom.

Zeke and Tone had a friendship that was beginning to transcend the simple bond between protector and protected. There were too many things that had happened in such a short time for this to be coincidental. Tone managed to find Zeke even though what he claimed was an imprint from Casadore. Zeke's power had changed Tone into something even greater than he had been when they first met. There were even traces of Tone within Zeke and Zeke within Tone. The healing of the phase not only left vestiges of angelic power in the human but left traces of Tone's touch within the angel. This bond would only get stronger the more they worked with one another. But so would Ezekiel's inability to be objective about Tone.

Michael knew that this was an angelic matter that was his responsibility. Ezekiel was well aware of Michael's concern and now so was Anthony. The human would not go quietly if he felt he was truly in danger but that could be handled in ways that even the knowledgeable Tone did not know about. The real question centered on the bond between Anthony and Ezekiel. Would that bond make Zeke defy an archangel?

"Arino, I'm sorry. I need you to do what needs to be done," came the sad command from Michael.

"Michael, please do not make me do this," there was pleading in Arino's voice. Her aura had taken on the hue of sadness and regret even before her actions were forced upon her.

Tone regained the power of speech. "What can I do to convince you I'm on your side? Everything I have done has been to help. OK, phasing Zeke wasn't; but that was an accident."

Zeke spoke up. "Michael, this is wrong. Do not make me choose. Not like this." There was a glow within the angel that showed his true inner conflict that would soon be forced into resolution.

"I think I'll take my chances with the demons. Later everyone." Tone winked at Arino, saluted Zeke and stuck is tongue out at Michael. With a bow and a flourish of his spirit he did not disappear. His spirit looked as if it straining against an unseen force. "Um. I can still see you. Tell me you can't see me."

Michael had a smile on his face. "Tone, did you think I was powerless to keep you where I needed you? You are not going anywhere."

"Now that is just cheating! I know because I cheat all the time and that is exactly how it looks! I expected more from an angel, Mikey." The bravado of the human nearly hid his very real surprise and fear.

"You will not be going back to Earth until this is removed or you are removed. I'm sorry but I have to look out for all humanity and angels." There was a sorrow in his words that gave pause to all who heard it.

"Arino. Now." There was a soft, sadness in the command. The momentary conflict in Arino was resolved as she slowly shifted into her amorphous form. Small beams of energy began moving toward a terrified Tone. He tried to move away but found himself rooted to the spot by unseen archangel power. Slowly the power inched closer and closer to the human. Anthony began to close in as if trying to protect himself from what was to come. The shades and tones within the spirit of Zeke were playing out showing his very real conflict. As the dangerous healing power came within touching distance a voice rang out.

"NO!" shouted Zeke as the power was deflected safely away from the huddled human.

"Atta boy, Zeke! I knew you'd come to my rescue!" shouted a momentarily relieved Tone. As he looked at his angelic friend he was filled with shock and awe. His mouth had shouted as his angelic power was straining to reach out and protect the human from certain, torturous death. His warrior form was in its full glory as it sought to protect an innocent human. Yet all that power was contained around him through the restraining of the archangel. Zeke's power was powerless to help. But the hurtful healing had been deflected.

"Good," stated Michael simply. The glow of pride shown on the aura of the archangel. The healer was also happily recalling her power.

"You sure waited 'til the last instance, Zeke," said Arino. "I was going as slowly as I could."

There was a mystified look on the face of Tone. "What the hell? It was a test?! People! There is only so much my underwear can hold! Please stop scaring the shit out of me!"

Zeke finally spoke. "Your management style really annoys me, Michael. I thought you were testing me but you are so hard to read."

Tone added, "I think he can be an asshole! You know OSHA would not approve of this work environment!"

Michael smiled. "That's why I'm the archangel, my friends. I'm sorry I had to do that Tone but I know what you two are about to face and I needed to be sure. You and Zeke have a bond that is going to get stronger and stronger. Be ready because I do not know what it is going to be like for you or him. But I need you two united to fight whatever we are going to be fighting."

"So you don't think I'm Bubba wearing a *Mission Impossible* mask?" asked a cautious Anthony.

"I know you are not Bubba. There was never any doubt." The frank and straightforward reply took Tone by surprise.

"Hey dude! I'm not a harmless little rabbit here! I can be a bad-ass bunny with really bad breath!" retorted Tone. He was pretending to breathe fire as he tried to hop toward Michael.

50

Laughter came out of the archangel that relieved the last of the tension of recent actions. He was really beginning to like the clowning nature of the human. But his laughter died away as he explained, "I knew you had nothing to do with Casadore or S'theno because you have an air tight alibi for the destruction of D'vrash. I was right behind you while you were fighting your way to Arino when he was destroyed."

"Not D'vrash! Please tell me that it wasn't D'vrash!" Tone paused. "Hey Zeke! Was D'vrash an angel or demon?" The look of shock and sadness that glowed throughout Zeke answered the question without needing words. "A little too far that time?" he asked to no one in particular.

Michael replied. "Yes. Over the top." Looking at Arino he said, "I'm sorry. I know you two were close."

Arino had almost lost her glow. The nearly perpetual smile that was as much a part of her healing as her power had disappeared. There was nothing but a silent stare from Ezekiel. The angels opened their minds to allow Tone to see what they were sharing. It left him speechless.

Raphael, the archangel of the healers, had found the fading form of D'vrash on the edge of the battle. Around him were the slowly fading bodies of four demons who looked as if they had been turned inside out and drained of every bit of essence they possessed. D'vrash was worse. He had been split into five segments and phased apart. There was no trace of his essence anywhere to be found. It was only by chance that Raphael had found the fading pieces of D'vrash before they were simply no more. Had he not been seeking all healers he wouldn't have noticed the absence.

"So there are at least five more victims? This is very not good." Tone had a gift for stating the obvious.

"Raphael is on his way to help with the healing of Tone. I'm going to prepare for a council of the archangels. We have to deal with this now." Michael had taken on the air of the authority that was his as leader of the archangels. "Zeke. Arino. Start getting ready. When Raph arrives he will want to get to work. You know how he is." And Michael was gone.

Arino was still silent as she contemplated the situation. Zeke reached out and held her more closely than Tone would have liked. "I understand. Casadore was like that for me."

"A little context would be helpful so I don't end up with my other foot in my mouth, too." There was a subdued air in the healing house that Tone had wisely chosen to honor by not being a flippant as usual.

The two remaining angels chose to keep their thoughts clear for the human. Each of them was the best at what they did. Ezekiel, the hunter and warrior, was second only to Michael in his battle prowess. Arino, the healer, was gifted in restoration of the wounded in ways that only Raphael could match. Each had trained many angels in the skills that they possessed; however, each had a star student. Casadore had been Zeke's best pupil while D'vrash had been the same for Arino. The bond between the angels and their protégés was beyond anything a human professor and pupil could muster. There are few angels who can find that bond. When it happens there is nothing on earth to compare.

For the warriors there was a relationship that allowed them to fight as one. They knew each other's moves and attacks so well that the normal link between angels to coordinate their battle was unnecessary. Both were master fighters. Each would take the lead in an attack and support the other based upon the situation and the skills needed. They were not identical fighters but more mirrors of one another. There was a sense of opposites attracting to allow their combat to work as one and while being two distinctive and polar opposite fighters. It is frightening even to other angels when the two worked in perfect offset synchronicity. Zeke would never have that bond again but he would persevere.

51

The healer connection was similar in many ways to the bond of the warriors. They formed a connection that would allow them to work more closely than others without the need of the link. Where the warriors used the differences to make them more devastating in battle, the healers were two who were as close to identical as possible. Their healing powers would mix and mingle as they healed those wounded in battle. It was this type of teaming that allowed many angels who had been phased apart to be restored to as close to the way they were before. Arino and D'vrash had even restored the archangel Adoneal who had been phased and had pieces removed to the far recesses of the spirit world. Now Arino would never have the same bond but she would survive.

The two angels held one another as their essences combined to find comfort in shared sorrow. "Would you two like some privacy?" asked a half joking Tone. "I can... ummm... is there a bathroom where I can freshen up while you two are doing whatever the hell you're doing?"

"Tone!" said both angels with mirth in their voices.

"It is not exactly like you are thinking. Come here," said Arino. She motioned for him to come closer. "Don't worry. I'm not going to touch you. This is how we share the greatest and worse moments. It is nothing sexual like you were thinking. We are not sexual at all. That is a gift only humans and other earthly beings have."

"I wish," said Tone chuckling to himself. "So what are you doing? It looks a little kinky to me."

Zeke was again aghast at his friend. Amused he said, "Arino and I are closer than most other angels. It is hard to put in human terms. She is my Omfrel. She is like a best friend but that really doesn't explain our relationship. It's complicated." After contemplating that, he continued, "Tone we are open to you. What are you sensing?

"I don't do the emotional stuff very well. This is a little too intense for me. Can we skip the touchy-freely crap? Now if Arino wants to go to Fiji with me, we'll talk." There was something about his words that unlocked another barrier to the walls around Anthony. "Is Raphael almost here? I want to get this demon turd out of my leg."

"I'm right behind you, Anthony." The voice was the most soothing thing Tone had ever heard, felt or sensed in any way. There was an instant sensation that all would be well. Everything would be fine. The problem with his leg seemed like it was just a minor issue that would now be brushed off. There was a sense of stoned, drunken euphoria being in the presence of that voice.

When Tone turned to look at the source, he realized the voice was nothing compared to the being before him. Unlike most angels he had met, this one has a very distinctive body. It was almost as if it were an androgynous person of undefinable pleasant appearance. Raphael was beyond handsome or beauty. Raphael simply was the most comforting being Tone had ever seen, heard, smelled, or sensed. Tone wondered how Raph would taste and then began worrying that he wanted to taste an angel.

"Tone, you do know you are saying what you are thinking, don't you?" questioned Arino.

"OK. That's nice," said a dazed Anthony. "So you are Raphael. I like you Raphael. You are a nice archangel. Am I the only one who feels like he drank a whole bottle of rum?"

"I have that effect on people," said the smiling Raphael. "Michael enlightened me as to the whole situation. Anthony, may I look at your leg for myself?"

"Anything you want." Clearly Tone was intoxicated by the presence of arch-healer.

Ezekiel spoke up. "I don't supposed you can stay with us all the time. He is much easier to tolerate like this."

"Yeah! We need Raph with us all the time. We can all get a house together and sit around and … ummm... sit around. That is good isn't it, Raph? Sitting is good and fun. I like you Raphael. You're a nice archangel."

Clearly amused but also patient Raphael responded. "Yes, Tone. Sitting is a good thing. Can you hold still for me?"

"Zeke! Raph called me Tone! He likes me. Raph is my friend. You're a nice archangel." The excitement was sincere in Tone's aura. "I'll try to hold still but I'm really happy you're my friend, Raph."

"I'm glad too, Tone. Now you need to rest. Sleep well." Without warning the human was out cold. "I take it he isn't always this agreeable?" joked the archangel.

"No!" said Arino and Ezekiel together.

"But he means well...mostly." added Arino. "Do you think it will work?" There was no need to explain since Raphael already knew the situation and the plan.

"We can drain the evil off and contain the fragment. But Ezekiel, you will have to remove it once we get the cold drained off and infuse him with some of your warmth. I do have a concern with containment. The hospital is being moved so that we will be away from everything that could have deleterious effects on this. We are as close to Heaven as I can take us without causing more problems for Anthony. But if this fragment still has some consciousness to it then we will have to use an alternate method of removal."

They all knew that meant leaving it in until they could find a way for several angels to be able to touch Tone. That could mean a much longer than planned stay in the spirit world for the human.

"Well let's get started, shall we?" Raphael did not like to waste time. "Ezekiel as soon as you are ready."

Zeke reached out and cautiously touched his friend's chilled leg. It was even colder than it had been before. Zeke knew that for the first phase he was merely the conduit for the process. He would not have to do anything more than allow power to pass through him. As Arino and Raphael reached out and touched him, the cold began to drain off of Tone, through him, and into the healers. No words or thoughts were needed as they slowly pull the cold out of the hurting human like venom from a snake bite. The cold had spread almost into his core.

The smiling healers had to fight hard to maintain their joy as the evil was being pulled off the human. Suddenly both healers' auras turned the blue of the demons as a sudden rush of demon chill flooded them. The shock knocked Arino back, cause her to lose contact with Zeke. The aura of the archangel was turned a shade of blue only seen in demons as he fought a battle with the demon within Tone.

"It... is... conscious!" grunted Raphael as his aura faded to an even darker shade of blue.

Chapter 13

"Let go of me!" shouted a voice from Anthony that was not Anthony. With a move that surprised Ezekiel, the human spirit twisted, turned and was inexplicably insubstantial as he slipped out of the angel's grasp. Wisps of blue demonic energy floated through the ether and surrounded the human. As the wisps of blue touched Arino and Raphael the demonic energy was drawn out of the healers and back into the source of the power.

Three angels reacted instantly to the onslaught of demonic power. Three angels surrounded the human spirit that now glowed the bright blue of the demon. Three angels were battle ready. Three angels paused waiting for the next move.

"Listen up, assholes! I don't have much time. This dumb ass is fighting me from the inside out and I know you won't let this last much longer." The voice and the feel were very demonic. There was a growl of pain that oozed out of the being before them. "Dammit, Tone! Stop the shit storm! I will give you your body back but – I can't believe I'm saying this – I need to talk to the angels."

"S'theno? How did you take possession of Anthony?" asked Zeke. "Release him now!" There was a fury in the angel as his warrior form blazed with holy fire.

"Cool off there, hot head. One stray bit of power and I'm gone, Tone here is in pieces and you are all phased. That would be a bad thing for us all, don't you think? I couldn't stay if I wanted to. Shut up and listen. I have information for you before I'm nothing." The voice of the demon was teasing them with knowledge they needed. "But before I give you what you need I want something from you."

Raphael stepped between the demon-possessed Tone and the hunter ready to kill. "S'theno, I can see that you are using up the power you had saved. You don't have long. Why play games with us? Either go into oblivion or help us. We are not going to make deals. I could just heal you out of him right now and you can spend your final bits of consciousness in agony. Or you can behave and I will allow you the mercy of fading out. No deals."

"Raph, Raph, Raph. You will all like this deal. It is a win-win for us all. But I want Zeke's word, not yours. When you find the son of bitch who destroyed me, return the favor! None of your 'mercy' as you call it. Take this bastard down and scatter it into nothing!" Looking at Zeke, "Do we have a deal?"

The fire in the eyes of Ezekiel blazed with power. "I will do everything in my power to send it into the same nothing that is your destination!" There was an intensity behind his words that even made the demon shudder.

"I'm glad I'm not him." The demon's glow was starting to fade. "OK, bitches. Here's the scoop. When that thing jumped me it shattered me. I was able to hide one shard of myself from it so now you know it's not all knowing. Or at least it's sloppy. What little was left of me I moved into that fragment. I was trying to get into Glomoq when Tone here decided to try for his field goal. It was just a hop, skip and jump into this body. What the hell is he anyway?" The demon paused in its soliloquy. "Yes, Tone. I am looking in your memories, you bad boy. Human with a little extra. Interesting. And look at that! That explains a lot. Also, you really need to delete your browser history when you get home. Now shut up. Momma has to talk to the grownups."

While S'theno has been rambling on Arino had moved into a sensory blind spot and was scanning Tone/S'theno with every sense she had. There was no doubt that the demon was dying quickly. Her healing power was ready to react at the slightest hostile move of the demon. She was uncertain of the side effects on the spiritual form and mind of Tone; but she knew what had to be done if the situation called for it.

S'theno continued, "Now where was I? Oh yes. You call it Bubba? Really, Tone? That's the best you can do? OK. So Bubba not only shattered me but the bastard also consumed the pieces. There is still part of me inside of Bubba. None of my glorious self but the essence of my power is in that son of a bitch! And you can bet your shiny, hot little asses that whatever it is, it's growing." The glow of the demon was starting to flicker between the blue of the hellion and the psychedelic of Tone.

"I'm truly sorry for you, S'theno. I remembered how spectacular you were once. It is a shame that you are going into oblivion." Raphael was always the comforter.

"No tears for me, Raphy. This nothing is better than Hell." The glow of the demon was fading away. "Just get the bastard, Zeke. Kick his ass like you have kicked mine so many times. I just wish I could have won against you once. But maybe this is my chance to win. I'm gone and you can't touch me. And it wasn't you who did it. Oh, I also now know who Tone really is. I wish I could see your face when you meet." A demon's laughter was the final sound that S'theno ever made.

The shard of demon drifted out of the collapsing Tone. All three angels attacked the tiny fragment that had caused so much trouble for so many. The healing of Arino, the crushing blow of Ezekiel and the containing and compressing power of Raphael made quick work of the already deceased fragment of the once powerful demon.

Zeke was quickly at the side of Tone. "Tone? Are you in there? Talk to me!"

"For the record there is nothing on my browser history. And do you have a soul shower? I need one really bad to wash that bitch out of my system." Tone was positively back to his old, obnoxious self.

"Raphael and I can help with that," said Arino. "There are no traces of her left in you, Tone. Any residual effects are simply your memories. Raphael, can you sense if Tone is safe to touch?"

The archangel had been silent and keeping his distance to allow Tone to focus without his natural intoxicating effect rendering him foolish. His abilities functioned even at a distance. His words came to all of their minds. *"There is still some danger to angels but the conduit method we used to draw off the power will work in reverse without any harm to any of you. I'm still not sure why he is so dangerous. It is a puzzle that we will discuss in the council."*

"Are you leaving Raph? Can you just talk to me one more time? I could use the buzz after the quill I've had." There was a pleading in his voice that was amusing in its child-like quality.

"I'm sure your next QUOLL will be better, Tone. Try to avoid the quills. Especially the demon kind. They're worse for you than smoking," joked the archangel as he disappeared.

The goofy grin was once again on Anthony's face. "I like Raphael. He's a nice archangel. He called me Tone. He's my friend," sighed the loopy human soul.

Zeke and Arino looked at one another. Arino spoke first. "While he is so calm I think we should try to transfer some healing power into him. He still looks a bit diminished."

Zeke placed his hand on his dazed friend. An amorphous Arino partially merged with the hunter and sent healing energy through him into the human. The effect was obvious as Anthony glowed brighter than he had ever glowed.

"Oh yeah, baby! Give me another hit of that! This is one strange threesome we've got going here." The dazed Tone was replaced by the abnormal flippancy that was normal for him. "So that is what healing is supposed to feel like. I feel warm all the way into my toenails. I think they are starting to curl! Nice! Wait. Do I have toes?"

"Yes. He's better. Now can you fix the attitude?" asked a teasing Ezekiel.

Smiling, Arino replied, "There are some things even I can't heal."

"Why mess with perfection, babe? I'm awesome! Now what shall we do next? I'm ready to kick ass and take names," Tone said. Then after thinking he continued, "Well, I'm ready to let you kick the asses and I'll write the names down on a scroll or something."

"Well Tone, I have others to help. But we have a link through the healing now. Just call me and I'll be there as soon as I can if either of you are hurt." Arino added, "Try not to kick any more demons in the nads." There was angelic laughter in the ether as Zeke and Tone were left in the middle of Spiritscape as Arino and the healing house were gone.

"She is amazing," declared Tone.

A rare unfocused look was on Zeke's essence as he said, "Yes, she is."

Tone decided to change the subject. "The dangerous duo together again. I guess we need to get back to work now that the play time is over. I miss them already. Well, I miss Arino and Raph. Mike, not so much." The constant chatter of Tone was back with a vengeance.

Looking around Zeke said, "Well it is time to start tracking Bubba again. I wonder how many angels and demons he has consumed. The archangels are checking on all the angels. No telling with the demons until Nasarg does a head count."

"Wanna know what I'm worried about?" asked Tone. Before he could respond Tone continued. "If one shard of a demon had me feeling like I should be dunked in bleach, what would consuming the five we know about do to whatever Bubba is?"

Tone looked around and realized something was different. "Uhhh. Zeke? Where are we? I know we were running scared but I don't remember the battle field looking like this. It's a little too bright and cheery. Also it's clearer than it used to be. Did Arino do a Lasik thing too?"

"Did she now? Interesting. She didn't let me know she was doing that. How do you like the view?" asked the angel.

The area of the spirit world where they found themselves was nearly a paradise in itself. There was a waterfall made of Burmese rubies that was a bright shade of pink, glittering with traces of silver and gold. It was crashing upwards into what looked like a spherical gem-filled lake that floated in nothing. A stream of stones flowed out of it back to the crest of the falls and created a continuous loop of beauty. There were crystal mountain peaks from six angles that crossed one another and created a prismatic display of colors shining beams that went in every direction as they crashed into one another. The mists all around them were bright reds and purples that shined creating an atmosphere with no shadows.

"It is spectacular! I really need to get your decorator to do something like this for my bedroom." Even in the beauty Tone found humor. He was amazing in the *joie de vivre* that was such an integral part of his very being.

"Merci!" said Tone who had been reading him.

"Raphael moved the healing house while we were in it. I think you were a little intoxicated at the time" answered Ezekiel to the first question Tone asked. If he didn't know better Tone would have thought that Zeke was smirking.

"You're smirking at me! It isn't my fault. He just makes me feel weird. Really weird." Tone was not feeling defensive. It was just that there were no words to describe the effect. "He is one of the nice archangels, isn't he?"

This time Zeke was definitely smirking. "'Him' is not the right pronoun but yes. You should see Raphael when mad. Not a pretty sight. I've seen Raph scare Hell out of demons."

Tone actually looked shocked. "Zeke! You bad angel. You just cursed, dammit! I need some soap to wash your mouth out!" Looking around he yelled, "Anybody got a scrub brush and some lye?"

Zeke laughed. "You don't get it. I was being literal, Tone. When I defeat a demon like I did with the unfab five, they have to go back to Hell to sleep off their wounds. It is a succubus sleep. They heal faster when they can sleep there. But I saw Raphael use his power that would heal an angel on a demon and it just collapsed right where it was. We had to step over it for more quolls than I counted. That is scaring Hell out of a demon."

"Shit! That makes me the only potty mouth around here. I was really hoping I was rubbing off on you." Tone did not really sound disappointed. He liked the friendship with the pure angel. Well mostly liked the mostly pure angel. He still wondered about what influence his traces would have in the long haul and was pretty sure Zeke had a slightly tarnished halo before they met.

Zeke jested, "Well I'm sure we could find a demon to give you come competition. In the mean time we have a job to do. Let's go take a look where we lost D'vrash."

"Time to put my bloodhound abilities to use again? Cool. Let's see if I've still got it!" Tone allowed Zeke to pick him up. "We going far?"

"Well it is a little ways away." Zeke seemed to be weighing Tone. He examined several aspects of the human. "You are different since you were infused with healing. I wonder..." trailed off the angel.

Tone gave him a look and said, "Why does the look of your aura make me want to say 'Oh shit'?"

"Let's try something." The angel set the Tone down. "Let me move a little bit away from you. Don't want to play games too close and get us both discombobulated."

"Nice word," said Tone. Zeke smiled. "You are learning well, cricket."

Zeke was channeling some of his power into a focused point ahead of them. "If you are expecting me to call you master you are in for a very long wait. This is a little complicated, but I've done it many times. Never tried it quite like this though."

There was what seemed to be a door made of mist slowly forming in front of them. The door was transparent but was becoming more and more opaque as it was gaining solidity. Tone was transfixed as a magic door seemed to be coming into existence in a place that had no doors, windows or even floors. Yet there it was. It was as out of place as a gourmet chef at a fast food convention. The door was becoming more and more solid all the time as the red mists become a semi-solid door with purple mists making a handle.

"OK. That is cool. You were right to add a domestic touch to this place. It is just too naturally beautiful. The whole door to nowhere gives it that homey feel." The human approached the door and moved around it, examining it from every angle. Tone looked at Zeke and said, "I'm guessing this is something other than a demonstration of your lack of interior design skills? Or I guess this is more exterior design? Or spirit-erior design? I really don't know how the hell to think of this place sometimes. Well... all the time."

"I don't even know if this will work. I have only used it to create a gateway to Hell when I need to toss several demons there at once. Think of it like a wormhole." The look of amazement on Tone's face answered the question without the need for words. "This is my version. I had to make a door to contain the power around you. But I'm pretty sure it should work."

Tone spoke up. "OK. Three things. One. Holy shit! You're into sci-fi!! Too cool. Second. Can we discuss the whole gateway to Hell thing? I'm as much a heavy metal fan as the next guy but from what you are saying I don't think I want to go spelunking there. I just got warm again and don't really feel the need to chill out, if you catch my drift."

"I'm not opening a door to Hell, Tone. This is a door to the battle field where D'Vrash died. It is a much faster way to travel than flying there. It is safer too since we won't run into any demons this way." Ezekiel was confident that this would be the best way to travel to keep Tone as safe as he could. He knew that one or a few demons would not be an issue for him and Tone could stay hidden. But why take the chance if it wasn't necessary?

Tone approached the door. Reaching for the handle he said, "May I?"

"Please do," replied Zeke.

Tone opened the door to reveal a hazy threshold that seemed to be a different place. He walked all the way around it but the opening looked the same from both sides of the door. "So this is a shortcut? Sounds cool. I'm all about shortcuts! But there is that third thing I wanted to talk about. You said you were 'pretty sure' it would work. Are you feeling a little more positive about it now?"

Zeke smiled. "Honestly, my friend, it works for humans when we take them from Earth to Heaven so it should work from one spot to another here, too. Plus, you are - in your words - 'special'. So there is a slight chance that it may interact strangely with your power. But I'm not worried."

"Of course you're not worried. You aren't the one who is going through the damn thing without a clue what will happen. Why do I have to be the guinea..."

Zeke pushed him through the door.

Chapter 14

"...pig?" Tone looked around. "What the hell?! Zeke? Get your ass over here!"

"I'm behind you, Tone," said a Zeke with a mischievous smile.

Spinning around, Anthony asked, "Do you know what that was like?" Before Zeke could answer, he continued, "It felt like I was taken apart piece by piece with a laser, then shuffled like a deck of teddy bear cards, shot like a spit wad through a green forty foot long straw into a bowl of Jell-O and put back together with duct tape!"

"Really?" asked a grinning Zeke, sensing that there was more than a little deceit in his words.

"Well no. It was like walking through a doorway to another room, but I could have been like that! You didn't know what would happen." A smile radiated through the whole being of Tone. "And I would've looked silly wearing duct tape. I do have a wallet made of duct tape with little mustaches on it though. You just ported here. You were afraid to use the damn thing, too!"

Zeke did the angel equivalent of shaking his head. "I would make sure you had some duct tape with starfish and sponges on it. Now if you are done making up stories for sympathy that will never come, can we get to work?"

"Thank you for being kind enough to consider deluxe duct tape for me and yes I'm done for now. But I will get sympathy out of you yet!" Tone looked around with his tracking senses. "And there is the scene of the crime," he said moving toward an area that was darker and colder than the surrounding ether. "What a mess!"

Tone saw that there had been very little movement from the bad guy. Bubba had just come upon the scene of four demons trying to jump an angel. Looking at the trails there were different spots showing different things.

"OK. This is strange. There are trails that are all mixed up around here but some are... well..." The eternally verbose Tone was having a difficult time finding a way to describe what he was seeing. "It's hard to put into words. Let's just say some are more faded than others." After pausing and looking thoughtful, he added, "Well, not faded. It is more like some is like a fresh piece of gum and others are like some that you've been chewing for a couple hours. There is even one that reminds me of this piece I chewed for six months until I found the record had to be continuous for three days. My jaws were so sore."

"So these gum trails are what? Different ages?" asked the angel trying to make the connection between gum and trails.

Tone was lost in reminiscence about his long lost gum. "Tone? The trails?" prompted Ezekiel.

"Oh yeah. Anyway, I think the more chewed the trail is the older it is and the newer the chew the younger it is." Tone said that with the air of one who was confident in a detailed analysis. He had no idea that Zeke was struggling to follow his way of thinking.

"So you are saying you can see the age of the trail? When did that start?" Zeke was confused that his friend would have omitted this information until now. "That would have been helpful earlier when we were trying to find the right trail of Bubba to follow."

Anthony looked at the angel as if he were a total idiot. "Dude, Bubba's trail is just snot. It doesn't dry up and clump or anything." He spoke slowly like someone talking down to a child "His trails looks the same. But that Dove-cash's trail has a chewed part and a less chewed part. And some of the oil trails look more dried out than others."

"D'vrash," corrected the angel. "Tone, how would I have known that?" asked a patient Zeke.

"Because I... didn't tell you, did I?" inquired Tone. "Well you need to listen to what I mean and not what I say. Haven't you figured that out yet?" He tried to laugh it off. Zeke was starting to learn how to read the human without actually being able to detect what was happening inside. Tone was actually troubled by this lapse. He pondered not pressing the matter. This was something that concerned the angel in more ways than one.

"What's going on, my friend? You're hiding something." Zeke had pieced together much of the secret identity of the human. This was something new that he was trying to decipher without hiding his efforts.

"OK. OK. I'll let you in on a little secret." Dropping his voice to a conspiratorial whisper, Tone continued, "On earth I don't remember very much of what happens here. But every time I come back it all comes back to me."

Ezekiel was sensing his friend with every sense he had and knew that this was the truth. "Why does that bother you? It makes sense. Here your mind is freed to have nearly limitless recall. On Earth your mind is bound by the Earthly limitations."

Tone's spirit fluctuated through so many simultaneous hues that even the angel could not read what was going through that complicated, human mind. "If you only knew," was all Tone said. "Now about these trails."

Zeke knew that the discussion was over for now. He made a mental note and continued to contemplate the mystery of Anthony as they prepared to track the elusive Bubba. "Do we really have to call this entity Bubba? Even the demon mocked your choice of names?"

"Hey! You can call it the 'Demon-Devouring-Angel-Eating-Entity-From-Parts-Unknown' if you want. I'm sticking with Bubba." Anthony elaborated his logic. "They are both fat, mean, evil and leave a slime trail. Seriously dude. That kid had some major hygiene issues!"

Tone was even able to make a discussion of a malevolent entity laughable. Knowing that arguing the point was pointless he let it drop. The hunter in in him was intrigued by the possibilities that Tone was creating with his tracking ability. "So about those trails?" asked Zeke trying to get back on track.

"Well the oil trails and the oil slicks are all over the place. I can see where Duh-Wash was fighting the four of them and it looks like he won. I can see what looks like oil splatter all over the place with just a little marshmallow cream here and there. It looks like they got in a few lucky shots." Tone looked more closely at one area. "Why wouldn't he have kicked their asses back to Hell? It looks like they were just lying there while he was waiting for something."

Zeke pondered that briefly before answering. "D'vrash was a healer. Not a fighter. It was his nature to look for ways to heal those who were injured. He may have been looking for ways to help those he was forced to fight. Arino is an impressive fighter when she needs to. I see that D'vrash was too, based on the shared memories."

"That is just weird," commented the human. "So based on these trails it looks like he was taking a look at the demons when he was jumped by Bubba." Moving a little ways away, Tone pointed and said, "Here is a puddle of fluffy stuff. This must be where Raph found him if I had to guess."

"That's right. I can see the memory." Zeke was surprised that Tone was able to take things so seriously even briefly.

"And over there is an oil slick where Bubba made a demon delicatessen. He must have made a hell-ham and terrible-turkey succubus-sandwich on cruel ciabatta with a side of deviled-eggs," joked Tone. So much for him taking things seriously. At least he avoided any references to the eating the angel. "Also that cheating bastard ate angel food cake before the demon dinner. That is just wrong eating the sweet stuff first. But it does tell us something that we didn't know before."

Zeke was almost afraid to ask. "What does that tell us?"

"The puddle of oil is just slightly fresher than the pile of marshmallow cream. After he attacked Don Rash he could have dined at his leisure. The demons were still fresh even though they were injured. He could have devoured them first but he didn't."

"Are you sure about that? You are making several assumptions based on trails. How can you be sure?" asked the angel.

"I'm sure. The demons were destroyed and devoured after the angel." There was no mirth in Tone's voice as he said, "He likes the flavor of angels better than demons."

"That is the first good news I've heard in a long time," sneered a voice from nowhere that was oozing evil.

Zeke went into full defensive mode reaching out into the ether to find this mysterious voice as Tone spun in every direction trying to find the source. There was nothing to fight and nothing to see. The two began moving in a circle with their backs to one another to prevent anything sneaking up behind them.

"Isn't that cute? The angel and his pet are all confused. If warms the cockles of heart. Or is it the other way around?" Laughter filled the ether around them that had none of the joy and mirth of true amusement. The voice was not like any demon voice Tone had heard. It had a smooth and silky quality that made one think of a sleazy, used car salesman. Hate and malice were abundant as the demonic laugh echoed off the edges of the ether.

Ezekiel's thoughts went out to Tone, "If I say 'blink' I want you to do your disappearing act. Stay visible for the moment. I do not want to give away anything if it is not necessary. Please try to keep your mouth shut and do not give it your name! This is someone I am not totally sensing yet but I think it is..."

"Zadrol? How unexpected to hear your voice," said the angel with a casual sound that he did not feel.

"Impressive Ezekiel. I'm flattered you remember me. Save me your sermon about not forgetting." The voice of the demon continued, "And no I'm not intimidated that you call me by that name. I'm thinking of taking it back as my regular name in fact."

Zeke reached out with his power and grabbed an area of nothing. As his power slowly closed around the nothingness he said, "I'm so glad to hear that. I always thought that Lordaz was too difficult to say without it sounding obscene. Do you want to appear before or after I close my grip?"

A being appeared in the middle of the grip of Ezekiel. It was small. Very small. It reminded Tone of the stories of imps he had read. It reminded Zeke of imps he had defeated. The demon was the smallest one that Tone had ever seen. There was a blue glow that was common to all demons, but this one had a very humanoid body. It was a shade of blue-gray that was not unlike an elephant's coloring. It looked like its wrinkled skin would be just as tough to pierce. It had two extra arms below its small arms that were even smaller and looked like they were meant for more intricate work. Its long thin legs were disproportionate to the rest of the body giving the impression they were made for running. Long fingers and toes made it look like it was meant for climbing and holding on to places that could be hard to hold. It was its head that made it look both odd and evil. There were four eyes that were evenly spaced all the way around its head allowing it to see in all directions. Three ears were spaced between eyes with a nose in the back in place of the fourth ear. Hairless and glowing, it wore nothing but its evil, jagged toothed smile. It surprised Tone that it looked like a doll in the area that he expected to see some kind of junk.

"You still have no sense of humor, Ezekiel." There was an arrogance about this demon that was strange considering it was surrounded by angelic power that looked ready to crush it. "Now before you show off for Rover there, can we just talk? I think we have something in common."

"Can we put a leash on him? I have always wanted a dog. He's just adorable in a so-ugly-he's-cute kind of way. Like a pug!" said Tone when he couldn't stay quiet any more.

"There you go. I knew you would talk to me sooner or later. From what I have seen you are the brains and Ezekiel is the brawn. Since my former friend is too rude to make introductions allow me to introduce myself. I am Zadrol!" The imp took a long flourishing bow. "Spawn of Hell and Chief Inquisitor of Denizens of the Demons. It is my great and mighty pleasure to meet you, oh miniscule minion of the effervescent Ezekiel. I didn't catch your name."

"He's Hell's spy," said Zeke without any enthusiasm. "He plays hide and seek with us and tries to find out what is going on. He is just barely worth noticing mostly. Now he's going home to sleep for a few decades of healing." The power that was holding Zadrol in place began to close around him. There was a momentary flash of panic in the aura of the demon before it regained its composure.

"Ezekiel. Ezekiel. Ezekiel. Why would I show myself to you if I wanted to cause any problems?" asked the demon with a false calm in its voice.

It was Zeke's turn to smile. "Because you knew I was sensing everything around here and you would not be able to hide much longer." He continued to bring the power closer and closer to the demon.

"True. True," said the demon with a trace of panic in its voice. "But consider this. What is my normal way of dealing with you? I usually kick you in the booty and then run away." Looking at Tone he said, "It is my way of counting coo, pet boy. What the heaven are you anyway? You smell human but look funny. You must be extra special to get such a coat of many colors." There was something in the voice that made both Tone and Zeke uneasy. It was as if he knew something that they did not. Zadrol continued, "Hasn't this lovely example angelhood explained the finer points of civility. It is rude not to share your name when you make a new friend." Looking at Zeke he said, "I would hope you would train him better."

"Call me Bob, new friend," said Tone thinking he had made a joke. Zeke's glow took on the shade that told Tone he was not happy at all. "What?" he said looking at the angel.

"I'll be glad to call you Bob, Anthony. But don't you think Tone would be better?" jeered the demon. There was laughter in the air as shock shown through on the entire being of Tone.

"How? What? Huh?" asked a confused Tone.

"You gave him a name. It was all he needed to find your real first name. It's a demon trick to get names so they can get more power over you. Please don't give him any more." There was exasperation in the voice of the angel. "He probably heard me call you Tone."

There was a look of false shock on the face of demon. "Ezekiel! I'm shocked and hurt that you would accuse me of eavesdropping. That would be rude and socially unacceptable and..."

"The kind of thing you always do for your masters down deep. Please stop with the drama. It gets old fast." Zeke's power had been closing closer in an attempt to intimidate the imp into giving away his game. There was not much more space to close before he would have to touch the demon with angelic power. "If you have anything to say you'd better say it soon."

"Well I'd like to know why you get a pet to follow you around and lick your heals out here when I can't bring any of the slugs in Hell out to play fetch?" Zadrol was fishing for answers and

Zeke was not about to play his game. "Come on! This is the first time I've ever seen a human soul get out of Heaven so I know things must be serious. Can you talk to your boss? I'd like my own minion following me around being impressed with all the cool things I can do, too!"

"Everyone who is confused please raise your hand now," said Tone raising his hand. Zadrol raise three.

"I'm really confused, Tone!" said the demon laughing.

"That's it," said Zeke. "Bye, bye, Zadrol!" His power finally touched the imperious imp. The effect was instantaneous. Gone was the arrogance and the humor. The smooth voice was replaced by speech that sounded like grinding stone against metal with indecipherable curses flying at the angel. There was a scream from the demon as his blue glow was dimmed to a barely perceptible shimmer. "Any last words before a few centuries of succubus sleep?" asked the warrior.

"I saw the monster!" bellowed the demon as it was writhing in pain.

Chapter 15

Zeke stopped his onslaught and pulled his power back to a safe distance from the demon. There was a look of anger and pain in the many eyes of the imp. With what sounded like major effort the smooth, silky sound of his voice was back. "I thought that might get your attention. Now, what is that worth to you? And don't even try to threaten me. We all know you need my information."

Tone who still had his hand up spoke, "Still confused here."

"So much for being the brains," taunted the demon. "Have either of you gentlespirits ever heard the saying, 'the enemy of my enemy is my ally'? I think we have a common enemy. Here is my offer. Five questions from you. Total honesty from me. Five questions from me. I know you can't help yourself, Ezekiel. And I get to ask Anthony one question."

Ezekiel spoke before Tone could say anything. "That is not going to happen, Zadrol. You overestimate your information. We can find this being without your assistance. Why would I give you any information? And there is no chance you get to ask my associate anything."

"How many more angels are you going to let die before you swallow your pride and share what you know?" The demon was making a valid point. "And I never said Tone had to answer my question. I just want to ask."

Tone tried to speak but Zeke cut him off. "Two questions each. We both can refuse to answer and get a different question. We will take turns. You will be in a spirit sphere. You will not ask Tone anything." The angel had taken on an air of authority that irritated Tone. "Those are my conditions. Take it or leave it. And if you leave it you will be crushed and sent back to Hell for as long as I can keep you there."

"Do I get any say in this?" asked an annoyed Tone.

"No!" said the two spiritual beings.

"Tough shit! I'm saying it anyway. I will gladly listen to your question after Zeke is totally satisfied with your answers," declared the human who thought he had settled the matter and helped his friend.

"Excellent Tone! And such language! That is fascinating." The demon was staring at Tone making the angel and human uneasy. "Zeke I accept your terms with one addendum. After we are done sharing information you will listen to my proposition before doing anything rash like... oh... I don't know... crushing me like a cockroach under a stiletto heel? Deal?"

The angel was looking at the human with a combination of frustration and admiration. If Anthony knew what kind of deal he was making he would be much more scared. He gazed at the demon. "Deal."

"I will even let you go first," said the demon with uncharacteristic generosity. "As a sign of good will."

"And also hoping he would forget about the spirit sphere," added Tone. "Hey Zeke. What the hell is a spirit sphere?"

Zadrol was continuing to look at Tone like a puzzle that was more complicated that he first thought. There was something about his gaze that was making Tone more and more concerned. His limited experience with demons made him think he had made a bad deal.

"Well that is also fascinating. Allow me to explain, Tone. May I call you Tone?" Without waiting for a reply the imp continued. "Tone, a spirit sphere is like a cage for demons or angels.

It contains our power so we can't do anything. While I am in the sphere that you were so kind to remind Ezekiel about..."

"I hadn't forgotten, "interrupted Zeke with some anger in his voice.

"Of course you hadn't. Keep telling yourself that." The demon turned his attention back to the human. "It also makes it so that any deceit is instantly punished by unbearable pain that..."

"Actually in your case it is monumentally unbearable pain," added the angel interrupting again.

"THAT makes it impossible to lie." The demon was actually getting irritated just as Zeke had planned. Seeing the pleasure it gave the angel, Zadrol regained his cool composure and continued. "That is also why, little human, that Ezekiel wants me in there to protect me from eating you."

"You can't..." began Tone.

"Enough talking," came another interruption from Ezekiel. *"You are giving away too much information about yourself by asking questions that you should know the answers to already,"* thought the angel hoping Tone was listening. The shift in the hues of Tone's multicolored aura told him he understood. *"I'm telling you! DO NOT SAY ANYTHING ELSE!"* Tone mimed zipping his mouth closed.

"Hmm. Fascinating. Yes. Enough talking..." trailed off the demon who had been watching them both. "So shall I get us a spirit sphere?"

There was a malevolent chuckle from Zeke. Pointing above and to the right behind the demon he said, "There is one arriving right now. I already called for one."

Tone had seen many things in his brief time in the spirit world, but he had not seen anything like this. There was a ball of energy coming toward them that was a prismatic array of colors that seemed to be constantly shifting and changing. It had many different symbols on it that seemed to shift in contrast to the colors beneath them to give them the appearance of opposite color. It made the runes look like a photographic negative of the color behind them.

As fascinating as the spirit sphere was to Tone, this was something that was even more intriguing. There were four beings carrying the sphere on what looked like yellow nylon bandages with blue spots that were wrapped around the sphere. The creatures themselves nearly looked like they had come out of a Renaissance painting. These cherubs were not exactly like Michelangelo had envisioned. They were as small as Zadrol. However, other than their size there was nothing to compare. They actually had wings! They were not the pudgy babies that so many artists like to portray. They were lean and well-muscled with those wings that were each twice the length of their bodies. And they were naked. No genitals but strangely they still made Tone feel embarrassed to be looking.

"Before you ask allow me to explain, little human," began the demon. "A spirit sphere has to be moved the old fashioned way. It can't be ported or portaled anywhere without absorbing the power being used to move it. Any being touching it will be pulled inside until the next being touching it allows it to be released. That's why the naked angels are carrying it that way." Waving to the cherubs, the demon said, "Hi guys! How's it hanging? Oops. Sorry. Nothing there."

"Said the junkless wonder," as Tone mocked under his breath.

The demon looked at Tone, "Well played, Anthony." There seemed to be an emphasis on the name. A shiver went through Tone that he unsuccessfully tried to stifle. Zadrol smiled a very evil smile showing many rows of jagged teeth.

The cherubs came to a halt beside Zeke. They all looked at him and nodded as he silently thanked them. In perfect synchronicity they moved a short distance away.

"Thanks guys!" said the imp louder than necessary.

"Are you sure want to torment them?" asked the angel.

"I do. I do!" laughed the demon.

Tone wanted to ask what the big deal was but knew better. "They do not like to talk. They do not like noise or voices and especially do not like the sound of demons. It causes them pain. He is trying to make them angry. Tell him that he won't be able to get at them like that," came the thoughts from Zeke.

"You won't piss them off. They are too cool for school! Chatting up a cherub will never get you to first base. They just aren't your type." Tone knew he should stop there but that was not in his nature. Zeke saw the shift in his aura but knew there was nothing he could do to stop it. "Although I can see why you would want to pick on someone your own size. I bet S'theno never gave you the time of day, did she?"

"That bitch would have been lucky to..!" raged the imp before catching himself. "Well played, ANTHONY." said the demon emphasizing the name. Tone felt a deeper chill trying to sweep over him that was deflected away.

"Nice try," said Tone. He had to remember to thank Zeke later.

"You seem to have an air of my deceased lost love about you. You have met her. That is very endarkening!" said Zadrol with an air of his own that seemed to smell of discovery.

Without warning the four cherubs moved with speed that made Zeke look like a sloth. They were upon Zadrol before he even noticed.

Seeing he was surrounded by angels he had previously been goading, he tried to be calm as he said, "Well since I can't stall any longer, would you mind backing off the power so I can get in that damn thing?" He was beginning to lose some of his pseudo-civility. A corridor of open space opened between the sphere and the demon. "You are so paranoid. I'm not going to steal your pet, Ezekiel." the demon moved right up to the edge of the sphere. "Is this really necessary? Can't we all just trust each other?"

The four cherubs shoved the demon who was swallowed up by the sphere.

"You really don't want to mess with cherubs. They are the fastest angels and have no sense of humor at all," stated Zeke.

"Mental note: do not piss off cherubs. Thanks for the tip," said Tone as he eyed the cherubs who were eying him right back. Tone tried to smile a friendly smile but seeing no reaction distracted himself with the sphere.

The spirit sphere was mesmerizing with the transformation occurring on its surface. It was slowing going through its array of colors until it settled on an opaque golden with blue runes that continued moving around the sphere in concentric circles. Each character moved in line with others as different sets moved in their own orbits. No grapheme ever touched another as they passed incredibly close in their movements. As the lines of runes moved faster and faster they became a blur of softly shifting blue lines on the sphere. Zeke approached and carefully waved his hand over a section of sphere where there were no runes moving. In that part, outlined by the runic lines, a pentagon shaped area became transparent showing an impatient imp with folded arms. Zadrol looked unpleasant.

"Was that really necessary? I was getting there. Can't we all just be nice to one another?" asked the demon in an attempt to save face. It was then that Tone noticed that the four cherubs were positioned in equal spaces around the sphere. He wasn't sure if they were guarding the sphere or guarding the occupant.

Zeke looked at the imp with something akin to amusement. "Well, as my friend said, it is not wise to make the cherubs mad."

"Close enough for angel work," chimed in Tone.

"Well now that we are done with the unpleasantries, I think I will go first with the questions since your little buddies copped a feel." The demon was doing all in his power to maintain the importance of his worth. "So Ezekiel... How many angels has this monster taken out?"

Zeke considered the question. He had expected this since it would serve so many purposes for the hellion. Not only would it tell the demon about the appetites of Bubba but it would also allow him inside information about the losses the angels had suffered. "There have been two," he said simply. He had considered sharing the fact that it had defeated both a warrior and a healer. To be fair, that was not information the minion of Hell had requested.

There was no reaction from the imp other than a smile that showed his pleasure at the death of some enemies. It was not a pleasant smile at all. Tone wanted to say something. He began but stopped himself. He knew that he had already caused himself more problems by saying too much. This was one arena where he was totally out of depth.

After taking a moment to savor the losses suffered by the angels, Zadrol continued. "Only two? That is a little disappointing. But I'll take what I can get. Now what would you like to know, Ezekiel?"

"What demons are searching for the monster?" asked the angel.

The imp looked surprised. "You don't want to know how many demons? Hmm. Well right now I am and," Zadrol paused for effect, "Je'relir." The look on Zeke's face said it all. "Yeah. It's like that." He was very pleased with the reaction.

Zeke stared at him in disbelief. Tone stared at Zeke in disbelief. Zadrol gazed at both of them truly enjoying the chaos that was caused. "I love it when they are speechless," mocked the demon. "Have you ever seen one speechless, Tone?"

"Once or twice," said Tone wishing that Zeke could read his mind. Turning to Zeke he asked, "You OK there, buddy?"

"Later," was all he sensed. Zeke turned to the imp with his composure reclaimed, smiled and said, "And what is your next question?"

Zadrol looked thwarted. "That's all I get? A look that says 'Oh my god! What the hell are you thinking?' and 'What's you next question?'. You are all about disappointing me." Zadrol gave them both a look that was obviously hoping for more. Seeing he would get no more entertainment he continued, "Why aren't more angels helping out with the hunt?"

Zeke had dreaded this question. In fact he had wondered about that himself. "Sorry but that is an off limits question. Try again."

"You don't know either. Or is it that you're the only one with the halo to take the job? That is fine. What I really wanted to know is, how are you planning on finding it?" came the real question from the little devil.

It was Zeke's turn to smile. "We will follow the trail he leaves." The look on Zadrol's face was priceless. It was like the shock of the angel at the name of the demon hunting the monster.

Tone broke his silence. "He is kind of cute when he has an 'Oh my god! What the hell are you thinking?' look on his face."

"What trail?!" demanded the demon. Both Zeke and Tone enjoyed seeing the ever cool imp loosing that cool. Zadrol looked from Zeke to Tone and back again waiting for an answer. The silence was driving the imp into a frenzy. "Dammit! What trail?! Spiritual beings don't leave trails here! Are you saying the monster isn't a spirit?"

"You didn't know it left a trail? Interesting." Zeke was not about to give any more information. "I think it is my turn to ask a question isn't it?"

"I do believe it is," echoed Tone.

The imp glowed blue with rage. "Ask" he spat at them.

"What did it look like to you?" inquired Zeke.

The demon was ready for that question. "Well it was not really describable." There was a sudden change in the sphere as raw energy flowed into the deceiving spirit. Bolts of golden energy hit the demon like lasers from every rune that was spinning around the sphere creating what looked like a wall of power crisscrossing the demon at angles that made it seem like Zadrol would be dissected into hundreds of pieces if it continued for very long. It mercifully stopped leaving the devil barely singed. "Ouch," it said trying to hide the pain.

"That had to hurt," taunted Tone who was enjoying the spectacular spectacle.

"Please be precise in your description of the describable," said Ezekiel who was finding an unusual amount of pleasure at the pain being inflicted. That bothered him but he would have to figure it out later.

"Well if you take a large ball of greenish gray slime and combine it with a spots of black liquid and streaks of white goo then you would have a good start. It did not have a defined form that I could see. It was flowing like your healers when they are trying to fix an angel." The demon paused. "Precise enough?"

"Thank you. Very picturesque." Zeke could sense there was something else. "Did you want to ask something?"

The demon paused as if thinking even though the angel knew it was merely for effect. "So have you got a battle plan?"

"Well, what are your plans for defeating it?" asked the angel.

A maniacal laugh filled the spirit sphere. "You don't know how to beat it either?!" The imp's laughter was joyless as it conveyed fear, panic and desperation. "We are all so totally screwed!" Zadrol was no longer thinking of answering questions.

"I guess that means they have no idea," said the human.

"No they don't. So ends the exchange of information." There was disappointment in the angel's essence.

Looking at the hysterical demon, Tone asked, "Can't we slap him around a little to get him back to his annoying self?"

"That is tempting. Normally, I'd be the first to do that. Fortunately for this demon, we have work to do and he has wasted enough of our time," replied Zeke. Looking at the laughing demon he asked, "Zadrol? Can you come back to us or shall I leave you in there?"

The laughter died down quickly as that caught his attention. "You wouldn't dare!"

"Try me!" challenged the angel.

The calm, cool, demonic spy returned to his normal self. "So now we all know a little more than nothing. Want one more question because I have several?"

Ezekiel was over the games of the imp. "No thank you, Zad." As the cherubs moved from the sphere to flanking points around Tone, Zeke touched the sphere one more time. The transparent window turned opaque and then matched the rest of the sphere. "Even though I never agreed to let him out, it is the right thing to do."

"Well, you didn't say when," offered Tone.

"Very true, but I have a hunch he may be of some use later," replied the angel as the spirit sphere began to become multicolored once again.

"I didn't know you had hunches. Any angel with instincts? That is too cool," teased Tone.

"I'm one of a kind," joked the angel with a glow that said there was some truth to what he was saying.

The sphere transformed back into is prismatic display as Zadrol was unceremoniously dropped out the bottom. His exit was neither dignified nor graceful.

"Did you make it do that?" asked the irritated imp.

Ignoring the question, Zeke stretched out his power around the demon again. "You have one chance to keep me from sending you home to heal for longer than you have ever slept. What is your proposition?"

Realization of his predicament was not slow in coming. Zadrol said simply, "The enemy of my enemy is my ally. You may not think you need me but what if you do? You know I get information like nothing else. Spare me and I will share the next information I discover without the quid pro quo."

"And you will keep your word because..?" asked the heavenly being.

"I am a stand up demon?" Zeke and Tone looked at one another and then looked at the demon shaking their heads. "Because you know how to find me and will totally kick my ass back into that damned sphere if I lie to you."

"Now that I believe," said the Tone. "It's all right. I have a trace on him, Zeke. I'll know when he finds something."

"A trace? What is that?" asked a curious and confused demon.

Zeke chose to ignore him again. "We have a deal, Zadrol. Now go before I change my mind," declared the angel.

"One last question for Tone." The demon paused, smiled and asked, "How does a human spirit get off the earth without dying?" And he was gone in the blink of an eye.

Chapter 16

"Is he really gone?" asked the human.

Ezekiel looked at the cherubs who then moved at blinding speeds all around them. They spread out in every direction examining the ethereal area for any unwanted company. After a very brief amount of time one returned and hovered in front of Zeke. With a nod the cherub verified that they were truly alone this time. "Yes," he said without any additional verbal eloquence.

"Good. Now, how the hell did he figure that out?!" asked Tone. His very glow showed his real confusion and a touch of fear.

As the cherubs were wrapping the spirit sphere with its unusual wrappings, Zeke was looking at Tone and considering all the possibilities. He was not happy with Tone at this moment. He really wanted to kick the human's ass. Anthony had not listened again when dealing with a demon. He tried to play games with an imp who was far craftier than anything Tone had ever encountered. Ezekiel continued to stare at him trying to decide the best way of dealing with this bad boy. Watching the cherubs fly away with the spirit sphere in tow the angel said flatly, "You told him."

The earthly soul was getting more agitated. "Yeah. Right. I said, 'Hey freakazoid with the funky eyes and strangely placed ears! Come on over to Te... ummm... Earth and see me!" He almost slipped and really gave away some information.

"Te? Texas? Tennessee? Tacoma? Timbuktu?" The rapid fire questions only had the effect of making Tone even more upset.

"Dammit, Zeke! What happened? I'm seriously freaking out here!" His voice was reaching a manic level. "A demon knows that I am here and on Earth. How deep is the shit I'm in?"

Zeke was torn between two options. As mad as he was he also knew that Tone was not as strong as he liked others to think. Speaking the truth in love was different than merely speaking the truth without any thought to the human's feelings. Tone needed to be taught the dangers he was facing but did not need to be scared to death. "You are buried over your head by about twice whatever your real height may be."

The tone of Tone dimmed. His normal psychedelic display became a monochromatic green. "I feel sick. Is this what being sick to your soul feels like?" There was no sarcasm in the question. It was a real and very serious inquiry. It was almost as if Tone had never experienced the feeling of disapproval that was his displeasure to feel.

"Most likely. I've never felt that." Zeke was still not letting him off the hook for his stupidity. He knew that he would not be able to take showing tough love much longer if Tone continued to look as defeated as he did now. "Do you really want to know how bad this is?" asked the angel already knowing what he would say.

"Lay it on me," said the humiliated human. "And don't sugar coat it. If I'm screwed I want to know how much lube I'm gonna need." The attempt at humor failed to amuse either one of them.

The angel used all his senses to examine his friend. Everything about him seemed to know that he was in a dangerous predicament. The only thing that could help him at this point was the truth. "Zadrol is brilliant even by angelic standards. He has a way of getting information as a superb spy. He could tell by the first time you spoke that you were not from Heaven as he first suspected. Since you did not know about a spirit sphere he also deduced you were not released

70

from Hell because most of the spheres are there for reasons you do not want to know. I could see he was trying to decide between a soul that was lost after death or a soul that was still living."

"But how the hell did he figure it out?" asked Tone who was just beginning to understand the gravity of the situation.

"S'theno was the last clue. As soon as you mentioned her he knew that you could not be lost. Had you had any contact with her and been a lost soul, you would have been dragged straight to Hell by her very capable and corrupting influence. When you said 'shit' was when he finally put one and one together. There was only one possibility and he wanted to make sure we knew that he knew. That is why he asked you that." As he heard those words from Zeke, Tone looked like he was going to fade away into nothingness. "And to be honest, if he had any doubts the look on your soul when he asked you that told him he was right. You may want to think twice before making any more deals with demons."

Tone looked at his friend with true remorse. "I'm sorry," was all he could say.

Ezekiel softened. "It could be worse, Tone."

"Um. Sure. I could have given him my address, phone number, Amazon account number, and my shoe size." That was enough tearing down. It was time to do something that most angels other than Zeke did all the time and help a human in pain.

Smiling with everything he had, Zeke continued, "Tone, if the legions of angels can't find you, do you think one little imp has a snowball's chance in Miami of finding you? Trust me on this. We have our own information detection teams who are even better at finding intelligence than Zadrol. They have tried everything they know but none of them even have a clue who you are on earth. I will be very popular with them if I ever meet you face to face."

"You damn near said 'hell' in a very inappropriate context for an angel." Tone actually smiled. "I promise you we will meet when all this is over. Just don't get your hopes up. I'm more impressive here than there."

"I'll be the judge of that." Continuing, Zeke elaborated, "Zadrol is also the most secretive demon you will ever meet. He does not give information away to anyone. Not even other demons. There is always a quid pro quo even for his masters. I doubt that he will follow through on his promise to share the next tidbit of intelligence he finds. Your secret is a piece of information that he will keep for himself as long as he can. I do not think hoards of devils are trying to find you. If we play him right they probably never will know." Zeke paused and added, "Nice touch with the trace comment. Good bluff."

Tone's aura began to brighten and started to add colors back. "Who says I was bluffing?" said the mischievously grinning human.

That stopped Zeke as he was about to build upon the foundation of positive energy he was trying to share with Tone. "What trace?" There was a combination of inquiry, hope and the beginning of joy in the spirit's core.

"Zaddy boy has a very unique trail. I can track him as easily as I can track Bubba." There was pride in Tone's voice as he continued, "The imp has an oil trail that has gray streaks. Most of the demon trails are hard to tell apart and so are the angels'. But I can see where he was hiding now that I know what to look for. I can also see he disappeared and then moved a little bit before porting away. He can't hide from us. When he is near I will just have to look for the trail." Tone had a very self-satisfied look about him.

The glowing angel glowed even brighter. There was a cautious hope in his voice as he asked, "Do you think you could discern trails of any other demons?"

71

"With some practice and time, I should be able to identify any of them just by their trail," said Tone with a renewed zeal for his position in the spirit world.

Zeke was glowing. He could see the truth in his friend's soul. He was bursting with joy. "Do you know what this means?"

"One of the biggest pains in your ass is no longer as much of a pain?" asked a smirking Tone.

"It means that you will soon be one of the most dangerous entities for demons in the Spiritscape!" declared Ezekiel.

"Say what?" asked Tone. He didn't understand the significance of this new revelation. "So I can track demons by their oil slicks. Big deal. That does not make me your pet blood hound!" He seemed offended.

Zeke was often amazed by his friend. This human had the most eclectic mind the angel had ever encountered. It was almost like there were some areas where his intellect was nearly on par with angelic mental processes. He could make deductions that were intuitive leaps beyond the norm for mortal minds. Yet there were some areas where he was lacking any trace of wisdom when applying his knowledge to situations. It seemed he could see others and outside influences with the most detailed clarity while being completely myopic when seeing how they applied to him.

"Tone, angels have been trying to track and trace the movements of specific demons in the Spiritscape since the beginning. None of us have had much more luck than being able to tell where they have been and only a few can follow them based on special sense similar but not exactly like you." He let that sink in before adding, "You may just have the ability to track and tell us who the demon is. That may make you extra special."

Tone's aura was back to its full, constantly changing luster. "So mom was right. That may be a first," joked Anthony. "Now for the sixty-four dollar question although I bet this one is worth a shit load more than that. Do you think I will be able to track Je'relir?"

There was a noticeable change in the ether around them. There was a new sensation that Tone had not seen in Zeke before: rage. The emotion was so strong that it felt to Tone like a momentary desire to see that demon devoured by Bubba. There was a history between Zeke and Je'relir that needed telling. For a brief moment Tone regretted the question, but soon changed his mind and decided that he had to know.

After contemplating this adversary for longer than truly necessary the angel spoke. "Don't go down that road, Anthony. You do not want to know."

"Let me guess. He stole your girlfriend on prom night while she was waiting in your custom sixty-five Mustang. He probably took your sweet ride too!" Tone was trying to lighten the mood with his wit. It didn't change the sense of foreboding that was permeating his very soul. Tone wondered out loud, "How are you making me feel as shitty as you feel? That is a cool trick I didn't know you could do!"

As quickly as it had hit him the feeling was gone. Ezekiel had regained his control. "I will tell you that story some other time. For now let's just say that it would not be wise to have Je'relir in the same locked room with me. Only one of us would come out."

"It would be you, of course. Right?" asked Tone. He observed every aspect of his friend. There was nothing to be seen and there was no answer forthcoming. "On a totally unrelated topic, what would happen if I started chatting with you while a cherub was around? Would that piss it off?"

Zeke looked surprised by the sudden change in topic. "It would be uncomfortable for the cherub. It would not get mad unless you were doing it on purpose." The unusual question made him inquire, "Why do you ask?"

Tone did not say a word. He just pointed. In the distance was a cherub moving at breakneck speed directly toward them. As it got closer there was a look on its face that told them it was on a mission of major importance. Zeke waited for the cherub and Tone moved behind his friend partially to stay out of the way of the cherub's and partly to have a Zeke-shaped barrier in case the diminutive angel could not stop on a dime. Tone's fears were unfounded. The angel went from full speed to stopped without seeming to pass through the speeds in between. Tone resisted the urge to say anything about how many G's the cherub had pulled.

Ezekiel opened his mind to allow his friend to hear the silent conversation.

"Greetings Ezekiel, warrior of Heaven, acolyte of Michael, Demonbane of the battle of Shraggel. May you be well and ready for battle with the speed of the cherubs to bring you victory," greeted the cherub to the warrior.

"Greetings Lom, cherub of Heaven, disciple of Iofiup, Swiftfoot of all Cherubs. May your speed be a gift to all who encounter you as the warriors protect you." The warrior returned the greeting.

"I come bearing news from my brothers, your brethren. As my three brothers and I were returning the sphere of the spirits to its rightful resting place, we encountered a being that was not unlike that which the blue glowing abomination described. It had no glow of its own but seemed to have a borrowed glow from others that was a revulsion to any who would gaze upon its visage. It was moving slowly by the pace of the cherubs and could be overtaken by a warrior's speed had one been near. If a being who is not naturally existing within this realm of the spirits were to pursue, it would find the pace of the other far too rapid for approach and capture."

Tone was not following the tedious conversation. He would have loved to shout to the tiny angel, "Please get to the point! Whatever the point is!" He knew that would not be the best choice so he waited as patiently as possible. There were ways to amuse himself imagining how cherubs would speak if they were on fire: *"Would you do me the honor of putting out the flames upon my ass?"* Or how would they ask for a bathroom key at a gas station: *"Perchance wouldst thou allowest me to useth the unlocking device since I have the uncontrollable desire to purge myself from the unwashed breakfast burrito that hath given unto me explosive bowel movements?"* Tone chuckled to himself.

As Tone looked up he saw both angels were looking at him. He realized he was laughing out loud and stopped. He mimed zipping his lips again. The cherub looked at him with a look that he could not decipher while Zeke's look clearly said, "Will you please behave for one minute?"

Zeke continued. "It is most gracious of you to share such vital information with those who are on such a mission as has never been undertaken since creation began. Might we inquire as to the location of the mysterious one who caused such revulsion?" After finishing he glanced at Tone who was doing his best to stay still while the all too formal conversation occurred in front of him. His aura was glowing in a way that Zeke knew he was laughing on the inside.

With what seemed to be great effort, Lom tore his stare away from Anthony and once again gazed at Ezekiel. "Mighty warrior, use caution in your endeavors. There is a new form of evil within this being. As it approached the waters of the river Fanjil, it drifted in and disappeared from our sight. It did appear to be flowing with the mighty current and not against it as its form was taken and stretched by the energy of fever." It looked again at the shaking human behind the warrior. "Perhaps the one who is not naturally here needs the ministrations of the mighty Raphael to cure it of the palsy that has afflicted it?"

Zeke knew better than to explain the true reason behind the humor-induced shaking of his friend. "May your speed be ever glorious to Heaven, cherub Lom. Farewell and many thanks for your assistance."

"May your battle prowess be ever glorious to heaven, warrior Ezekiel. Farewell and may your mission be a success." The cherub went from still to full speed and was gone before any words were spoken.

"Is that how they always talk?" asked a giggling Tone.

Zeke was beginning to create another portal so they could travel to the place where Bubba had been sighted. "Yes. That is how they think. That is the longest communication I have ever had with a cherub," said Zeke almost to himself. He looked at Tone and clarified. "They don't like to communicate more than a greeting since they are usually just bringing an item that can't be brought through porting or portals. When they brought the spirit sphere they just greeted me. Nothing else. The fact that Lom stopped moving the sphere to come back and tell me they saw Bubba is astonishing."

"What's more astonishing is that its name is Lom. What kind of name is Lom?" ask the human.

"Well your name is Tone? Do you really want to cast stones?" asked a teasing Zeke.

"Touché!" replied the smiling Anthony. "So may I ask a huge favor?"

"You can ask anything you want. Do I have to grant the favor?" retorted the hunter.

"You are such a smart ass sometimes. I like it!" goaded the humored human. "Can you please translate what Lom said into something I understand? I kind of tuned him out after the first... let's see... five words? But I did think of some funny ass related humor about him."

Zeke looked at his friend shaking his head. "I'm sure I don't want to know. Basically he came back to tell us he saw Bubba getting into the river Fanjil and heading downstream. I could see in his mind where he saw it."

Anthony was at a loss for words. "Why couldn't..." He paused. "He said..." His aura was vacillating between so many colors and shades that Ezekiel almost laughed. "You have got to be bullshitting me!"

Zeke actually laughed. "I'm afraid not. That is how they communicate. They are the second-most formal of the angels."

"Then I sure as hell don't want to meet the most formal!" declared Tone. "I'm serious! If I had to talk to whoever the hell is more serious than that little turd I would get in so much trouble I'd be nuked angel-style."

"You're probably right," agreed the angel. "But this is the best lead we have had since we started. Are you about ready?"

A new doorway had appeared before them that looked just like the previous one. Tone looked where the old portal had been and found it had disappeared. He approached the door and opened it to reveal the gateway.

"You know if we are going to a river I'm not a tracker anymore. I'm a fish finder!" joked Tone.

"As long as neither of us are the bait. Fishing never ends well for the bait," said Zeke.

Laughing, Tone quipped, "Once more, into the breach," as they stepped through the portal.

Tone emerged ready for anything. A hoard of demons? Been there. Evil possession? Done that. Surrounded by pissed off angels? Got the t-shirt. He had seen more than any other human since creation. He was convinced that nothing could surprise him.

"OK. That is surprising," was all he could say.

"Don't ever say I don't show you new things," said the amused angel. It was a treat to see Tone without some kind of witty repartee. Zeke was savoring the moment in a most unangelic kind of way. That disturbed him but he brushed it aside.

"So that is what passes for a river around these parts. I didn't see that coming," said Tone.

The River Fanjil was not a river in an Earthly sense. It was a bluish, greenish, gray with hints of gold. The unusual thing was there was no water in the Spiritscape. It was a flowing of the ether that seemed to move even faster than the ether that was around it. As the ethereal world of the spirit realm moved as the thoughts of those around it moved, the river moved in the opposite direction. It snaked its way opposite of the flow of the world around it. There seemed to be no river bank as the flexible tube of ether was taking a random path through this strange world. While Tone watched it he saw it seem to move back and forth, thickening and thinning at random intervals. He looked what he would have to call upstream and it seemed to go on forever. There seemed to be no ending point for downstream either.

"Zeke?"

"Yes, Tone."

"That is so bitchin'. But I was kind of wondering... What the hell is that?" asked Tone.

"That is the Fanjil. It is what we call a river. You may not have noticed but there is an energy to the spirit world around us. But our energy doesn't disperse. It just gets absorbed into the ether. When there is too much energy in one area, it naturally flows to an area that doesn't have as much. A river is born when that happens. This river comes and goes as it is needed to balance out the energy. It has been flowing for three-thousand, one hundred and eight-five quolls. I was at the battle that caused it." He considered the river for a moment. "It is my fault there is so much blue in it. Demons depleted themselves fighting me."

Tone almost thought there was some pride in his voice as he explained his role in the creation of the river. "It looks like my garden hose but without the hose. So what happens when equilibrium equals things out? And is there a lake at either end? I would love to go for a swim."

"When the power equals, the river disappears until it is needed again. This river has come and gone more than a million times throughout the battles that have been fought. It may be more accurate to call it the Fanjil Region River. There is something like a lake upstream where there is too much energy where it begins. As to swimming..." Zeke smiled at the innocence of the human. "I don't think you would want to swim in that lake or the river. Too much demon power floating around. At the downstream end the power is spread out. You could compare it to a delta at the end of a river like the Mississippi. To be honest you are not going to enjoy riding on the river that much."

"We are going boating? Awesome! It is a fast boat? Please tell me it will pull a skier. I have always wanted to learn how to ski on a river made of used up energy from a battle caused by my buddy while slaloming around floating demon body parts! It is right here on my bucket list." Tone pantomimed holding a piece of paper and made a check mark in the air.

"Michael, I'm going to need a skimmer," thought Zeke. *"And I could use a couple more eyes."* He looked at Tone. "Trust me. You will have to put a note next to that one on your bucket list saying, 'Zeke said no!'"

Tone pretended to write. "'Zeke was an old fart and party pooper.' Check!"

"I have never had gas," replied Ezekiel. Tone was not sure if that was a joke or not. He decided it was a funny even if the angel meant it seriously. "The residents of the river would definitely enjoy your company."

"Fish?" asked Tone, certain that there were no trout to be caught. "I didn't being my fly rod."

"Do you remember what I said about bait? I'm sure the pha'ards would love to try you," said Zeke knowing that would catch his attention.

"What the pha'ard?" joked Tone. He waited for a response. Zeke just looked at him. Tone stared back. The battle of wills was short lived since Zeke knew that Tone would break as he asked, "OK. Ezekiel, warrior of Heaven, hunter of demons, minion of Michael, ass kicker of imps, what the pha'ard is a pha'ard?"

Smiling at the small victory, the warrior of Heaven replied, "It is a fragment of power that has temporary consciousness. It depends on the source and how much power was used if it is helpful or harmful. Most of this river was originally demonic power so I am not counting on any helpful pha'ards. That is why it's so blue. There goes one now."

Tone looked as a dark blue spot appeared at the edge of the tube of power. As the dark spot got closer to the surface of the river, the form became clear. It looked like a mouth with large, sharp teeth. "It looks like a nightmare of a windup clicking teeth toy I have." Calling out the pha'ard he said, "Are those your real teeth or did you have crowns?"

The river flowed toward Tone unexpectedly. Though not touching the energy, the human felt dangerously close to it. The pha'ard flew out of the river, jaws opening and closing at a speed that made the teeth a blur. Just as the malevolent mouth was ready to latch on to Tone's face, angelic energy split it into a thousand pieces.

"They don't like to be teased," said Zeke calmly as he pulled his power back.

"H-h-h-holy sh-sh-shit!" stammered Tone. "Th-th-thanks."

"Look at it," ordered the angel. As Tone looked at the pieces of the pha'ard they were quickly fading into a bluish, greenish, gray mist that was pulled back into the stream. "Most of them have the look, intelligence and personality of a piranha. I hope we can find one with just a little more residual intellect that can tell us if they have seen Bubba."

Tone was still regaining his composure. Finally he asked, "Could Bubba be one of these things? Maybe he is one of them that got hungry. He did go for a swim in there."

The angel replied, "We have considered that. It could be possible, but they can't last very long out of the energy river. Bubba would have to go back in one regularly. If he is one of these then we may have found a weakness." There was a notable lack of excitement in the angel's voice.

"That would be a good thing. Right?" asked Tone, sensing there was something he wasn't being told.

Zeke smiled weakly. "A weakness would be a good thing. A pha'ard that has grown to the point that it is hunting would be a very bad thing. Bubba also seems to be very intelligent which is also a conundrum, if he is a pha'ard. Before I met you I would have said a pha'ard as big and smart as Bubba would be impossible. But you are impossible too. There are so many things that are now possible that nothing seems impossible anymore." Zeke seemed to feel the weight of the changes to his perceptions in ways that were beyond Tone's ability to understand.

"You know the Bubster could just be hunting in there. The pha'ards would be easy prey compared to angels and demons. They probably taste like tofu compared to the deep-dish demons and airy angel food cake." Anthony was trying to find a way to encourage his friend who seemed to be getting more and more pessimistic. "Or maybe he just wanted to get cleaned up. I bet he has demon oil all over his best shirt."

"Those are also possible," admitted the angel. "But even if he is eating the pha'ards that still means Bubba will be growing and getting more power. Or he could be trying to absorb some of the power flowing through the river."

76

Tone wondered out loud. "So how are we going to travel on this toxic river? I didn't bring my waders or hazmat suit."

"Our ride is arriving right now. You are going to love this." Zeke smiled for the first time since they had been considering the options of the beast in the river.

An enormous portal appeared nearby. It looked almost like the river could have flowed right through it. Instead of the river flowing into it, something came out of it. It looked like a gigantic crystal ring.

"Our ship has come in," said Zeke. Tone just looked at it with his mouth hanging open.

Chapter 17

The crystal ring was called a skimmer. The skimmer was a unique form of vessel made to ride the energy currents of the rivers of the Spiritscape. The hollow ring was large enough for an angel to be upright within it. There were two angels inside of it seeming to guide it to a halt in front of the unusual detectives.

"I take it you're impressed?" asked Ezekiel, knowing full well the answer.

The look on Tone's face and shining of his spirit told all since words seemed to have abandoned him. He was trying to take in the enormous crystal ring before him and it seemed to be beyond his comprehension. Zeke let him struggle for longer than he should. Eventually the angel came to Tone's aid.

"This vessel is the *Hajile-R*. Would you like to know how it works?" Zeke waited for the head of Tone to make something like a nodding motion. "It skims along the surface of the river. Since the river is a floating tube of energy without a bank, the skimmers have to float all the way around the river. The Fanjil will be in the middle of the ring and the ring itself will be on surface of the river. We will be able to walk all the way around the inside of the ring and see what is in the river more clearly. Think of it as a glass bottomed and topped boat."

Tone had not yet regained the power of speech as he looked from Zeke to the *Hajile-R* to the Fanjil and back. Smiling, Zeke asked, "Do I need to call Arino? Is your voice broken?"

"I get to ride in that... on that?" asked an incredulous Tone, pointing first to the *Hajile-R* and then to the Fanjil.

Laughing Zeke replied, "Yes you do. We need your help to find him, you know. Even I try to avoid going in the Fanjil any more than I must. These boats are made so we do not have to get covered in demon slime when we need to check on the rivers. They also work perfectly for someone who would be pha'ard chow like you."

"Odysseus, eat your heart out! Anything that keeps those little monsters away from me is a good thing." Tone looked thoughtful and continued, "I'd rather face demons than their leftovers."

Zeke looked at the *Hajile-R* as it was being moved into position. "You seem to have forgotten the gauntlet of demons I carried you through."

"OK. Maybe not those demons, but Zadrol wasn't as nasty as the pha'ards. At least he hid his fangs until he smiled. So how do we get this thing in the river?" asked a curious Tone.

"We don't. You get inside while I get it in the river. Let me give you a hand." Ezekiel touched a section of the crystal ring and then lifted Tone right through the wall of the *Hajile-R*. Releasing his grasp on both the ring and his friend, the wall was once again solid as Tone knocked on it and stuck his face to the side. *"Perhaps on earth he is a child,"* thought the angel.

Both the angel and the *Hajile-R* moved close to the river. With a thought from Zeke the flow of the river stopped and created an opening in the tube of energy just wide enough for the crystal ring to slide in. Zeke passed through the wall of the energy skimming vessel as the flow was restored and the *Hajile-R* began moving with the current.

"Nice parting of the river!" said the human who had the look of a kid in a candy store. "This is so cool! I don't supposed we can get one of these with a sundeck?"

The river was flowing through the center of the crystal ring as they seemed to be drifting with the current. Tone was looking at the river in the center of the ring that was much clearer through the crystal of the *Hajile-R*. As he looked at the Spiritscape around him he realized that it was both clearer and magnified as well.

"What is this thing made of?" inquired the curious human.

"This is the same material of the streets in Heaven. In Heaven you can look through the streets and see all kinds of interesting things." The angel had to add, "But you will have to wait a while before you get to see that."

Looking at the cryptic angel, Tone considered pursuing the topic. The human could tell from the look of the spirit and the few random thoughts he could detect that there was no hope of finding any answers. He decided to ask a new question. "So why did you think I wouldn't like the ride? This very cool. It is a nice leisurely cruise along the river Fanjil. The break from the fast paced spirit world is just what I needed."

Chuckling at the question, "You'll see," Zeke replied. "Tone, allow me to introduce you to our pilot and our spotter. You will understand if they keep their distance." The two angels who had been guiding the crystal ring approached from odd angles. "This is Nazilaq, our pilot. Nazilaq has the most experience on the rivers of the spirit realm. He has taken the *Hajile-R* in places that I don't even like to think about."

"Hello, Anthony. It is a pleasure to be helping you on your quest," said the simple looking angel. Nazilaq looked better than any human could ever dream of looking; but he was different than the other angels Tone had met. He was not as breathtaking as Arino and Raphael or as awe inspiring as Ezekiel or Michael. However, there was something that was difficult to explain that made Tone want to trust him. He exuded confidence and competence. He seemed like the angel version of the ship captain who makes you want to sail with him for the adventure alone.

"Naz, you have a great boat here. Call me Tone. Belated permission to come aboard, sir?" Tone saluted and smiled his most ingratiating smile.

Laughing in a way that made Tone even more confident in the angel, he replied, "Belated permission granted, Tone." Nazilaq returned the salute.

"And this is our spotter, Irkja," introduced Zeke.

The spotter nodded to the human without taking his eyes off him.

"Hi there, Irk. Do you ever get tired of people asking you if you are Irked at them?" asked Tone, trying to get the angel to speak.

"You are the first," said Irkja who was neither smiling nor frowning. The angel was not unfriendly; but it did not have the warmth of Nazilaq. Tone felt like he was being dissected under the gaze this unusual angel. "He'll do," said Irkja to Zeke as he turned his attention back to the river.

"What?" asked Tone as he looked at the oddest angel he had ever met. "He's not much of a talker. Is he a really big cherub or something?"

Raucous laughter came from the gregarious Nazilaq who said, "He is more of a looker than a talker."

"He's not that cute," retorted Anthony.

Zeke explained, "Irkja has senses that are more detailed than any other angel. He just looked you over down to the tiniest parts of your soul. He likes you."

"I can tell by the bear hug and the warm way he invited me over to his place for daiquiris when this all over," jested Tone.

Nazilaq laughed at Tone's sarcasm. When he stopped laughing, the pilot said, "If he didn't like you, you would know. 'He'll do' is about as good as it gets. That's all I get and we work together all the time. Arino only got, 'She's not bad.' Let's be honest, you've got nothing on Arino!"

"Back off sailor! She's going to Fiji with me!" laughed Tone.

Zeke was watching the banter between the angel and human. "Do either of you really think you have a chance with Arino? Naz, are you ready to get going?"

"Just tell me where you want to go," said the smiling spiritual ship captain.

"Tone, do you see any traces of Bubba in the energy stream?" asked Ezekiel.

"Bubba?" asked Naz.

"You never link do you?" laughed the warrior.

"It is more fun to hear your stories. I suppose I'll make an exception this time," said Nazilaq as he linked minds with Zeke. "I'm glad we don't need underwear," he said after learning the story.

"You should be glad. Boxers are not meant to be thongs!" declared Tone. "Zeke, I can't tell which way he went. Are you sure Lom saw what he thinks he saw?"

"I'm sure." Turning to Nazilaq he said, "Lom thought it was going downstream so let's head that way. Irkja, you know what we are looking for. Are you ready?"

"Ready," said the sighted spirit without elaboration.

"Hit the power and let's go," ordered Ezekiel.

Naz began to glow. "Power up! Here they come!" Tone screamed as pha'ards surrounded the *Hajile-R* trying to eat through the crystal to get at him. "Here we go in three! Two! One!" shouted Nazilaq.

Then the pha'ards were left far behind them as they moved at speeds that made everything seem to be moving in a blur the human couldn't process. Tone screamed louder and called for his mommy.

The disorientation of the human was not shared by the angels around him. Quite the contrary. Ezekiel seemed to be enraptured with the ride as he continually looked deeply into the river of energy seeking his elusive prey. Nazilaq was smiling his jaunty smile. The pilot was also moving his entire body as he controlled the amazing ship as it skimmed along the surface of the Fanjil. Irkja had the focus of an obsessed captain relentlessly pursuing a white whale with a look on his face that Tone would expect from Captain Ahab.

Tone was trying to wrap his mind around what was happening. He had seen this spirit world in so many different ways but this was truly the most astounding. There was nothing to hold as the *Hajile-R* traveled on the river of energy. He was just floating in the middle of a crystal ring that had a river running through it with hundreds of little pha'ards floating past. That river seemed to be carrying them to the far reaches of this endless world he had been discovering.

"I really wish I had introduced myself to you angels sooner. This is the coolest way to travel ever!" said Tone. "Do you get used to this?"

"Part of being an angel is that you are always accustomed to everything. We were created knowing all about all these things that you are seeing for the first time. However, it is a pleasure to experience them through your eyes," said Zeke looking at a group of pha'ards trying to keep up with the speeding skimmer. They were soon left far behind.

Nazilaq chimed in saying, "Well Ezekiel, some things are new to us. Right Tone?" There was a smile on his face as he looked at the unique human.

"What can I say? I'm a character," replied Anthony.

"Agreed." The agreement came from Irkja. The other three looked at him. He nodded and went back to his scanning the energy flows for clues to the elusive Bubba. He only saw a few pha'ards.

Naz, after staring at Irkja for a long time, looked at Tone and said, "You have made an impression!"

"Because he agreed that I'm a character? Let's be honest." Tone paused for effect. "I'm all about character. I know I am one. Do you think I have some character?"

Zeke answered first. "You are one and you may have a little. The jury is still out on that,"

"Tone, I have worked alongside of Irkja on and off since creation. I'm as close as he gets to having a friend. But I have never heard him make anything close to a joke. When he said, 'agreed' that was as close as I have ever heard." Nazilaq looked at his friend. "Irkja is finally starting to loosen up."

"No," said Irkja, not even looking away from his work as a pha'ard bounded off the wall of the *Hajile-R*.

Zeke and Naz laughed. Tone didn't get the joke so he asked, "Am I missing something?"

"Yes you are. That was actually funny for Irkja. It's an inside joke. I don't think you would understand," answered a lightly laughing Zeke.

"I hate jokes like...Stop!" yelled Tone.

The *Hajile-R* came to an abrupt halt. It was like the cherubs stopping since they didn't even slow down. The three angels were all on alert. Zeke was battle ready. Naz was altering the vessel so that the smooth sides of the ring morphed into sharpened blades on seven angles ready to slice anything in or out of the river. Irkja had changed from a calm, cool angel into something that made Tone more than a little unnerved. The sensory superiority took on a new look as Irkja became all eyes and ears. There were eyes and ears on every surface of the angel making him look monstrous. There were also strange dots of several different colors that seemed to be glowing brighter and brighter.

"What's wrong, Tone?" asked an energized Ezekiel.

"Something is wrong. I don't know what; but something is wrong. It's not a feeling or anything." Tone was confused. "Do you see anything, Irk?"

"I sense nothing," stated Irkja flatly.

"Skimmer spinning beginning," said a very efficient sounding Nazilaq. "Outer skin is battle ready and hardened. Charging with angel fire."

The outer skin of the *Hajile-R* began spinning while the interior stayed still. The entire boat was now a seven bladed saw that was having a churning effect on the energy in the river. There was no cavitation or aeration of the river since there was no water or air for that to occur. The effect was stunning to Tone because it caused a disruption in the flow of the river. A widening bubble of energy formed behind the ship as the river was squeezed through the blades of the ring. It reminded Tone of a garden hose with water backing up behind a narrowing spot. Now nothing could pass through the center of the ship without being sliced and diced. The river of energy was now a death trap.

"That looks painful to swim through. Like getting sucked through a propeller," observed an impressed Tone.

"I sense nothing other than the energy flow," repeated Irkja.

"It would be more like getting sucked through the turbine of a jet, but you have the right idea," said Naz. "This is more than a pretty crystal doughnut that rides a tube of energy. It is a battle ship as well. Those blades are as close to unbreakable as I can make them and they are powered up with my angelic power. The *Hajile-R* will make short work of anything in its way."

"This is such a bad ass ship!" declared Tone.

Zeke, who was still on full battle alert, spoke up, "I don't know what this would do to Bubba if he is out there. But if anything can affect him it would be the crystal!" He was still scanning the energy river but finding nothing but ever more rapidly flowing river due to the battle power of the ship.

"I sense nothing other than the energy flow," Irkja said a third time. To Tone it sounded like the angel has a trace of frustration in his voice.

Tone looked disappointed. "I guess I'm just jumpy. Sorry for the false alarm. I was sure there was something."

"Before you give up, see if you can sense Bubba's trail in the river. That may be what you are sensing," suggested the hunter.

The spiritual sailor added, "Never apologize for being safe. It is better to be ready for something that doesn't show up than not ready for something that does." There was a simple wisdom about Nazilaq that made Tone comfortable.

Tone began searching for the trail of the mysterious Bubba. Regrettably, the energy of the river had diluted any trail he may have left. Briefly, Tone thought he sensed something of his adversary in the river. He used his tracking talent, straining for all he was worth. The hint of his prey faded too quickly to be helpful. "I've got nothing," he said feeling even more dejected than before.

"I sense nothing other than the energy flow," said Irkja. Tone now saw that the angel was trying to draw their attention to the river.

"Yes Irk. We get it. You don't see anything out there. Even I don't see anything other than energy flowing. There is not a damn thing!" Looking more closely, Tone realized, "There is nothing out there. Hey guys? What happened to the pha'ards?"

Irkja actually smiled as he said, "They are conspicuous by their absence."

"Dude, you could have said, 'Did any of you dumbasses notices that the pha'ards are gone?' Would that have been that hard?' asked Tone.

"Yes," replied Irkja.

Interrupting before Tone could make any more remarks that could be inflammatory, Zeke said, "It seems likely that Bubba has something to do with this. Has he eaten or absorbed them? Are they following him trying to eat him? Did he scare them off somehow?"

"Is he pulling their teeth to make them less scary?" added Tone.

Naz laughed. "They are disturbing for you I'm sure, Tone. But you do get used to them."

Tone continued to look into the river. "I doubt it. Maybe Bubba is eating them all so they won't eat me. This means he may serve some purpose for the greater good! Or at least lesser bad."

Zeke was about to debate Tone when Irkja shouted, "Incoming!"

Chapter 18

Irkja's warning was too late! The incoming was all over the *Hajile-R* before they had time to react.

"That is what you were warning us about?" asked a laughing Nazilaq. The downstream facing section of the ship was covered with pha'ards. They were holding on to the sections between the blades and seemed to be trying to eat their way in. Most of them had been pulled through the spinning projections and been shredded. There were enough of them clinging to the outer hull to give Tone more than enough nightmares for years to come.

"You know this place may just kill my body. Between the full underwear and the heart palpitations, I may just end up stuck here." Tone was only half joking.

"You're fine, Tone," said Zeke. "Naz, why are they doing that? I'm sure Tone looks like a tasty morsel but this is ridiculous."

Nazilaq was still piloting the skimmer and manipulating the shredder. "I have never seen them willingly go into the blades. They usually run away. The only thing I can guess would be..."

"Incoming!" shouted Irkja again.

A gray blob came into view. It seemed to be pursuing something and had not noticed the skimmer with its spinning blades. Most of the pha'ards leaped out of the river and over the outward facing curve of the ship only to be caught by the outer blades and forced back into the river with not much remaining of the fragments that had been. A few glided over the hull and dropped back down into the river on the upstream side only to get sucked into the blades and made into tiny pieces. Some just tried to swim upstream through the blades with the same result.

The fragments of the pha'ards were speeding downstream into what looked like a mouth on the gray blob. There was a pause as the being stopped to take in all the pha'ards that had been shredded for it. The three angels and the one human looked transfixed at the being gorging itself on the remains of an angel and demon battle.

Zeke found his voice first. "Who and what are you?!" he demanded of the being. It stopped its feast and turned its mouth toward the *Hajile-R*. The mouth went from a gaping maw that was devouring all in its path to a toothless smile. The smile was even more terrifying than the mouth.

One word thundered out of the hideous mouth: "Dessert!" The blob lunged forward toward the crystal ring causing all within it to prepare for battle. Zeke was ready with his powerful angelic touch. Irkja was ready to relay weaknesses and use his own precision fighting style. Nazilaq caused the blades to spin faster and glow with even more angelic fire. Tone hid behind all of them since he was no use in battle. It was almost upon them when it stopped. The waves of the river of energy passing through the spinning blades in the center of the ship caused the being to be stretched out against the currents. It was not the rapid flow of river that had stopped the creature. A tendril of gray fought against the current to the outer reaches of the spinning crystal blades. "Human?" came the voice only slightly less thunderous than before as it looked right at Tone.

Zeke moved between this malevolent, malformed monster and his friend. "Who are you?!" demanded the warrior. The question was more of a command than an inquiry.

The tendril examined Zeke, Nazilaq and Irkja. A voice boomed, "Warrior. No threat. Skimmer pilot. No threat. Watcher. No threat." Moving so it could see Tone, it said, "Human. Not like any other human. Unknown."

"I get that a lot!" said Anthony. "Hey Bubba, feel free to eat all the pha'ards you want. I really don't mind."

Again Zeke moved to protect the human. "Who are..." he began.

The blades of the skimmer sounded like a garbage disposal trying to chew an entire place setting for twelve. The entity had enveloped the ship on all sides and the blades were eating into it.

Nazilaq was straining. "We are cutting it!" he yelled over the horrendous racket of the ship. "No damage to us yet. I don't know how much damaged we are really doing to it though!"

The *Hajile-R* began to shake all over and then, without any warning, it was back to its normal silence. The entity had passed over, around and through it and was moving upstream.

The ever efficient Nazilaq reported, "No damage. Changing course. Beginning pursuit." The skimmer began moving at its amazing speed as the first ever high speed chase of Bubba was underway.

"It is just ahead of us. We are gaining," came the calm voice of the ever watchful Irkja.

"And we want that, right?" asked Tone who was still not certain what had just happened.

Zeke looked at his friend. "You do know that you are what scared it off, don't you?"

"It was afraid of my rapier like wit!" said Tone. "It's just not sure what the hell I am. That's all."

The angel looked at the human. "Maybe."

"Firing at target!" shouted Naz. A ring of power went out from the ship that narrowed as it reached the being. When it touched the edge of the creature, it was absorbed. It almost looked to Tone like it glowed a little brighter as it slowed allowing them to close the distance. "That slowed it down. Firing again!" Another beam shot out toward the monster that was again absorbed. This time Tone was sure it glowed brighter.

"Hey Naz. I don't think..." Tone was saying.

"Stop firing. That makes it stronger," said Irkja over the top of Tone.

"...that is helping," finished Tone, glaring at Irkja who just nodded and kept looking at the being they were pursing.

"Try again," boomed the voice. It was taunting them. "I could use the snack!" The same laughter that Tone had heard after the death of Casadore echoed through the ship. "No? Thank you anyway. That is enough for this."

"Incoming!" shouted Irkja at the same instant that the being turned and faced those pursuing it. The amorphous blob had taken on a new look. It was no longer flowing but looked like a solid wall of gray. Tone had one of those rare moments for humans when everything seemed to be moving in slow motion. As he looked at the wall in their path he saw a face in it that reminded him of something he had seen in a movie. A man had gone face first into wet concrete and looked up with his features distorted by the quickly drying cement as those around him laughed at his misfortune. This face was not comedic at all. Evil personified would not be too strong a description. The mouth smiled. The eye winked. The skimmer slammed into it at full speed.

The ship was sent spiraling out of the river as pieces of blades flew in all directions. There was a scream from Nazilaq as they all tumbled due to the loss of weightlessness. Ezekiel surrounded Anthony as Irkja flew past and around the edges of the *Hajile-R*. Naz landed on Ezekiel and then went spinning off in the direction of Irkja. Tone was enveloped in a cocoon of angelic power that cushioned all the chaos around them.

The ship came to rest far away from the river on what seemed to be a rock floating in the ether. The skimmer had seen better days. Zeke thought it looked as if it had been through a war.

All the blades were broken or bent. There was a crack in one section that still had a pha'ard trying to eat its way through. The entire section that had been facing upstream had traces of decimated pha'ards and something akin to scratches.

"Get off of me!" came a muffled shout followed by several inaudible colorful phrases from the still enfolded Tone. "What the hell are you doing? I don't need this much protection!"

Releasing his hold and allowing Tone to move about, Zeke replied, "I wasn't just protecting you. What if Nazilaq or Irkja had crashed into you when we were falling?"

"Boom?" asked Tone.

"Big boom! Or at least a colorful substance where you used to be. There were hungry pha'ards around too," reminded Zeke. "This is where you say, 'Thank you for not allowing something bad to happen to me, Zeke.'"

"Thank you for not allowing something bad to happen to me, Zeke," parroted Tone. "Seriously, thanks. You saved my ass again."

"That's what I do. Now that we are both safe, let's see how bad it is." Zeke sounded worried.

"Come here," they heard the monotone of Irkja calling.

When Tone and Zeke made it to the far end of the skimmer they saw what had concerned the watcher. Nazilaq was injured. Both of his hands were separated from his body and floating in the ether outside the ship. They had drifted out through the hole in the side of the *Hajile-R* that had not been there before.

"That hurts," was all Naz could say as he tried to smile.

"Arino!" called Tone. "Get your cute little ass over here!"

"She and Adoneal are both on their way," said Zeke.

"Who? What is an Adoneal?" asked Tone.

Before anyone could answer, a voice said, "That would be me."

"I really hate it when you angels sneak up on us poor defenseless humans like that. It's not good for my heart and it's rude," Tone said while looking for the voice. Zeke shot him a look that glowed showing what would have been a raised eyebrow on a human. Tone ignored his friend as he looked and saw a simple angel standing near the *Hajile-R*. There was nothing special looking about the spirit. Tone thought this angel must be a boat mechanic.

"My apologies young human. How may I serve you today?" asked Adoneal.

"Our boat is broken and so is our Nazilaq," stated Tone. "Just as a side note, who the hell are you and where is Arino?"

Irkja looked at Tone with a strange glow about him. Zeke gave him a look that said, *"Behave!"* Naz just looked at him with no real reaction since most of his energy was going toward being conscious.

Moving to Nazilaq while looking at Tone, Adoneal replied, "I have nothing to do with Hell. My name is Adoneal and I am the archangel of those who serve. Leading them is my great honor."

"You're Naz's boss. Got it. What's your special mojo?" asked Tone. The ever calm Irkja looked like he was about to lose his composure as his steady and steely gaze was nearly shooting lasers at Tone.

"Please pardon Anthony, Adoneal. He does not understand our ways." Looking at Tone, Zeke continued, "He needs to learn to show more respect to one of the most honored and powerful ARCHANGELS in creation."

There was a concern that Tone had not seen when dealing with Michael or Raphael. *"Perhaps since he is not named after a ninja turtle he is more sensitive,"* thought Tone.

"It is understandable," said Adoneal. "I have neither a mo nor a jo, young human. I exist to serve."

Tone looked from the archangel to the warrior to the watcher and back again. "Was that a joke?" he asked not sure if he should laugh.

"Humor is not a concept that I am able to address. Please forgive me if I do not comprehend your statements." With those words from Adoneal Tone decided to have some fun.

"Please accept my apologies if I have offended you," began Tone amicably. Then the mischievous glow shined brightly. "It was not my intention to piss you off." Irkja began moving toward Tone after that inflammatory remark. Ezekiel stepped in the way.

"Since it was not your intention to 'piss me off' then I shall choose not to be pissed off," said the archangel. Tone froze in place unable to believe what he had heard. "And since I have no idea what pissing someone off is, I will trust that one of you will explain that to this human. And yes, I am the leader of both Nazilaq and Irkja. I have work to do. Irkja?" Without another word of acknowledgment, Adoneal and Irkja moved to the battle-scarred ship and began the process of examining the blades that had been broken in the attack.

Tone moved to be right next to Zeke and the injured Naz and asked, "Did an archangel just say 'piss me off? Please tell me I heard that right! If he really said something else, I'm begging you to lie to me and tell me he really said 'piss me off'!"

"Adoneal is unique," replied Zeke with some hesitance. Tone could tell he was holding something back. "He does not concern himself with human issues or human idioms. He is all about taking care of the amazing and the mundane things that are needed to keep things working. Without Adoneal doing what he does the others angels could not do their jobs. He takes care of those who take care of the behind the scenes items like ships. He is the archangel that both Nazilaq and Irkja follow."

"Dude! He said the word 'piss'! What the hell?!" asked a still astonished Tone. Ezekiel was trying to avoid explanations and had determined not to allow his friend to nose his way into something that was not his business.

"It is our fault," said a very sweet voice nearby. Arino had appeared when Tone had been distracted. She was in her amorphous form healing the injured Nazilaq. "Allow me to coordinate the healing of Nazilaq and I will answer your questions."

"But babe, he said 'pissed off'! You gotta tell me now! It's killing me!" said a very excited Tone.

Zeke intervened. "Then you will have to die. Tone, it's none of your business." He paused as he gazed sadly at the healer. "But if Arino wants to tell you she will. Right now just please be quiet and watch. This will be interesting. Trust me."

"Thank you, Zeke," said a glowing Arino. "Tone, can you please move back. I don't want any accidents."

Zeke and Tone both moved away from the healer and the ship. "Why are they just looking at the skimmer? Shouldn't they be putting it back together?"

"Watch," said Zeke.

Arino moved her patient to be near the damaged *Hajile-R*. No words were spoken as the three angels knew what to do and began to work simultaneously. As Arino began reattaching the severed limbs of Nazilaq, the archangel and the watcher moved the broken blades back into place. Irkja moved three of the broken blades into place and looked like they were ready to be repaired. It was Adoneal that was truly amazing to watch. Every other broken blade was being moved into place by the blurred form of the archangel moving his arms to place them where they needed to go. It was then that Tone noticed that either there were more arms on the angel than he had noticed earlier or they were moving so fast it looked like there were more arms. Even as he watched the amazing spirit work he was still not certain.

The more than a hundred broken blades and the two hands reached the point where they became whole at the same instant. Somehow Adoneal had made them all arrive in the reattachment point at the same instant. Arino glowed with healing power on Nazilaq as Adoneal glowed with repairing power on the *Hajile-R*. A transparent shield of warrior power came up between Tone and the odd healing and mechanical work happening courtesy of Zeke just as a burst of angelic power sealed the severed hands and the severed blades.

"That was cool," said Tone. "I think." Looking at the now recovered Nazilaq and repaired skimmer he asked, "Are they connected?"

Zeke looked at his friend with renew amazement. "Very good, Tone. Yes they are. The skimmer is an extension of Naz. He has total control over it. On the down side, while he is linked to it, when it is damaged so is he. But on the reverse end, without Naz the skimmer has no power. It is just a crystal ring. Keep watching. Adoneal isn't done."

Almost on cue, the archangel approach the skimmer as the blades morphed back into the crystal of the smooth skin of the ship. With no exertion, Adoneal lifted the gigantic crystal ring in one hand and began to spin it around. It moved faster and faster as his other arm took on the appearance of several as it moved all over the ship repairing the hole in the side and the many cracks and crevices created by the crash. The skimmer spun faster and faster as the angel removed the remnants of pha'ards and the many dents and dings that made it look like it was the last used skimmer on the lot. When he was done he released the floating skimmer and looked at the angels and human.

"I am needed elsewhere. Is there any other service I can provide?" asked the archangel.

"Thank you for all you have done, Adoneal. I appreciate your time," said a now recovered and smiling Nazilaq. Without another word the archangel was gone.

"Well I feel good. Thanks Arino." Nazilaq looked at Irkja. "Let's get back on the river. We have a Bubba to follow." Irkja followed the pilot back through the solid wall of the ship as it moved back toward the river.

"We better get back in there too, Tone," said Zeke moving toward the river hoping that his friend was not going to press the issue about Adoneal.

"Hold your horses there wing-boy. This lovely example of feminine angelhood promised me a story with fairies and unicorns and ogres and goblins." Tone was looking at the now angel appearing Arino. "So why is mister mechanic such a savant?"

With more than a little trepidation, Arino began, "Adoneal was once just like any of the angels and was created to be the ultimate servant of all. He created so many of the devices used in the Spiritscape that we take for granted. You have already seen two of them."

"The skimmers and the spirit spheres, I'm guessing?" said a now serious Anthony.

"Correct. Anything you see that is a tool that we use was created by Adoneal. He still has the most amazing way of creating whatever we need. Any of us can make things that we need from time to time but he is extraordinary. He always has been and always will be," said Arino with admiration in her voice.

Zeke reluctantly took over the story. "He was repairing a spirit sphere in the field because we needed it to contain a particularly nasty demon. Six warriors had it surrounded while he was placing the last rune on the sphere. Adoneal called out to me to let me know it was ready and the demon took that moment to strike. I wasn't ready and when it hit me I was stunned. The demon was on me in before I knew what had happened and struck. Adoneal threw himself in the way and took the hit meant for me. He was phased apart worse than any angels I had ever seen. This demon was brutal and very powerful. He is one of the worst of the archdemons." Zeke stopped with the story truly saddened and ashamed of what had happened.

"Zeke it wasn't your fault. You couldn't have known that abomination had that much power. None of us did." Arino was trying to comfort the warrior. Turning back to Tone she continued, "The warriors were jumped by over fifty demons who took the phased pieces of Adoneal to all parts of the spirit world. A couple even tried to get back into Hell with them but Zeke intercepted them and left them in tatters. All the phased parts of Adoneal were recovered but Raphael had been injured that day while trying to recover a piece of Adoneal. It fell to D'vrash and I to heal the phased Adoneal before his parts had degraded too much."

"Well it looked like you did a good job. He is amazing at what he does," said an uncharacteristically caring Tone.

There was a dimmed sadness in her normally glowing eyes as she continued. "We restored his spirit, but I had to make a choice. There was a piece that was damaged in his essence where his inventing power resides. It had degraded too much. Without it there was no chance that he would ever be able to serve in the way he had. I knew what he wanted and I had to use part of his personality essence to fully restore his inventing power. It made him even better at invention and repair..." Arino's voice trailed off. "...but he lost so much." Arino paused, gathered her composure, and continued. "He can never again link with any other angels. He will never know all that we know because that part of him is damaged. He cannot recall the time before his accident other than perfect recall of all he made. He doesn't even know most of our names anymore."

Tone was in shock. No smart ass remarks came to his mind. There were no words to comfort the two angels who had helped him the most. After looking at the angels all he could think was to ask, "Did you ever get the demon?"

Zeke glowed with rage. "No. But we just may have a chance soon." There was an iciness in Zeke that Tone had only seen one other time.

"You don't mean that it is Je'relir do you?" asked Tone, hoping and praying that he as wrong.

"Yes. The demon that's tracking Bubba is the one who caused all this pain," said a barely contained Ezekiel. "I would gladly feed Je'relir to this beast before we destroy it."

Chapter 19

"We need to get back on the river," said Ezekiel as he moved away from Tone and toward the *Hajile-R*. The discussion was over and the demon hunter was not going to allow any more words.

"Hey Arino. What just happened?" asked Tone. He had seen his friend in a new light.

Arino was nearly as befuddled. "I'm not sure, Tone. I knew there was some animosity toward Je'relir, but this is something new. Let me check something. I will be right back." Arino ported away but was back before Tone had caught up with the quickly moving Zeke. "Please stay out of this no matter what happens."

"Why do I not like the sound of this?" asked a very wary Tone.

Smiling at the human, Arino said, "Because you're not stupid." She laughed as she approached Zeke with Tone in tow. "Good news, oh great hunter, you now have your own guardian angel." Arino's eyes glowed even brighter as she bowed.

Zeke looked at the healer with a combination of happiness and leeriness. "I'm glad to have you with us Arino but aren't you needed elsewhere? I'm sure there are several battles that need your skills more than we do." Zeke was aware that there was more to her presence than helping them with wounds.

"We all have our orders. Yours are to find the mysterious beast killing angels and demons and protect our favorite human in the process," replied the feminine spirit. She glanced at Tone who was doing his best impression of a blush. "My orders come from Raphael. I am to keep you all functioning and healthy and to fight if necessary. You, my dear Ezekiel, are stuck with me."

"And this way you can check on me to find out why I am not acting like myself?" asked Zeke.

"Now Zeke. We both know what's going on. Have no doubt, I will do whatever it takes to keep you safe no matter what the danger may be." There was a fire within the healer that took both Tone and Zeke off guard. "And for my first order of business I will be to sense you and make sure that you are still truly you."

The tension between the two best friends could be sensed even by Tone as Irkja and Nazilaq watched from within the skimmer. Zeke stared at Arino for a moment but said, "You are the healer. Please sense me and let's be sure this is what we think it is. But can we do this once we are underway? There is a dangerous Bubba on the loose."

Arino giggled hoping it would have a calming effect on Ezekiel. Tone loved that giggle. It made him think rather unholy things about this holy angel. He was still wondering what the hell they were talking about right in front of him and still managing to leave him in the dark. Angels could be such pains in the ass sometimes.

"Of course Zeke," beamed the healer. "Let's go ride the wild river! I'll get Tone and myself in the skimmer if you will do the honors."

Arino and Tone passed through the walls of the skimmer. To Tone it seemed to be taking more time than before. Zeke once again split the river to allow the *Hajile-R* to get in position. He ported and appeared beside them as the current took the ship.

"So we are now a five-some? I must say the additional crew member is definitely an improvement over the three of you!" said a charming Nazilaq.

"Arino," said Irkja, nodding to the healer before turning his attention back to the river.

Tone spoke up. "I think that is Irk's way of saying, 'Hey pretty angel. Glad you're here! Wanna do some tequila shots?'"

"I have a feeling that you may have done a few more tequila shots than Irkja," said Arino, laughing. Irkja looked up, nodded at Arino and shot an ambiguous look at Tone. Turning her attention to Zeke she said, "Please give your orders and I will start my work." She transformed into her healing form and moved to examine the warrior.

"Follow that blob!" said Tone. "Did you get a license number cause I didn't. Irkja, did you catch the tag on what hit us?"

"No," was all the watcher said.

"Are you still pissed at me for playing with your archangel? Dude, you really need to lighten up." Seeing that was not making any headway with Irkja he added, "For what it's worth, I'm sorry. I didn't know the whole story. But I really do understand and did not mean anything by it. It's just the way I am."

The watcher was watching Tone carefully and intently. After a tense silence he said, "Forgiven." He then returned his penetrating gaze to the river before them.

"Now that you two are buddies again, let's get moving," said Zeke. Turning to Naz he said, "You heard the human. Follow that blob."

Laughing, Naz reported, "Moving upstream in three, two, one." The skimmer shot off after the killing machine that had nearly destroyed them. "By the way, this is the improved model. Adoneal made some... changes. Let me share." Naz opened his mind for all of them.

The *Hajile-R* was not the same as it had been. The angels had noticed that it was different but not the full extent. Tone hadn't even noticed but that was not surprising since it required senses he did not possess. The skimmer was now hotter than it had been. Adoneal made it able to take more of the angel fire of the pilot to be able to attack with more power. Since the angel fire had only charged the creature for attacking, the vessel was now able to transform angel fire into a reverse of that attack. It could pull angelic power out of anything it touched. That draining power was an experiment to find out if that could be used to battle the beast. A new part of the mission was to try the new weapon if they had another encounter.

There was also a new defensive capability of the skimmer. The entire hull had been thickened and strengthened explaining why Arino and Tone had taken longer to pass through. Not only was the outer hull thicker and stronger, there was a medial hull that would have to be breached before another hole could be punched through the inner hull. The outer hull blades had been repaired but the number and length of the blades had been doubled. The blades also now moved in eight circles but alternating directions. It was truly a battle ship ready for battle.

"When did he do all that?" asked an impressed Tone.

The captain winked at the human, "You watched him do it. He also created all that on the spot when he saw the damage. That is what makes him Adoneal."

"Damn! He's good!" said the human.

"He's great," corrected Irkja. Tone and the watcher shared a look that truly solidified their reconciliation. Agreeing about the archangel was rather timely since he appeared beside Zeke.

Adoneal addressed Zeke. "Warrior. Your archangel requested this for the human. It may be something he needs in the very near future. Please use caution. It needs to be placed on the arm of his choosing." The inventor handed Zeke a crystal case and ported away without another word.

"That was unexpected," stated Zeke. "Tone, I think this is for you. Is it your birthday?"

Tone was bursting to know. "What is it? What is it? What is it?" Looking at the crystal package and then looking up with a bewildered look, he asked, "OK. So what is it?"

Nazilaq spoke first. "You have to open it, Tone. I wonder what kind of device they have made for you."

"Tone, you just have to touch the top of the crystal. It will only open for the one it is made for. That would be you, my friend." Turning to Irkja, Zeke asked, "Are you seeing anything Irkja? I don't see any pha'ards."

"Only energy flow. Nothing else yet," said the watcher. "I will alert you."

Tone reached out and touched the case. It slowly dissolved revealing one of the most amazing things Tone had ever seen. Floating in the ether was a crystal knife with all kinds of runes on it. As he looked at it the runes seemed to be continually morphing into different forms. The crystal was different from the walls of the skimmer because there was lightening inside of it that seemed to be ready to fly out of the blade.

"Cool knife! That is for me?" asked Tone. He looked around at the angels and saw them all staring at the knife. The ever efficient Naz had stopped the skimmer and looked like he wanted to hold the knife. Irkja was in his full sensory, slightly creepy mode with far too many eyes and colorful spots all focused on the blade. Arino had returned to her normal angelic form and was smiling and giggling like a little girl who had caught Santa Claus putting gifts under the tree.

"Tone, you have no idea what that is, do you?" asked the awestruck Ezekiel.

"Well it looks like a very cool knife with lightning bolts shooting around inside of it," declared Anthony. "But based on your reactions, I'm guessing that there is something that I'm missing."

"You are missing something," said Irkja. "I have only seen one of those before today. That is a H'tes."

"First, you must be impressed because that is the most words I have ever heard you say at once!" said Tone. "Second, let's assume the human is a dumbass and does not have access to all the knowledge of the angels since you keep thinking too much for me to read you. Third, can someone please explain to me what a Heat-S is?"

Zeke looked at Tone with a leery look that went all the way through his spirit. "Have you ever wanted a weapon that could send a demon straight back to Hell?"

Ezekiel was beginning to enjoy seeing Tone speechless. It was happening more the deeper he got into the Spiritscape. Now things were changing rapidly. Michael had commissioned a H'tes from Adoneal which meant that the situation was becoming more dire. What had happened while they had been on the trail of the beast?

Arino approached Zeke and Tone smiling. "You wanted him to be able to defend himself. Now he will be able to."

Zeke looked at her with his glow showing his disbelief. "Do you know what that can do?" he asked pointing to the blade. "If he bonds it to himself he is committed. There is no going back." Turning his gaze on Naz he said, "Get the skimmer out of the river. I need to make a call and I don't want to leave you shorthanded."

The skimmer was steady as Irkja moved through the wall and stopped the energy river to allow it to slide to the side. With Zeke porting away to talk to Michael the remaining angels were all gazing at the H'tes. Tone was still mesmerized by the floating knife that was meant for him. He found himself both drawn to it and afraid of it at the same time. His hand reached out to take the weapon when another hand came between he and the blade.

"My friend, you may want to wait a moment. Let Zeke come back before you take the blade," said Nazilaq.

Tone yanked his hand back quickly to avoid touching the angelic sailor. "Dude! Be careful! I have a bad habit of making angels blow up!" Looking back at the H'tes he asked, "What's the big deal? It's for me. Why can't I just touch it? Will it hurt me or something?"

Arino's calm voice soothed the very ether around them. "Tone, it is not as simple as all that. That is not a pocket knife. That is a very dangerous blade. Zeke was not kidding about sending a demon to Hell. It will do that and much more. But it is not my place to tell you all about it."

"But why can't I just touch it?" nagged Anthony, bouncing in the ether. He looked like a kid who had just gotten a birthday present he wasn't allowed to touch.

Irkja added his commentary. "Trust me. Wait for Ezekiel." There was something in his voice that sobered Tone up immediately. Looking at the quiet watcher, he saw there was something about the glow of Irkja that had changed. He seemed both amazed and afraid.

"Irk, are you okay?" asked the concerned human.

"Yes," replied the watcher without elaboration. The two gazed at each other as if they could read more from their essences. It seemed to be a meeting of the minds and spirits that was something that could not be expressed with mere words. At last, Irkja nodded to Tone as he turned his attention back to the river flowing past them.

Zeke's voice startled Tone as he reappeared while speaking. "Tone, you may touch the H'tes. But you need to know what it is first. I will clear my spirit to allow you to truly understand what this gift can do. But you need to know that it is dangerous for you."

"Enlighten me!" said Tone with his enthusiasm returning.

Sharing knowledge was becoming something at which the odd detectives were becoming adept. Tone saw it in the mind of the warrior. H'tes blades were something that no angel or demon could use. Even touching a H'tes was something to be avoided. It was made of the crystal of heaven but had the power of angel fire within it. If it was used against an angel, it would be painful but not devastating. Stabbing an angel or merely touching it caused a draining of angelic power that would be stored within the blade. Stabbing or even prolonged touching could lead to severe depowerization causing a fading and eventual phasing.

It was demons who feared the sight of these blades. Angel fire could be sent at a demon from a distance that would be as ferocious a warrior's attack. That attack was enough to hurt all but the most powerful demons. The true power in the H'tes was as a slicing and stabbing weapon. The slice from the H'tes would send those same angelic flames into the wound caused by the heavenly crystal. Even the most powerful archdemon would be infected with slowly spreading angel fire that would eventually consume the demon causing it to speed back to the deepest recesses of Hell to heal for at least a century. However, a straightforward stab would cause the same angel fire to be sent to the very core of the demon causing instant ruin. That demon would be sent to those same recesses of Hell, but for an even longer stay for healing.

The truly frightening feature of these angelic blades was the owner. Each of the first two blades had been used by two humans throughout the history of the universe. But each blade would bond to the human for a lifetime. Once bonded the blade would never be laid aside. It was attached as part of the spirit of the human. When the human's life ended and they entered their eternal reward the blade would be surrendered and the human would retire from their role as blade keeper for a special place in Heaven for eternity. This was only the third H'tes ever created. And it was made solely for Anthony.

"Are you shitting me?" asked Tone. "This is really a blade that drains angels and kills demons? How totally freaking cool!"

Zeke formed a new crystal case around the blade to prevent Tone from making any rash decisions. The angel placed his hand on his friend. "The archangels have decided that you need this. It is for defense only and they are not going to make it an eternal bond. Just a temporary one...for now."

"For now?" asked Tone. "How long do I get to keep the H'tes? And why don't I get to keep it for the whole lifetime bond thingy?"

Zeke smiled. "You keep the H'tes as long as Bubba is on the loose. I doubt that it will do much good against whatever Bubba is; but it will be helpful against any demons. As to why you don't get to keep it," there was a glint in the angel's entire spirit as he said, "they don't know who you are. It will be up to me to decide if you get an eternal bond when we meet face to face."

Turning on all the charm Tone said, "Zeke, old buddy, old pal. Can I get you anything? A sandwich? A nice ale? A date with Arino?" Looking at the healer he said, "I know you want me but it's for a good cause, babe!"

The warrior ignored the insincere flattery. "Tone, you are only the third human to ever be offered this honor. If you touch the H'tes it will never be used by any other being. It is dangerous to all of us. That is not what concerns me. It will make you a target once the demons know you have it. Are you sure? Please think this through."

That caught Tone's attention. "Wait a sec! What the hell are you talking about? By target do you mean that they will be looking for me here and on Earth?"

All four angels saw the change in the glow of the human. It transformed from its usual psychedelic shifting colors to a solid shade of teal with his love level dropping significantly lower. It was unusual for Tone to wear his feelings and thoughts on his aura. It was usually glowing and changing as he constantly showed his smart ass nature throughout every mood. This time he was showing real fear.

Arino looked at the human and asked, "Are you all right, Tone?" She was genuinely concerned. She was also curious about his identity on Earth and believed there may be a clue in this change of character.

"I'm fine. Just answer the damn question!" demanded Anthony.

"Yes. If they discover you have the H'tes they will make you a target. And if they discover who you are on Earth you will be a target there as well. We can prevent that from happening." Ezekiel, the second greatest warrior of the angels, touched his friend's hand. "You do not have to take it. It's all right. I can protect you."

Nazilaq and Irkja were watching the reaction of the human. Tone looked from Naz to Irkja with a near pleading in his spirit. "What do you two think? I honestly don't know what to do."

Nazilaq spoke first. "Considering that you may be a target already anyway thanks to the imp, what harm can it do? At least you can defend yourself if needed." Tone nodded to the angelic captain, acknowledging his thoughts.

Irkja added, "You do not have to keep it past this adventure." That was all he had to say.

"You are both right," said a somber Tone. "But I really don't want the demons after me. But you really are right. I'd rather have it for now. If I need it and don't have it I'll really kick my own ass before the demons can."

The warrior turned to the three other angels and said, "We will be right back. I'm taking Tone to the Council."

"Are you sure you want to do that?" asked Arino with a giggle. "You know how he gets around archangels."

"I resemble that remark!" declared Tone. He had regained his usual colorful appearance. "How many archangels are there anyway?"

"Ten" said all four angels in unison.

Zeke replied, "I have some reservations about this but I want them to meet Tone. He does make an impression."

"I can do a good Groucho, too!" joked the human. "Dude, you have to take me there now. I will behave."

There was something in his spirit that said he was telling part of the truth. Even Irkja was curious about this when he asked, "Really?"

There was a look of mock offense on the human. "Of course I will. Everything I do is behavior of some kind."

Nazilaq laughed. "Always ready with a loophole. I wish I could watch this. Zeke, pay close attention for those of us who have to get back to work."

Zeke looked at the other angels as he began making a portal. "We will be back by the time you have the skimmer back on the river. Do not leave without us."

"You got it, warrior," said the captain.

"Tone, please try to behave and avoid some of your more colorful euphemisms," said a smiling Arino. She knew her words were meaningless to the human. At least she had tried to do her part,

"Later," was all Irkja said to the duo as the portal finished forming.

Zeke turned to the human and said, "They are expecting us. Are you ready?"

Tone's excitement was palpable. "After you, warrior," he said with a bow. Before Zeke could respond or even move to the portal, Tone winked, opened the door and was gone.

"Lovely," said Zeke as he followed his friend.

Chapter 20

The portal took Tone where he wanted to go. It was nothing like he anticipated. He had expected the Council of Archangels to be in a grand cathedral with ten angels sitting in a circle in tall, ornate chairs. In his imagination, the archangels were robed in glorious white robes that gleamed so brightly it was nearly painful to stare at them for more than a few moments. He would be placed in the middle of them in some kind of special circle that would limit his power on them while they were trying to delve into all his mysteries. He would be forced to turn constantly to answer the plethora of questions they would use to uncover who he really was on Earth and why they could not discover it.

Or perhaps they would try to lull him into relaxing around them by having a great room. There would be walls that looked like they had been made from centuries old cedar logs laid upon one another. The focus of the room would be the stonework fireplace that was large enough for eight Tones to stand side by side without touching one another. The blazing fire would create a warmth to the room that would heat his soul in ways that he had never known. The fuel for the fire would be burning without being consumed by the flames. The log walls would be filled with works of art from all of Tone's favorite artists. From Monet to Degas to Escher to Vincent and Leonardo. All would be there for his perusal and enjoyment to distract him as they asked him all the questions to secret out all his secrets.

The council was not like either of those paradigms that Tone had imagined. The council room was dark with only the glow of the portal to light it. There was no one and nothing to be seen. As Zeke came through the portal behind him the gateway closed leaving them in complete darkness.

"Don't worry. It's not as bad as you think, Tone," reassured Zeke. "But you didn't give me a chance to tell you what was going to happen."

A soft hum began all around them. It was gradually growing louder as Tone replied, "I thought you said that we were going to the Council of the Archangels. Are we really in a theater? Please don't tell me I missed the previews. That is the best part of some of the movies I've seen."

Zeke pondered Tone's nonsense as the hum was growing louder. "No, Tone. We are not in a theater. We are in the Council of the Archangels, but there is something else we are in, too." Tone looked confused so Zeke explained. "Adoneal has made you your very own, specially made, one of a kind, spirit sphere. You are inside of it."

Tone tried to look stunned. He failed. "I take it that they don't trust me not to do something silly like... oh... I don't know... blow them up?" The sphere began to vibrate lightly.

"It has been known to happen," answered the warrior.

"You blow up one angel, phase him apart, and have to put the pieces back together and you're branded for life!" joked the human as the humming and vibrating stopped.

The walls around them were becoming a lighter shade of black. The darkness faded to be replaced by a gray with golden highlights. Quickly the highlights became the primary color and the gray became the highlights. The gray faded to reveal golden walls with green lines crossing at odd angles. As Tone looked more carefully he saw that the walls of the spirit sphere were not golden but it was the area around them that was. Unlike the spirit sphere that Zeke had used on Zadrol, this one was transparent on all sides with the rotating runes making the lines around them. The room containing the spirit sphere containing Tone was a sphere in its own right. Up and down; left and right; in front and behind; everywhere was a brightly glowing gold. But as expensive as the room looked, it was still missing something that would be handy for a Council of Archangels.

"Hey, Zeke. Shouldn't there be more archangels here?" asked Tone. "It is a little lonely with just the two of us. Not that you're not excellent company; but I do so enjoy meeting new archangels to piss off."

"They will be here in momentarily. I just have to do something first," said Zeke as he touched the wall of the spirit sphere and was suddenly on the other side. He smiled at his human friend and said, "Now you try it."

Tone reached out and touched the sphere just as Zeke had done. Nothing happened. He knocked on the wall and still nothing happened. A kick at the wall sent him flying backward only to hit the rear wall of the sphere and bounce back to where he had begun.

"You enjoyed that one, didn't you?" asked the human.

"Oh yeah. Count on it." Zeke was smiling. "Now if you would be so kind as to read my essence. I am not doing anything to make it too busy to read,"

Tone tried to discern what was going on within his friend and was frustrated in every one of his senses. "Now that is just not nice!" declared Tone. "So this is how you feel around me all the time? How annoying!"

"Welcome to my world," said the amused angel. "In more ways than that." The smile was one of mischievousness that Tone was getting accustomed to seeing on his friend.

Tone didn't even tried to hide his delight in his friend's amusement. "You sneaky little bastard! You have come so far so fast!"

Tone turned involuntarily to face an area of nothing as an unknown and invisible archangel spoke up. "Does Anthony know that we are not creatures that worry about parentage?"

Another voice spoke up as Tone was spun by some invisible force to again face nothingness. "Perhaps he does not understand our origins."

Tone spun a new direction to face another voice saying, "Don't worry. He understands. That was his way of bonding with Ezekiel. I have seen him do it before."

"Raph? Is that you old buddy?" asked an excited Tone. "So that is how you sound when I'm not stoned out of my gourd on your voice. Very relaxing tone, if you'll pardon the pun." After thinking a moment he said, "Even if you won't pardon the pun!"

The archangel of healing spoke again as Raphael faded into existence nearby. "Hello Tone. It is good to see you and be able to carry on a conversation with you." Raphael laughed a musical laugh that made Tone laugh in response even though there were no mystical affects manipulating his. It was just that kind of laugh.

Tone spun down and to the left as another voice spoke. "So this is the human who can break all the rules. He does not look like any human soul I have ever seen and I have seen all of them after they have died." The speaker became clear as the voice seemed to echo through the spirit sphere. This angel was gender neutral; but in spite of the androgynous nature there was obviously an aggressiveness about it. "Hello Anthony. My name is Gabriel. I am the archangel of the messengers. We are the ones who are having such a difficult time locating you on Earth. I do not suppose you would care to tell me where you are."

"Gabe! I have read about you! How are the wings? Why don't any of you have wings? It's kind of a letdown without the wings and halos." Tone was deliberately avoiding the question by trying to goad the angel. It did not work.

Zeke faced Gabriel. "I'm sorry, Gabriel. He is very protective of his secret identity."

"It is not your fault, Ezekiel. Some humans are just difficult to deal with," replied the messenger.

"I am not difficult to deal with!" declared Tone. The three angels he could see all looked at him with the same disbelieving look. Zeke and Raph also looked amused. Gabriel didn't. "OK. Maybe I can be challenging on rare occasions, but it has been a rough day."

Another familiar voice rang out as Tone was spun in yet a new direction. "I had no idea that rare occasions happen so frequently, Tone," said a quickly forming Michael.

"Hey, Mike. What can I say? I'm a rare one all on my own!" joked the human. "By the way, why am I spinning like I'm in one of those concentric ring spinney things? I'm starting to get dizzy and I didn't take any of my roller coaster meds. Is this one of those rides that try to make you sick?"

Michael looked at him with amusement in his voice. "It is how things work here in the Council. You are not on trial. You are being examined. We are all here but some have chosen to remain hidden for the moment. Gabriel, Raphael and I will be asking you questions. If any of the other seven choose to show themselves they will when they speak to you. But you are forced to face the angel addressing you. That way we can see your reactions to the questions."

"Because how I react is as important as what I say. Makes sense," agreed Anthony. "But could you three at least be in a line so I don't keep going upside down? Or is that disorientation part of the procedure?"

A new voice and new angel entered the conversation. "He is much more intelligent than he likes to portray. There is also a child-like wisdom combined with a well read, or possibly well experienced, intellect. He sees far more than many of us suspected."

The new angel was feminine in appearance. Her body was not unlike Arino's that was a lithe and lean build that Tone looked at with more pleasure than he should. Her long strawberry blond hair was flowing all around her making her look like she was radiating some kind of power out of her attractive head. She was smiling at Tone in a way that made him uncomfortable. He felt like she was reading him in a way that was unlike any of the others.

"Tone, allow me to introduced Vret," introduced Michael. "She is the archangel of knowledge and wisdom."

"I am so glad to meet you. There is something you could tell that I would really appreciate if you don't mind," began Tone. "The end of *2001: A Space Odysseys*, what the hell was that about? I have been wondering about that one for years!"

Gabriel looked both amazed and disgusted. "He is at the Council of the Archangels in the presence of the archangel of wisdom and he wants to know about a movie? Unbelievable!" It was obvious that Gabriel was not impressed.

"Gabe, you have your questions. I have mine," defended Tone. "So Vret, about that movie..."

The smiling angel of wisdom replied, "I'd be glad to explain all the nuances of the entire movie if you would be so kind as to explain the nuances of how you are able to leave your body."

"You are so sweet to offer to exchange information. But I do not know how or why I do what I do. I just do it." Tone looked at her and asked, "Does this mean I don't get to find out what happens to Dave?"

Anthony found himself spinning again. He turned upside down in this process. As he faced his interrogator, he was certain it was an intentional attempt at discombobulation. "How about a city where you live?" asked Gabriel. "I'm certain Vret would be happy to share the entire thought processes of the writers for that little hint of information."

"Dude you are persistent!" exclaimed Tone. "I told Mikey that I will meet Zeke when all this is done. But not a nanosecond before."

Tone was again facing the wise angel. "Nanosecond? You are computer literate and possibly more than that. That is not a word used by many in the commonality of humanity." She was smiling that same smile that made Tone nervous.

"You are sneaky and clever. Plus you have the looks! I'm really starting to like you, Vret." Tone was not as comfortable as he tried to portray and he was pretty sure Vret could tell. He knew that if he spent too much time around this angel that all his secrets would be an open book.

Vret was beaming at Anthony, but looking at the other angels. "The feeling is quite mutual. I can see what you all like about Anthony. He is quite the charmer." Looking back at the human, "May I call you Tone?" she asked knowing the answer.

"You can call me anything you like, beautiful!" flirted Tone.

"He also uses flirtation or insults to divert us depending on the situation. Very clever, Tone. There is so much more to you than you want others to see. I would be willing to make a leap of logic to say that you enjoy being underestimated by those near you on Earth as well as here," declared Vret. The look on the very essence of Tone told her she was absolutely right. Smiling she turned and asked, "So shall we get down to business, Michael?"

"Absolutely, Vret," said Michael. "So Tone, are you ready to take on the H'tes or shall we find someone else?

Tone gazed at Michael as his fear returned. "You know I am usually the first to laugh in the face of danger or at least in the face of an archangel," began Tone. Gabriel was still not amused as he looked at the human with what could easily be mistaken for disdain. "But I'm just not sure about this. Zeke says it will make me a target here and on Earth."

"Very true words, but it will also make you able to defend yourself." Michael was attempting to see through Tone's facade of sarcasm and bravado and intuit what was really troubling the human. "What would be the issue?"

"What if I get attacked by a butt-load of demons on Earth and there is no one to help? What if I can't use the knife on Earth as well as I could here?" asked Tone.

Vret joined in the conversation saying, "Are you concerned that you may not be able to wield the H'tes on Earth? Interesting. Why would you be afraid of that?"

Tone examined every bit of Vret he could sense. He knew she was fishing for more information. "I like you Vret, but stop trying to get inside my head. I'm just worried about that whole target thing. If I take the H'tes I want to be sure that I can give it back after we are done here." Tone considered his options and looked at the archangel of the warriors. "Is it possible for me to use it only when I'm here? Let's be honest. You may need me again someday if we survive this whole Bubba disaster."

Raphael's words came into play, "We should ask Adoneal what he thinks about that. Adoneal?"

The archangel of service faded into view. "I have been listening," came the monotone of Adoneal. "I can change four of the 100 runes on the H'tes and augment it so that it bonds only for as long as the blade keeper desires. One additional rune will make it capable of being taken back up should the need arise. It can be done without any measurable effort. Would that be satisfactory?"

Smiling, Raphael turned to Tone, "Is that more to your liking?"

"That is perfect! Why didn't you say you could do that before?" he asked no one in particular.

"No one has ever not wanted a lifelong bond to a H'tes," said Adoneal simply.

Michael raised his hand motioning to Ezekiel. "Would you mind if I took the blade now?" It was not really a question. Zeke approached and handed over the crystal case containing the H'tes. The case dissolved with a look from Michael, leaving the blade floating in front of all of them.

"Council of Archangels, behold the H'tes," began Michael. "During this time of the unknown I have chosen Anthony as a blade keeper. My warrior's instincts tell me that there is a reason for his special ability to leave the Earth to assist us. I am aware that not all of you share my confidence in Anthony due to his lackadaisical attitude and the unknowns as to his nature on Earth. However, I ask you to trust me and my instincts as we present this honor. You need not agree with my decision. I only ask you to honor it. Are there any objections which cannot be overcome?"

"I honor your decision and support it," came the words from Raphael. He reached out with his finger and touched the H'tes causing the fire within the blade to glow even brighter.

"You are a nice archangel," joked Tone, winking at Raphael.

"I will honor you decision," came a voice that surprised Tone. Gabriel was there supporting the goals. He reached out and touched the blade imbuing it with his power creating more fingers to the lightening within the weapon. "My angels will continue to seek Tone on Earth to protect him while he wields the dagger."

"And I thought you didn't like me," smiled Tone. Gabriel gave him a look that clearly conveyed that he really did not like the human. Tone tried to smile at the messenger as the angel turned away.

"I honor and support your decision," said Adoneal. At his touch six of the runes on the blade were erased to be replaced by new runes that were even more complex than the ones that had been there.

"I honor thy decision," came a disembodied voice. "And I support it." An angel appeared by the blade unlike any angel Tone had seen. This was how an angel was supposed to look in the human's mind. It had the wings, the halo, and was dressed in white that glowed too brightly to be stared at for long. When this angel touched the blade the color of the fire became whiter than any human could make it. The angle faded away.

"Thank you, Uriel," said Michael. Zeke, who had been trying his best to stay out of the way, looked at his friend and mentor and saw that Michael was genuinely surprised by Uriel's action. Michael sensed his protégée examining and communicated silently that he was surprised by the actions of Uriel. Michael had not expected support, only honoring of the decision.

Another angel appeared beside the blade. This one had no clear form. It seemed like a blurred photo that was moving too quickly. As part of the angel brushed the hilt of the blade its voice echoed out. "I honor your decision." It then faded away. The blade of crystal now had tints of silver along the edges giving Tone the image that this blade was far too sharp to be a mere toy.

Zeke had moved to be next to the sphere to give Tone commentary on what was happening. "That was Halalio. Archangel of Miracles. With his support all the others are not needed. He only needed five of them to agree."

"Because he settles the ties?" asked Tone.

Zeke looked at his friend, "You are quick. Yes, Michael settles ties,"

"You have my support as I honor your decision," said Vret as she smiled at Tone. At her touch the H'tes gave off a warm feel to all nearby. Tone wished he were not in the damn sphere so he could be closer to all the action. But he understood the reasons.

A cherub next appeared by the blade. "Honor," was all it said. It touched the H'tes causing the exterior of the blade to gain a shine it had not previously possessed. The cherub faded away

Tone looked through the wall at Zeke. There was an expression of pleased amazement on the face of the warrior. Tone asked, "I assumed that you are dancing the happy dance on the inside?"

Zeke looked at the human and replied, "Iofiup was the one mostly likely to not honor a wish of the archangels. Cherubs tend to follow a different path as you have seen. Not only did he honor the decision, but he said it instead of thinking it. That was for your benefit."

"I'm honored?" asked Tone.

"You should be," replied a serious Zeke. "They hardly ever use their voices and Iofiup says even less than other Cherubs."

Another angel was resolving itself into visibility. This one looked like it had been through many battles. There was something in its gaze that made Tone glad there was a spirit sphere between the two of them. He got the impression that this angel would enjoy taking him apart if it was necessary.

Looking at Michael he said, "Michael, I trust you. I honor your decision. You have my support." Turning to the spirit sphere encased Tone he said, "Human, I do not trust you. If you are deceiving us I will make certain you are locked away in the deepest, darkest, coldest, mind-raping depths of Hell. You will stay there for all eternity alone and in perpetual torment from the moment you arrive. Am I clear?"

This angel scared the hell out of Tone more than all the demons he had met. "Y-y-y-y-es," was all he could stammer.

The angel smiled and said rather pleasantly. "I'm glad we understand each other. Good luck." As this angel touched the H'tes the point seemed to elongate and sharpen giving it a stiletto look on the end. The angel was gone in a blink.

Tone tried to speak. He moved his lips but nothing came out. He was still too scared to find the words. Zeke saved him saying, "That was Nasarg. He is the archangel in charge of guarding Hell. And he can do what he threatened." Looking at the trembling form of Tone he tried to reassure him. "Relax. Once we defeat Bubba he will be impressed."

"Damn, he's scary," said a meek Anthony.

"Think about what he deals with. He has to be," replied the angel. "We only have one more. Do not say a word unless you are spoken to. Understand?" Tone had never seen his friend as serious as he was now.

"Understand," said Tone, who was still shaking.

A very pleasant looking angel appeared looking in the spirit sphere at Tone. The human suddenly felt like he was an animal in the butcher shop window who was being considered for slaughter. This angel almost had its faced pressed against the sphere as Tone was examined in infinitesimal detail. This angel was almost as lovely as Raphael. It seemed to have the spiritual muscles of Michael. It's long flowing blond hair that seemed to be bristling at the ends reminded Tone of wave after wave of crashing surf. The eyes of this archangel were the darkest shade of blue Tone had ever seen.

The angel spoke first to Tone in a very soft voice that made his blood boil with pleasure at the beauty of the pitch while simultaneously running as cold as ice with the words spoken. "I am Samael, archangel of death. If you are lying to us, I will find you and end you and hand you over to allow Nasarg to do with you as he pleases." Tone nodded at the cold words spoken in such a pleasing way. Turning to Michael, the angel of death said, "You have my honor and support, Michael." This angel smiled as it touched the blade giving it new bolts of black lightening intermixed with the white. The angel vanished as fast as it had appeared.

"I guess that's it," said a relived Tone. He had now met all ten archangels and had not been destroyed. It was a good day to be Tone.

"Not quite," said Michael. He approached the blade, looked at it for a moment, and grasped the hilt. The blade glowed more brightly than ever as power from the most powerful of the archangels was transferred to it. He held on to the blade unlike the others who had merely touched it. The power placed within that blade would be beyond any that had been before. After what felt like an eternity, the archangel released the H'tes. His glow had diminished slightly as the blade glowed so brightly it hurt Tone's eyes. "Now, that is all," said Michael.

Looking around the golden sphere, Michael said, "I dismiss the Council of Archangels. Thank you for your honor and service." With those words, all were gone except for Michael, Raphael, Zeke and Tone. "And now we need to bond the blade."

Chapter 21

With a thought from Michael the spirit sphere dissolved leaving Tone in the midst of the angels. Michael spoke. "Tone, this will be a bit uncomfortable at first but that will soon pass. That is why Raphael remained. I'd like to use his effect on you to ease the pain. Is that all right with you?"

"You mean you want me stoned on angel-voice so it doesn't hurt? I'm cool with that," said Tone. "Just make sure he keeps talking. I'm not much into that 'no pain, no gain' stuff. I'm more of a 'no pain, no pain' kind of guy."

"Don't worry, Tone. I will help you as much as I can," said a reassuring Raphael.

"I missed you, Raphael. You're such a nice archangel," slurred Tone as his rapid, prismatic coloration slowed to a lethargic set of softly shifting hues... "Why don't you stay with me forever? We can have chicken wings and marshmallows and supreme pizzas."

Michael turned to Zeke, laughed and said, "I see why you like him like this." The two warriors began the processes of the bonding while Raphael continually spoke to Tone.

"So Tone, you like chicken wings? How spicy?" asked Raphael. Zeke took Tone's hand and wrapped his fingers around the blade. There was a shock that caused Zeke to pull away momentarily. He quickly returned to place two hands around those of his friend's clutching the blade.

"Sweet and spicy. But not too spicy. You are so nice, Raph," said the human dreamily. "You know, I can get bunk beds if you want to come live with me. You're such a nice archangel. My arm hurts but I don't mind." Michael tapped a series of runes that caused the H'tes to glow brighter with each touch. As the last rune was touched, there was a flash of light as the hilt of the blade seemed to fuse with the palm of Tone's hand.

"You are nice too, Tone. So what all do you like on your pizza?" asked Raphael who was trying to keep Tone's mind away from what was happening. The blade had now become part of the hand of the human. With a nod from Michael, Zeke reached out and touched a rune on the bottom of the hilt and the blade spun around and buried itself inside Tone's arm leaving not trace on the surface that is was hidden within.

"I like pepperoni and sausage and ham and mushrooms and olives and pepperoni and mushrooms..." trailed off Tone.

"You already said pepperoni and mushrooms, Tone," said Raph. "How do you feel?

"I feel great. You are a really nice archangel. Can I have a marshmallow?" asked the delirious Tone. There was a rune on Tone's wrist where the blade had disappeared into his arm. The blade spun back around and was firmly lodged by in his hand as Zeke touched the rune again.

"That wasn't as bad as I thought it would be," said Zeke.

Michael looked at the glazed human. "Let's get him sobered up and then see how it feels for him."

Raphael looked at Tone, "I have to go now, Tone. Be good for Zeke."

"Oh don't go. I just ordered marshmallows for us from that green unicorn over there at the concession stand." Tone was getting more drunk the longer Raphael spoke. With a blink, the healer was gone.

"Tone, I need you to snap out of whatever this is now," said Zeke. "Wake up, old buddy."

Tone looked at Zeke through a haze. "Raph is such a nice archangel. I wish he would stay longer. He never stays long enough. Why won't he stay longer? I like him. He's such a nice archangel."

"Zeke, touch the rune," said an impatient Michael.

The blade spun back into Tone's arm and out of sight. The strange sensation made Tone come out of his stupor and look around.

"Are you done? That was fast. I didn't feel a thing." Looking at his hand he asked, "So where is it?"

"There is a small rune on your wrist. Touch it," ordered Michael.

"Mikey. Mikey. Mikey. You got to stop giving orders like that it only makes me want to..." Tone touched the rune and the H'tes spun out of his arm and into his hand. "Holy shit! That was too cool!"

Michael and Zeke were pleased at his reaction. "Now touch that rune at the bottom of the blade that matches the one on your wrist," said Michael. With a touch the blade spun into his arm disappearing from sight. The look on Tone's face was priceless. It was a combination of shock, amazement, delight and horror.

"OK. That is just too damn weird. So now I have a spirit knife in my arm. Do I have to touch the rune or can I just think it into my hand?" asked Tone. As he asked, he thought of the touching the rune and the blade spinning out.

Michael began, "You actually have to touch the..." The blade came swinging out of Tone's arm without the rune being touched. "Interesting. You do NOT have to touch that rune apparently. Tone you are always full of surprises. The two previous blade keepers had to use the runes."

"Mike, when will you learn to stop underestimating me?" laughed Tone. Looking at Zeke he stage whispered, "Quick. How the hell did I do that?"

"Think of that rune again, Tone," said Zeke. "Let's see if that's how you did it."

With a thought of the rune and H'tes swinging, the blade disappeared again. Another thought brought it back out. In and out the blade went several times. Tone giggled with joy at this most simple yet amazing thing.

"Now you need to learn how to use the blade. The main thing you need to learn is the angel fire throw. It will send the angel fire we placed in it at one or more demons." Michael pointed to one rune in particular. "Look at the rune that is on the shoulder of the knife. It looks like lightening. Aim the point of the knife away from us and press it."

"How about I think of it?" asked Tone, aiming the blade away. Nothing happened. He thought of it again. Nothing happened. Reluctantly, he reached out and pressed the rune. A blaze of white and black fire shot across the golden room bouncing off several walls before being caught and absorbed by Ezekiel.

"That is powerful," said Zeke as he touched the H'tes returning the power to it.

Tone was excited. "That was fun! I almost want to see a demon now. Can I try it again?"

"This time when it bounces back, hold up the blade and absorb the power." instructed Michael.

Tone pointed the blade and tried again to think of the rune. Nothing happened. When he thought of the rune and the flames they once again shot across the room to bounce off one wall, then a next, then a next, to finally find their way back to Tone. He held the blade in the path of the fire and watched in awe as it was all taken back into the H'tes.

"That was good. But let me try this." Tone just thought of the blade swinging back into his arm without picturing the rune and the H'tes obeyed his command. The thought of it swinging back out of his arm had the same effect, "I just have to think of it doing what I want. The runes don't matter."

Zeke was confused. "How can they not matter? They are what controls and contains the power. Without the runes it would just be a crystal knife."

Michael was silently staring at Tone. He seemed to be thinking and examining the remarkable human with new respect. Finally he said, "I suspected this. Thank you, Tone. You just proved me right."

"It was an accident, I assure you," jested Anthony.

Tone and Zeke were both looking at Michael waiting for an explanation. Michael continued, "Every one hundred generations there is a human soul that has uncommon abilities. One out of every one hundred of those 'Uncommons' is a 'Remarkable'. There have only been two discovered in the past; although, several others have slipped by only to be discovered after their deaths. As soon as I knew you were telling the truth about leaving your body, I suspected you were a Remarkable. Now let's see if you are even more."

Suddenly, Zeke found himself inside a spirit sphere watching Tone and Michael preparing for battle. The hunter knew what was about to happen and wished he could help his friend. Michael had put him in the spirit sphere because he knew that Zeke would not be able to stop himself helping Tone. In the very core of his spirit, the hunter knew that this was a trial that Tone had to face on his own. This would tell if he could truly handle the H'tes. If he failed the weapon would be stripped from him and he would once again find himself defenseless.

"Um, Mike? What ya doing?" asked a nervous Tone.

A spirit sphere appeared around Michael that only partially covered him. He tested and confirmed that he could pull himself fully within it if needed. "I'm preparing to attack you. Ready or not, defend yourself!" said Michael as angel fire shot out of his hands toward Tone. Reacting instead of thinking Tone moved the H'tes between himself and the flames. They were all absorbed as if the knife were hungry for it.

Smiling with his whole soul, Tone was proud of himself as he said, "How was that?"

Michael glowed with power as he said, "Good start. How about this?" Five different balls of fire came from the archangel's hands, feet and head, rolling out and converging on Tone from five different angles. Tone first tried to spin in several directions at once; but seeing the place where the fireballs would meet, he raised himself out of the way, flipped upside down and placed the blade in the path. All five flaming orbs were taken into the blade. "OK. That was a sweet move if I do say so myself. How the hell did I do that?" asked Tone.

"Move around this!" said Michael, who was really enjoying himself.

A sheet of angel fire flared out of the archangel and flew toward the human at a surprising speed. Tone moved down and then right, but the sheet of flame seemed to follow his every move. He looked at the fire and, smiling, moved his hand in a spinning motion charging toward the wall of angel fire. Before breaching the wall of flames he pulled back and began pulling the flames into the blade like a tornado sucking up debris.

"I don't think we're in Kansas anymore, Zeke-to!" said a winking Tone.

Zeke was confused. Tone had never shown that kind of prowess before. His movements were as fluid as a seasoned warrior and his anticipation of the attack was like that of Vret. His speed was like Gabriel. Granted, he was not as efficient or on the same level of any of the archangels. Somehow, he was doing things that he should not be able to do. Tone was inexplicably accessing the power of the archangels within the blade and using them to his advantage. This was yet another thing that should not be possible, but with Tone seemed to be second nature.

"Let's see what happens with this," said Michael. A blast of power burst from the core of the archangel that was like an enlarging ball of fire heading every direction at once. Michael retreated within the spirit sphere around him as soon as the attack was launched. *"Let's see how he handles this one,"* thought Michael as he watched beside Ezekiel.

Tone considered many options rapidly. It seemed that thoughts that he had never considered in the past were flowing as freely and quickly as a waterfall while a torrent of options cascaded through his mind. He considered trying the cyclonic move again but there was too much power going too many directions. The idea of moving all around with the speed of the messenger to capture the edges of the attack and then return them to the attacker was dismissed as impractical within the confined space. Tone finally just moved behind the protection of the sphere containing Zeke as the power passed harmlessly by. With a simple move he had found a way to avoid an attack instead of looking for a way to stop the unstoppable.

"I'd say that is enough for now, Tone." Removing both spirit spheres with a thought, Michael called to Zeke. "You know what he is doing, don't you?"

"Accessing the power of the angels who touched the H'tes. But how can that be? Why can he do that?" replied the warrior.

Michael just smiled as he said, "Who knows with Tone? It is his gift along with annoying us. Let's make the best use of his abilities." Zeke suspected there was something that Michael wasn't telling him. He knew better than to ask. Turning to Tone, the archangel continued. "The H'tes can do other things, Tone. But you have to discover them for yourself. I'm not trying to keep secrets. It is just the other two had very different powers based on the abilities of the holder. With you, who knows what it can do?"

"I don't suppose it can roast hot dogs like these nails did when I plugged them into the wall? I could really use a chili dog!" laughed Tone.

Zeke chimed in, "I'll try to find you a hot dog to try it on."

Michael ignored them, saying, "One previous H'tes keeper had the ability to slow down the actions of others. He could use it on angels and demons alike. Another could hide himself but you don't need a H'tes for that. Each rune has access to a slightly different power. With you, I wouldn't be surprised to find you using them all in one way or another."

"It is such a totally freaking cool gift. I feel bad that I didn't get you anything. When is your birthday? You deserve a card at least. Or how about an angel food cake with lots and lots of candles? That will have to be one big ass cake." joked Tone.

"Just help us take care of Bubba and we can call it even," said the archangel, bringing the discussion back to the topic. Michael created a portal with just a thought and ended the discussion. "Now it is time to get you back on the trail of the beast. I am only a thought away for either of you now."

Walking through the portal together, Zeke and Tone emerged just as the *Hajile-R* was being placed in the river. The other angels were working in the same way as when they had departed. To Tone it looked like they had barely even moved while they were gone.

"How did it go?" asked Arino.

"It went very well. The..." began Zeke.

"We have company," interrupted Tone.

Chapter 22

Tone looked right where the imp was hiding as he spoke. "There are some demons who actually may keep their promises. Who knew? How's it hanging, Zadrol?"

"Impressive," came the voice of the demon as he allowed himself to be seen. "And here I thought that trace was a bluff. We should really go out for drinks sometime so you can tell me how you do it. The next time I'm in New York I will be glad to look you up."

Tone's face betrayed a smile. "Nice try Zaddy. You're not going to get anything else out of me. Zeke?" While the imp had been focused on Anthony, the warrior had ported right behind it. With one quick movement the demon was in his grasp.

"Why Ezekiel, how nice to see you. You are as charming as ever." The imp tried to remain calm even though all could see he was nervous about his precarious predicament.

"Why Zadrol, how horrendous to see you. You are as slippery and slimy as ever," chided the hunter.

Zadrol actually looked at Zeke with surprise. He looked at him very long and hard. It seemed like he was trying to dissect him with his senses. "You are... different. How are you different Ezekiel?" Tone shot a look at Arino who did not take her eyes off the imp. She was staring at him with something that Tone had not seen from her before: anger.

"You only wish I were different, imp. What do you have to keep me from sending you where you deserve?" asked Ezekiel.

The demon smiled his toothy smile that made Tone think of a shark ready for a feeding frenzy. "First, I want the word of all of the angels present that I will be allowed to leave if what I share is of value. Otherwise, feel free to send me to the depths of Hell now without knowing why I am willing to risk so much to share some information with you."

Nazilaq was the first to speak. "As much as I hate to say so, it does have a point. We can always blast it to Hell later if it has lied to us." He turned to Irkja and asked, "Don't you agree?"

"Yes," said Irkja simply. He was glaring at the imp who had been able to sneak past his ever watchful senses. There was something in his gaze that made all of them certain that if the demon did not live up to its promises that Irkja would be the first in line to deal out punishment.

Zadrol saw the animosity in him as he regarded Irkja. Trying to hide his discomfort, he joked, "Irkja, you have such a way with words. It is always amazing how you can convey so much with so little. It is truly a gift!" The laughter of the imp was not echoed by any of the others. "You all need to grow a sense of humor. I thought you were helping them with that, Tone."

"Anthony," corrected the human. "Only my friends call me Tone." Then looking at Zeke he said, "We do have that tee time to get to and we already have a fivesome. Did you want to use him as a tee or the golf ball?"

"A tee would be fine with me. I am concerned that his mouth is so big he would swallow the ball," replied Zeke,

"And that is a problem?" asked Tone.

"I'm fine with that," said Naz.

Tone turned to Arino and said, "What do you think, babe? Would you like to drive the golf cart or the beer wagon?"

There was menace in her voice as she said, "I think we need to find out what that thing wants to tell us so it can go away or we can make it go away." She glowed with a power that Tone had not seen before. She was ready for battle with this insignificant demon for reasons that were beyond Tone. Her mind opened up as Tone heard, *"It is up to something. Let's get this over with before it gets anything from us."*

"Agreed," said Irkja to both the spoken and mental messages.

Ezekiel took over, "You have the word of the angels that you will not be harmed if your information is reliable. You had better be convincing. What do you have to say?"

Zadrol looked at them all and then focused on Tone for a bit longer than the others. "We never just talk anymore. Why don't we all just sit around and have a nice cup of tea?" Looking at the faces of the angels who were now far too close for comfort. He sighed and said, "No? Fine. Let's keep this business-like. So how is the search for Bubba going?"

"Fine. What information do you have?" snapped Zeke.

The imp tried to look hurt. "Ezekiel, you are getting rude in your old age. I merely have the most delicious bit of gossip about the beastie you are pursuing. One of my fiendish fellows met up with him some time ago when he didn't look like something from a twisted gelatin commercial. Once upon a time, he looked very different from how he does now."

Arino was intrigued. "What are you saying? How did he look?"

"Well, he was not as big as he is now. I suspect that he has been gorging himself and has put on more than a few pounds. When Kmulax knew him he was only a little bigger than I am."

"Kmulax? You must be joking if you think we will take anything that comes out of that beguiler as worthwhile?" asked Nazilaq. It was obvious that there was a history between the two to make the normally jovial angel have that kind of animosity.

Taking on a placating timbre, Zadrol gave his proof. "Normally I wouldn't have even bothered asking him but since he was in a situation that left him, shall we say - vulnerable, I took advantage of it." There was an evil grin on the imp's mouth.

Zeke clarified, "Kmulax was in a spirit sphere when Ladnon beat him recently. He was left alone briefly and, I presume, Zadrol found him and chose that time to interrogate him. Am I right?"

"Why Ezekiel, you are well informed!" said the demon with sarcasm in the compliment. "Yes, I found him in a rather unseemly situation. He asked me to help him get out before his captor returned and I made a deal with him. He had to give me any information about the beast that is killing our kind and I would help him out."

"Liar," said Irkja.

The mock offense on the demon was nearly comical. "My dear Irkja, I would have gladly helped him out of the dire situation he faced but for two minor issues. First, the angel had just appeared. Second, I don't like him." The imp looked around at all of them as if that settled the matter and made perfect sense. "You cannot tell me that you are unhappy that Kmulax is going to be in a succubus sleep for a couple decades are you?"

"Please continue," said Zeke.

"As I was saying," continued the imp, "when Kmulax met him he looked much smaller. There was also the form of Bubba. He looked less like a blob and more like a well formed spirit with the basic arms, legs, body and head of any of the spirits."

Nazilaq looked at him in disbelief. "You can't be serious. That thing cannot be a demon. That is just not possible! You are lying so prepare for a nap." Naz looked ready to blast him with everything he had as the floating *Hajile-R* glowed brightly behind him.

"Calm down, Nazilaq. I never said it was a demon," there was fear in the demon's voice. "But you are not going to like this part any better so I must remind you of your promise." Looking around at them he emphasized, "All of you,"

"We understand, Zadrol. What are you saying?" said Zeke trying to keep the imp from being devastated by the other three angels before they got any useful information. Zeke looked at the each angel and silently communicated, *"If he is lying, I will know. He is in my hands literally and figuratively. I will handle this."* Looking back at the imp, he said, "Spit it out. What are you saying?"

There was almost joy in the imp as it said, "Well, my caged associate described it as something that was almost like a human spirit that had gotten lost, but not lost. It was different in that it had the glow of one that still had a hold on earth." Zadrol paused and then looked at Tone. "In fact, if I didn't know better, I'd have thought he was describing our friendly, helpful human right over there."

Zadrol was enjoying the chaos he had caused. All eyes turned to Tone. At first it seemed as if none of them knew what to think. But then all turned and stared at the imp, each of them glowing an ominous glow. He had prepared for anger, disbelief, frustration, fear and a desire to kill the messenger. The demon was prepared for them to break their word and send him to Hell for a long time of healing during which he would have the satisfaction of knowing that they would spend eternity with a broken promise weighing them down. Or they would release him, turn on their human ally, and end up alienating him until he had nowhere else to turn but his old friend, Zadrol. Either scenario he would win. There was a third option that the demon had not contemplated that changed everything. The house of cards that Zadrol had constructed came falling down around him as that one thing that he had not considered happened all at once.

It was Irkja who spoke up. "Another human? Just what we need."

"How can there be another one like me?" asked Tone. "I thought I was special."

Zeke replied, "Get over yourself, Tone. You are special. But let's think this through," Zeke paused and released the demon, "but without the extra company. Zadrol, I appreciate all you have done. You have earned your free pass. Next time I see you I hope you have something that is half as helpful as this. Now you need to leave."

Zadrol was in shock. This could not be happening. All of his eyes were wide with horror as he realized what had slipped passed him. "But you don't think it was Tone, do you?" he asked as it all soaked in.

"Anthony," corrected Tone.

"Shut up, ANTHONY!" screeched the demon trying to inflict pain on the human. The hidden blade protected Tone from the assault causing surprise in the imp. His failure to hurt Tone increased his rage... "How can there be another human like this tool? How can you have this human with you in the first place?! What the heaven is going on here?!!"

Arino approached the demon, glowing with righteous rage and ready to assist the imp in its imminent departure. "Now would be a good time to go. Or shall I try to heal you of that terrible color you seem to have taken? Indigo seems so unhealthy to me."

"Bye, bye, Zaddy. Have a nice day," jeered Tone.

The imp was gone in the blink of an eye. All the angel eyes turned to Tone who said, "He's really gone." Then he added, "Damn! I love being able to see their trails!"

"So do we, Tone," said Nazilaq. "And that was very well played, Zeke."

"Thank you. I'm just glad he didn't know we had all encountered Bubba. I'm sure he wouldn't have shared anything if he hadn't thought it would tear us apart."

Tone raised his hand. "Question?"

"Yes, Tone? And why are you raising your hand now?" asked Zeke.

"First, thank you for allowing me to get in here before the conversation goes over my head." Tone looked at each of them. "Second, how do you know it's not me at a later point in my time? Isn't it possible that I am Bubba, but just an older version of me? We are not in my time line right now. If I understand where this is, we are outside of time. Right?"

Naz spoke first to no one in particular, "I wish Vret was here for this one. It is so hard to explain this to them."

"Come on sailor. I'm pretty good and I have watched a lot of *Star Trek*. I have seen you guys time shift before since I've been watching you. I know you can move around outside of time on earth."

All four of the angels looked at Tone. They were impressed. Arino began speaking to explain. "Tone, it is not quite that simple. Yes we can moved back and forward in what you call time. There are ways to do that in this spiritual world that involved us jumping into the water of time. Time for you is very linear. For us it is circular. We can visit any time and exist there for as long as we need as often as we need. When we leave that time on earth, we come back here. But we never totally leave this place behind. We are anchored here. Imagine going deep sea diving but having a line that can pull you back to the shore. We have a line that pulls us back to here.

"Since you are right here with us, the energy of a human soul holds us to the time your body is in. It is essential that anyone in your proximity stays in your time stream. We could move about in time but it would cause your spirit damage. No human soul can handle that. It will basically kill your body or at the very least rip this part of you out of it. Now, if you were here from a different time then you would have not had the power to affect us in the river. You would have been a shadow that passed us that was disconnected."

Tone looked at her and then looked at Zeke. "So basically, I can't be here in two different times?"

Zeke said, "You can and you might be right now. But you cannot see or touch yourself. The ether of Spiritscape has too many levels to allow that to happen. It automatically moves you to a different level. There are an infinite number of levels right here within the Spiritscape. But this level is locked onto your time stream while you are here. Even if you were right here you would not see yourself or any of us. Think of it as another dimension within the Spiritscape."

"Right," said Tone. "So basically I can't be here in two different times?"

"Yes," said Zeke giving up trying to explain angelic temporal mechanics. "And we call it time jumping. Not shifting."

"Because you jump in the ocean with the rope tied here to bring you back," said Tone, proud that he had gotten that part right.

"Close enough," said Irkja. He had been scanning the river for any signs of activity. There was none.

"All that Zadrol did was give us a clue to the nature of the beast. Based on what he said, Bubba was some form of human soul at some point." Arino looked at Tone as she continued, "Could there be someone with the same power to leave their body as you do, Tone? Ever seen anyone else?"

Tone gave her his best smile as he said, "I'm one of a kind, babe!" Then he added, "As far as I know."

"What if there's is another or many more?" asked Irkja.

"Dude, you are using up your word quota. Don't you have a limited number of words you are allowed to use this quoll?" teased Tone.

"I've been saving them," said Irkja. Tone laughed at the joke. He looked around and saw no one else was laughing. "Really," said Irkja, as if that settled the matter.

Tone looked at the other three angels and they all nodded their heads. "I don't even want to know," said Tone flabbergasted. Changing the subject, he continued, "So do you really think Bubba is like me? I mean, how many amazing guys like me can there be?"

Zeke took the bait. "I had always hoped there was only one. But as annoying as you can be, you are at least a good man. What would happen if someone had powers like you that was not that good of a person? Or if the first being they encountered was demon instead of an angel? Do you think a demon could have corrupted a soul like Tone's? Based on what happened with S'theno, I'd say it was absolutely plausible."

Nazilaq spoke up. "And if a demon tried to take over someone like Tone, would they have been shattered like you were phased, Zeke?"

Arino added, "And if that demon were shattered and Bubba were to take in some of the remains, would that cause a change to begin? Let's be fair, there are traces of Zeke in Tone and Tone in Zeke from their encounter. But Tone wanted to help Zeke. If Bubba didn't care about saving a demon, then what would happen?"

"Anyone who is not scared shitless by this situation please raise your hand now," asked Tone. Three angels had the same concerned look on their essences. Irkja raised his hand. "Really?" asked Tone.

"I do not have that bodily function," said Irkja with the barest hint of a smile. They all laughed.

Chapter 23

The *Hajile-R* was speeding along the tube of the river once again. Nazilaq was his jovial self. It seemed he was the most joyful when he was controlling this vessel moving along a river at ridiculous speeds. As Tone watched him more closely than before he saw that there was something that on the surface seemed haphazard about the angelic sailor. However, if you looked at his essence more carefully, there could be seen a focus that was beyond the norm. Recalling his calm during the battle with Bubba and his peace after his injury, Tone decided that his initial appeal was well founded. Now he just knew why he liked the angel.

"So Tone, do you like your H'tes? Do you have any special talents you want to show off?" asked Nazilaq. He already knew since Ezekiel had instantly shared everything when they portaled back. He just wanted to give Tone the chance to share.

With a thought the blade came swinging out Tone's arm. "Like it?" The gleaming blade seemed even more powerful as it glowed brighter in the ether. It reminded Tone of a brightly shining lighthouse that was a beacon to all around it. Now he was holding the beacon. He held it high to allow all to see it.

Zeke smiled and said, "I think he is going for a Statue of Liberty look."

"Dammit! I was trying for the Luke Skywalker look from the original *Star Wars* poster," countered Tone.

"Either way it looks good on you," said a complimentary Arino. "I am so proud of you."

Tone beamed at her. "Thanks, babe. Does it make me look sexy?" The blade disappeared back into his arm as he winked at the healer. She smiled shaking her head. Zeke did the angelic equivalent of rolling his eyes.

"There is something ahead of us," stated the ever calm Irkja. "It is a pha'ard that it is different than others."

Zeke was trying to sense the pha'ard. "Angel or demon?"

"Demon," stated the watcher. His gaze was like a precision laser looking past a bend in the river. "Coming into view now."

"Slowing," said Naz. "Rings are charged if we need them. Deploying net." Tone looked and saw a crystalline net growing out of the riverside section of the ship. It seemed to be reaching out to other sections as they all met in the center of the *Hajile-R*. As Tone watched it flexing and flowing with the current of the energy river, he noticed the net was as transparent as the ring but had a plasticity that the ring did not. The net would allow them to capture most things that might be flowing past and hold them as long as they needed,

The pha'ard came drifting down the river as Tone called out, "Thar' she blows!" The others turned their stares from the pha'ard to Tone who said, "Someone had to say it. Irk has already made his one joke for this eon so I figured I had to." Zeke shook his head. Arino laughed. Nazilaq beamed at Tone in pride of his nautical nuance. Irkja just looked at him and then slowly turned his gaze back to the pha'ard. Tone could have sworn that he almost saw a trace of a smile on the watcher,

The pha'ard was quickly entangled in the crystal net of the *Hajile-R* as Tone got his first good look at it. Even with his limited experience with the pha'ards he could tell it was demonic by the blue tint and the teeth. Most of the pha'ards he had seen were little more than teeth-filled mouths that were ready to devour anything in their path. This one had the same kind of toothy mouth with slightly more to it than that. The mouth was attached to what could have been a small part

111

of the torso or abdomen of the demon. His imagination was beginning to conjure up all kinds of scenarios where a mouth would be blasted off the face and embedded in the ass of the demon by Zeke's powerful battle touch when the warrior spoke.

"So that's what happened to Lijenad's mouth. I wondered where it went when Krewob hit it. That demon went to hell to grow a new one when we were done with that battle." There was a hint of pleasure at the recollection.

Arino looked closer. "I thought those teeth looked familiar. It is so hard to tell when they are separated from the essence of the demon. Do you supposed there is any residual intellect left?"

"Yes," croaked a voice from the net. It rasped, "But not much."

"OK. That is freaky!" said Tone who was both captivated and disgusted by the pha'ard. "Can it do any other tricks?"

"Not many," said Nazilaq. "Let me see." The angel drew the pha'ard to the wall of the skimmer and began looking at it. "Let me bring it in."

Tone was suddenly alarmed. His H'tes swung into his hand showing he was ready for anything. "I hate those things! They are just too...mouthy."

Laughing, Nazilaq continued what he was doing. "Relax, my friend. I'm making a pha'ard bowl for it. Don't you want a pet?"

"No thanks. I'd rather have something safe like a cobra or a hippo with bad attitude and loose bowels," joked Tone without returning his blade to its hiding place.

A portion of the wall wrapped around the pha'ard and part of the energy. The crystal enshrouded demonic fragment was slowly pulled through the wall of the ship until it emerged on the interior still covered in a crystal shell. To Tone it looked like an evil crystal ball that was inhabited by demon ass with a mouth instead of an asshole. It could have been his imagination or just paranoia, but he thought it looked happy to be inside. He kept his blade ready to defend himself in case it somehow broke free.

It came to hover before Ezekiel. "Do you understand me?" The warrior angel had taken on the glow he used in battle. Zeke was trying to intimidate it into telling him what he wanted to know. To Tone it looked impressive. The pha'ard looked at him and looked away unaffected. It was clear that if it understood it was not about to speak to one who had taken part in its destruction. "Tone?"

"What?" replied Tone, realizing that he knew what his friend wanted. "No way! Forget it! I'm a snack to that thing. I do not have pleasant conversations with sharks, piranhas, giant squids or pha'ards. They all have the same goal."

Zeke considered just throwing the crystal globe at Tone but knew he had to use some subtle encouragement. "Don't you want to show off your new H'tes? This thing can't tell any demons you have it. Think about how much fun you can have scaring it!"

"Well..." said Tone, holding his blade between himself and the pha'ard terrarium. He closed the distance, gaining more confidence as he neared the beast. As it turned within the sphere it saw him. The jaws flew at the wall of its crystal case as the mouth screamed in a guttural, nonverbal noise that chilled Tone to his soul. "SHIT!" screamed the human. Tone did not think. He reacted. A blast of angel fire shot out of the tip of the blade to hit the crystal globe containing the pha'ard. The blast bounded off the sphere and separated into six separate strings of fire bounding around the interior of the skimmer. Tone caught one with his H'tes while Irkja caught two and Arino, Nazilaq and Zeke each captured one. The angels each touched the tip and returned the power to the blade.

"Maybe that was not the best idea," said Naz, laughing at the reaction of the human. "But that was a very powerful demonstration of the angel flames. Please don't do that again in here. I just got this skimmer working again."

"Sorry," was all Tone could say. He looked at the other angels who were still looking at him. Zeke and Arino looked amused. Irkja just looked. "It scared me!" said Tone, giving the only defense he could give.

"Obviously," said a teasing Zeke. "I think we better try something else. Naz, any ideas?"

The pilot looked at the captured pha'ard. He had more experience with these anomalies than any other angel. He spun the crystal case to look at it from every angle with senses that Tone could only imagine. "I don't think Irkja's eloquence is the right method to reach this beast. Arino, shall we try your more subtle approach?"

Sharing a smile that made them all smile back, Arino looked at Tone and then the pha'ard. "I will be glad to try as long as Tone agrees to be my bodyguard," said the healer. There was more than a trace of humor in her voice.

"Gladly fair maiden. I, Sir Tone-alot, will happily slay any dragon that may trouble thy countenance," replied a bowing Tone. "Or at least kick its ass with this cool switchblade I have." He either missed the joke or chose to make his own in response. Either way it got laughs from all but Irkja.

The sphere moved to Arino. She looked it over carefully while examining all the battle marks and scars on the remains of the demon. It looked at her with an interest it had not shown as it had regarded Zeke and more subdued interest than it had shown to Tone. After the angel and the pha'ard had looked at one another for longer than Tone felt necessary, the healer spoke, "Hello Lijenad. I'm sorry you are just a shard of what you once were. Can I help you?"

The mouth moved and a rasp echoed through the curved walls of the skimmer causing Tone to grip his H'tes tighter. "Go to Hell, angel. You did this to me!" Its teeth seemed to be dripping something that Tone could not identify. He thought it was bleeding something blue until he realized the mouth was beginning to lose some of its connection to the fragment around it.

"I was not at that battle. It pains me to see you hurting. How can I help you?" asked the healer. Arino was trying with all the love in her being to get the pha'ard to speak. She knew that there was not much time before any communication would be pointless. This pha'ard was fading fast.

The mouth grimaced as if it were in pain. It moved but did not say anything. Arino was about to speak when it made sounds. "End me!" it begged. "Now." Its mouth moved again but nothing came out. As it tried five more times nothing but groans escaped the mouth. "Pain," came the word it had been struggling to say.

Arino wanted so much to help the hurting demon but knew there was too much at stake. She pressed on. "Did you see a gray blob? Where was it?" It was obvious that there was pain in Arino letting anything suffer.

The pha'ard began quaking within the globe. "End! End! End! End!" it screamed over and over. It bounced around within its prison like a perverse pinball until it came to rest beside the healer. Arino was looking longingly at Zeke, wordlessly begging him to let her end the suffering. Ezekiel felt bad that she was hurting for the demon's pain but one look from him said it all: wait. The connections between the mouth and the fragment of demon were held together by strands of blue threads that seemed more fluid than actual spirit. The mouth moved once, twice, and thrice without a sound. On a fourth try one last word came out of the mouth. "Lake!" it screamed as the mouth came off of the rest of the demon spirit. The remaining piece split into many smaller mouths that began devouring one another.

113

Arino placed her hands on the sphere and filled it with her power causing all the pha'ards within to evaporate into the blue energy around them. Lijenad's pha'ard was no more. But it had given them the location of the elusive Bubba: the lake.

Without waiting for orders Nazilaq had the skimmer was moving at top speed along the twists and turns of the Fanjil River. He and Irkja were focused on their duties as the speeds took much of their concentration to ensure the passengers of the *Hajile-R* remained as safe as possible. Naz had deployed the new blades which were making short work of the a few pha'ards that had escaped the maw of Bubba. It was truly astounding to see such a beautiful yet deadly display of power. The blades moved in their opposing circles surging the river through the center of the ship creating an amazing display of colors and textures than Tone had not yet encountered. Occasionally the pilot would send a gentle wave of power through the ring to travel upstream to assist the watcher by lighting up anything that may be trying to hide in the shadows while riding the currents. Irkja was vigilant as his many eyes and glowing dots along his body seemed to be seeing and sensing far more than any of the others.

"Irk, do you see around the bends?" asked Tone, curious about his silent friend. He really wanted to ask about the extra colored dots along his body and pondered subtlety, but finally just asked, "And what is the deal with all the dots on your body? They look bitchin' but also pretty damn weird." Tone was not one for subtlety.

"Yes," answered Irkja to the first question without elaborating. "The 'dots' are my extra sense eyes." The watcher never turned toward the human. Tone waited for more information about the extra sense eyes but soon concluded that there was no more detail forthcoming without some serious prompting.

Tone decided to nag. "So extra sense eyes? That sounds interesting. What do they do?"

"Sense things," replied Irkja, still not turning to Tone.

Arino came to the rescue since neither of them seemed as though they were going to let the other off the hook. "Irresistible forces and immovable objects should not be confined in crystal rings," laughed the healer.

"I knew you found me irresistible!" beamed Tone. "And we all know Irkja is immovable."

"True," said the angel who never stopped watching the river. "Thank you," he added taking that as a compliment. Tone had not really intended it as one but chose instead to focus on the much more appealing Arino.

"Tone, you are incorrigible," sighed Arino. "Irkja obviously has heightened senses even for an angel. The extra sensory sites on his body allow him to fully access all his abilities. The reds are for the warmth and cold, green is to sense the essences, yellow is for aura, infrared is for mental print, ultraviolet is for love and hate. Irkja also has another sense that is beyond words to easily describe. He sees the future flow. It is like a precognitive ability where he can see something slightly before it happens. On Earth it is a ghostly pre-image. Here it is like another version of what is there. Sometimes he has a hard time telling which one is the precognitive image and which one is the real. Most of the time he gets it right but he has been known to confuse them from time to time. That is the challenge of working in the Spiritscape."

Tone was intrigued. Looking back at Irkja, he asked, "So you can see the future in a place where future, present and past are all the same, but on different levels? Doesn't that give you a headache?"

Irkja actually looked at the human. "No," he replied. "It can be challenging."

Zeke jumped into the conversation. "He has a gift for understatement."

"Ya think? I hadn't noticed!" jested a sarcastic Tone. "That would make my head explode."

114

"Probably," replied a smiling Zeke.

"Wave," said Irkja calmly. Tone waved to Irkja without knowing why.

"Hold on!" shouted Naz. The skimmer began spinning as a large wave of energy came toward it along the stream. The wave nearly doubled with width of the river. Tone had seen the ship do some amazing things. He was prepared for the ship to expand to allow the wave to stay underneath the crystal hull so they could continue the observations of the flow. As it seemed to Tone that everything was again moving in slow motion, he took the moment to consider the possibility that the wave would wash over the top of the skimmer allowing them to see all sides of the river from every angle. What happened was neither of those and both.

The skimmer began to elongate on two opposing ends while narrowing at the others. The now oval shaped ring turned so the longer section went into the river as a forward facing bow. The five passengers found themselves at the forward end of a ship that no longer skimmed along the surface of the river but traveled in the middle of the stream. The *Hajile-R* continued its transformation until it was a conical shaped submersible cutting through the energy of the river with blades out the back that reached the surface of the river which continued to shred anything that passed through. The point of the ship was glowing with Nazilaq's power that was moving the few pha'ards away and into the blades behind. The skimmer was now skimming under the surface of the river.

The angels were all calmly looking forward at the river before them. Tone was dying to say something. "Hey guys. If you don't mind me asking... WHAT THE HELL?!" shouted an excited Tone. The angels looked at him with mild confusion until Zeke realized why Tone was so exuberant.

"Sorry, Tone. We're used to that." Looking around at the transformed skimmer he said, "It is still a skimmer but we are skimming under the river. It is handy for situations where we hit waves or lakes. And since we are getting closer to the lake, it was time." He glanced at his friend. "You are so much a part of our team I sometimes forget you haven't seen all of this before."

Tone was still amazed. "Can it change into anything else like an SR-71 or a semi?" He had just considered it a ring to skim the river. It had never crossed his mind that it could be anything else; but the more he thought about it the more it made sense that the ship could be reconfigured. It grew blades and a net. *"Why not become a bad-ass sub with a salad shooter on the back?"* he thought to himself.

Nazilaq smiled at Tone and asked, "Do you want a Blackbird or a Peterbuilt?" There was pleasure in the angel as he stated, "I can make the *Hajile-R* into anything I can imagine. I can reconfigure it into anything you can imagine. The only thing I want is to have the best ship for the situations we face. The native form is the ring and that is what it returns to if something happens to it or to me. But it really has no limits. Did I mention that it doesn't have to stay in the river or lake? We can use it anywhere."

Tone's face went from amazed to disbelieving to pure pleasure. "So we can go anywhere in this very nice ship and use its capabilities to chop salads or demons depending on how vegetarian we are feeling? We will talk, Naz, old buddy. You see I have always wanted a Tesla."

"Car or coil?" asked a laughing Nazilaq.

"Both!" joked the human.

"I'll see what I can do." Nazilaq turned serious as he said, "We are coming up to the battle field. The lake seems strange. Irkja?"

"Something is causing it to have turbulence," stated the watcher. "Sensing. Silence please." All the parts of the angel were glowing with even more power. Irkja was more focused than Tone had ever seen. He was not moving but everything about him screamed attentiveness. The angels were tuned into the mind of the angel who lowered his defenses to allow Tone to share in his sensations.

The sudden onslaught of senses was overwhelming. From Irkja's perspective the lake was a tumultuous cauldron of colors, temperatures and essences. Irkja could see in the energy ebb and flow the traces of angels and demons; the pha'ards of both kinds of spirits and the intermixing of the ether of the spiritual world with the fluctuating of the remains of the battle energy that caused the lake and the river. The heat and cold, mental images of the battle, the love and the hate, all mixed with something that Tone could not define. It was like there were several copies of everything he could see and they seemed to be moving in slow motion but with one version following behind another. It was too much for Tone to take.

"No more!" shouted Tone. Irkja immediately put his defenses back up. "That is how you see 24/7? How can you take it?"

"I don't talk so I can focus on it," explained Irkja.

Tone looked at the angel with renewed respect. "The next time I give you shit about not talking, open your mind for a millisecond to shut me the hell up! OK?"

"OK," said Irkja. "You all right?"

"I'll be fine. That was incredibly intense." He looked around at the others. "I may have missed it because my spirit felt like it was on fire and ready to explode; but did you notice something missing from the lake?" asked Tone.

Zeke had noticed too. "There is a notable absence of Bubba? Anyone see him? Naz, are you ready?"

"Don't worry. New draining weapon is ready to be tried." The angelic sailor was as prepared as always.

Irkja began, "I sense nothing here that even..." He stopped in mid-sentence.

"What's wrong?" asked Zeke, on full alert.

"Where is Tone?" gasped Arino.

Chapter 24

Tone was floating in the middle of nowhere. The skimmer was gone. Zeke, Arino, Naz and Irkja were gone. The lake of energy was gone. The gray blob they had been looking for was there, far too close to Tone for comfort. It had made itself smaller and changed into something that was somewhat like a spirit but still was very different. There was something that looked like a head with vacant eye sockets, no nose, and a mouth that was a rip in the flowing gray essence of the beast. The body of the beast still looked like an amoeba from hell with no real steady, solid form.

"Hello, Bubba. How are you today? I'd love to say it's nice to finally meet you and if I can find a way of saying that without sounding like a total liar, I will." Once again Tone was trying to portray more self-assurance than he truly felt. "If you don't mind me asking, where the hell are we?"

The gap mouth moved into a twisted version of a smile. "It is nice to meet you, Tone. I have felt so alone until I discovered you. We are safely away from the angels who have been getting in our way. You actually haven't even moved."

"Tone, are you hiding?" called a concerned Zeke as Nazilaq held the skimmer in position. He waited for a reply. The angel knew the bizarre sense of humor of the eccentric human but this was out of character. Sarcasm and an aggressive verbal style would not be unusual even in this situation. Even disappearing for reasons that only Tone could comprehend would not be that out of the question. But not replying to the angels who had been given the task of keeping him safe was not like Tone. He would reply in such a dire situation.

"Tone?" called out Arino. "Where are you?" She looked at Zeke as all four angels linked their minds, perceptions and senses. They could not find the human. All but Zeke froze in position as he moved at top speed covering the entire skimmer in a blink.

The group mind realized that their human companion was no longer on the ship. As Irkja began sensing the last place he had been, the others began spirit-storming the problem. It was not possible that he had traveled back to his body since Michael had not released his hold on Tone even though he was no longer in possession of a demon fragment. He was not hidden since Ezekiel would have touched him unless he could become incorporeal. That was possible with the H'tes but he had not said anything about it.

Nazilaq sent out a draining pulse wave to cover the lake. It covered the expanse of the pulsating energy lake in no time at all. There was no feedback from the drainage pulse indicating there was nothing to be drained. All the minds concurred on the meaning behind the absence of anything to be drained: no Bubba. The absence of both could not be a coincidence.

Irkja came up with the lead that surprised them all. There was a residual love glow where Tone had been. There was also an afterimage that only Irkja could sense that showed Tone shifting within the Spiritscape. The only time that kind of shift occurred happened when an angel would...

"We shifted to a different layer of the spirit world. They are right here but not," said the beast.

"And you did that because you wanted to have a chat?" asked Tone. "What shall we discuss? Art? Literature? The flavor of demons as opposed to angels?"

There was a laughter that echoed through the ether. "That was cute," came the voice that was becoming more friendly each time it spoke. "You have me at an advantage at literature but I'd love to discuss the differences between the abstractions of Monet over the surrealism of Picasso." The look of the beast showed something akin to lust as it added, "And angels have a much fluffier taste. The demons tend to be so greasy." There was something that was both wrong and right at the same time but Tone could not put his finger on it.

"I prefer van Gogh," retorted Tone. There was something going on here. He felt like Bubba was trying to pry knowledge out of him with this playful banter and kidnapping him was all part of it. He needed to stall until Zeke found him. *"Let the games begin!"* thought Tone.

"You actually like that trash? Vincent is so overrated. Why the hell would he paint haystacks?" debated the beast. "And would you please call me something else? Bubba is hardly flattering considering all I have done. How about Beast? Or Behemoth? Or..."

"Or Barbie? You do have the curves!" taunted Tone. "So Bubster. To what do I owe the dubious honor of an audience with your immenseness? Seriously dude! You're fat! Lay off eating the angels. They will spread out your waistline so fast!"

"I really like you, Tone. You make me laugh!" teased Bubba. "I know I shouldn't but after the first dozen demons you really want to try something lighter."

"Nice pun but you are still an asshole!" retorted Tone. He was not trying to get a reaction out of Bubba. He was trying to discover where this discussion was going. It didn't seem to be working. It was time to take it up a notch. "On second thought I take that back. At least assholes serve a purpose."

The new laughter that came at Tone contained a cruelness. He knew information beyond basic psychology from several textbooks but that was enough to discern that Tone was dealing with a sociopath. "Now your implying I'm not worth a shit?!" asked the devourer of demons.

"I refuse to take responsibility for anything you may or may not infer from something I may have implied." Then Tone added, "But, no you are not worth a shit."

The beast bantered, "Well I never have to let go of anything I take in unless I'm blasting your pathetic asses out of the river so not being worth something that I don't give a damn about means nothing."

Tone was bored with the banter so he decided to take a page out of Zeke's playbook. "What the hell do you want? Why are you doing this?"

"The direct approach? Really, Tone? I had such high hopes for you and now you sound like the warrior. You are so much more than that." Bubba was trying to fake a real sense of disappointment. He was very convincing. Unless he was not faking the disappointment. Tone knew there was something about this creature but could not narrow it down. What did Bubba want?

"It's been a long day. I saw a Bubba kill Casadore, had to track down an angel to report the crime then..." Tone had a laundry list of innocuous things to share to try and get the beast to reveal more. He was interrupted.

"You saw me take down Casadore? You have to admit it was a sweet move scaring the Heaven out of him like that. The poor bastard never knew what hit him!" bragged Bubba. "So you heard him call Ezekiel? Is that your guardian angel?" Without warning, Zeke appeared next to Tone. "Hello, Ezekiel!"

"What? Beast? How do you know my name? Tone?!" asked Zeke. Also without warning he disappeared again.

The three angels were ready to begin shifting through the near limitless levels to find both Tone and Zeke when the warrior reappeared. The sharing was immediate and the decision was as decisive. Three angels set off alone as Nazilaq took the *Hajile-R* to the next layer down. They had to find and rescue Tone before Bubba destroyed their biggest hope for defeating him.

"Good job, Tone!" complimented the gloating beast. "I'm actually impressed! How did you find him? Was there an interview processes? Did you play *The Dating Game*?"

"You moved him too? Wow! That is impressive. How did you pull that off?" asked Tone with genuine curiosity and even greater fear. The menacing crooked smile told him no answers were about to be shared unless he played along. "Yes, I had to ask all kinds of questions to find just the right one. Be glad I didn't choose Michael. He can be a major pain in the ass when you piss him off." Now it was just a matter of time before the angels caught up to them.

"I'm looking forward to meeting him. I've always wondered what archangel tastes like," said Bubba with a hunger to his voice. "So you want to know why I'm doing this? The real question should be, why aren't you? Haven't you seen what it's like for me? We are not all that different you know."

"Don't flatter yourself. You only wish you were like me. I have things you could never have. A personality. Devastatingly good looks that make the girl angels swoon. Abs of titanium that make the warriors ask about my training program. An ass you could bounce a quarter off of. Also, there are angels on my side," boasted Tone.

"I see that. They will make a very nice snack. The healer looks particularly tasty. The one that I tried was delicious! It charged my spirit and got rid of the awful taste of the whore demon." The desire in the voice was mirrored by the glow of the spirit. "She tasted like she had every VD out there. Really disgusting but she had power that was worth it."

"I hope you are not dying of anything you caught from her. It could make your dick fall off you know. Oh wait. You're a dickless blob. Too late!" tormented Tone.

A genuine laughter came bursting out of the beast. "Any dick around me is not your concern, little man. But you did not answer my question. Why not try a feast of the feeble? We could dine together and take on the angels of Heaven and hounds of Hell. It would be a dinner party for two!"

Tone was amazed that this perversion of a human could even suggest that. "Well there is the small matter that I don't eat other things! We are not talking about cattle here, dude. Do you hear them mooing?"

"No. I hear them grunting like the pigs they are. We are so much more than they are, Tone. Why can't you see that we are the next generation of spirits? We are as far above all of them as other humans are above beetles!" sneered Bubba. "They may be nice pets but I plan on eating mine!"

That was the piece of the puzzle Tone had been waiting for. There was something working with Bubba that he considered a pet. "Mine are friends. Not pets. They are very handy, too. They are great at coming up with things to make your life into a living hell. Or dying hell. Or just a hell since I have no clue what the hell you are anymore." The H'tes glowed with power ready to be used on the gray oozing creature that was almost within reach.

Bubba was unimpressed with the nobility of his counterpart. "I am what you could be but are too afraid to become. Don't worry. I'll help you." There was pause that hung in the ether than make Tone more than a little nervous. "I think I need to remove a few obstacles that are coming between us."

Tone glowed with anger. "Don't even think it! I'll take you apart if you come near any of them!" Pausing he said, "Let's play, Bubba. Just us humans. What do you say? I'll bring the potato salad and you bring your ass to get kicked. We'll make it a party."

This time the laughter was arrogant and sounded very human. "I wonder who would have what's left of their ass in a sling when we were done, Tone. Keep trying there, little boy. You have no idea who you are dealing with, do you? Oh the things you still need to learn. One of them is discipline." Bubba began to expand toward Tone as the glow of the beast became more and more powerful.

"OK. This is not good" thought Tone, as he brought his H'tes up between them. The beast paused looking at the unknown weapon. *"Let's find out how good this little pocket knife is."*

There was suddenly in between the two bantering boys a rather feminine presence. Arino was shocked to see both Tone and Bubba chatting so calmly yet ready for a fight. She was instantly ready for battle as she prepared to lay down her very spirit to save Tone.

"Run!" she ordered as Bubba surged toward her, mouth wide ready to envelope the angel. Arino knew that there was nothing she could do to stop the beast but she could buy time for Tone to escape. She was at peace as she faced her doom with the bravery of a warrior. Her last thoughts were of her Zeke and Tone as she sent a message to the other angels so they would find him.

The beast was upon her as she prepared to strike out. The blast was beyond anything she had imagined. There was a two toned howl of pain as Bubba screeched while being blasted back, stunned by the contact. Arino had not attacked or even touched the beast. With the speed of Gabriel, Tone had rushed between his friend and his nemesis determined not to let her die alone. Striking out with his H'tes he made certain not to send the angel fire for fear of helping the beast. Arino turned in time to see Tone flying backwards mirroring Bubba. The two had hit one another with power unknown to any other human only to find themselves repelling each other. The core of Bubba was spinning wildly away while fragments of the beast seemed to be flying off in all directions.

Arino followed her nature and flew after Tone to make certain he would be safe while hoping that her message had found her friends. As if in answer to her hopes the *Hajile-R* materialized out of nowhere with the blast of a draining pulse going in all directions. Irkja was there in a blink scanning the area with a dangerous looking glow emanating from the quiet watcher. He had the look of an angel ready to take apart an entire hoard of demons. It was Zeke who was truly frightening. Had Tone been alert he would have been terrified by the display of his closest angelic friend. Ezekiel, second to Michael, Demonbane, was in his full angelic glory as a mighty warrior of heaven. His spirit glowed with a kaleidoscope of colors and shades that were spreading in every direction following the pulse from the skimmer, searching for beast who had attacked.

The minds of the angels were instantaneously linked in battle readiness, prepared to destroy the beast or die trying. It was a shock when the three newly arrived found a fourth mind joining them. It was Arino who explained that Tone had stepped in and attacked the beast, saving her from destruction. She was soaring after Tone who needed them now more than ever. The mind of Zeke took charge, ordering Irkja to follow the beast but to stay hidden and at a safe distance. They needed to know what was happening and if it was injured.

Tone had slowed to a gentle drift in the ether of the Spiritscape. Arino arrived first, wishing she could risk touching the heroic human. What she saw made her frightened for the brave man. Tone was flashing with different kinds of power than she had never seen in him before. It was almost like there was something trying to take him over. A thought from Arino and Zeke ported directly there holding his stunned friend in his arms, wrapping him in angelic warmth. Tone was not unconscious but he was not sensible either.

"Darkness. Darkness. Darkness," repeated the human over and over. Zeke held him tighter wishing he could heal as well as Arino. Healing power began flowing through the warrior as Arino touched him to allow her loving power to wash over them both. She could sense it through the warrior. Tone had been touched by the evil of over a dozen demons that were within the abomination. Zeke felt it too as Arino began drawing off the evil; but she stopped.

"What is it?" asked Zeke, knowing that Arino would not stop healing Tone without a good reason.

"I can feel angel mist inside Tone," said a surprised Arino. "Not just the pieces of you that are always there. It is part of Casadore and D'vrash that was in Bubba. There is also some of Innod in there too. I didn't know Innod was gone."

"Neither did I," admitted Zeke. "Can you tell which demons have been devoured by that thing?"

"No. They are too intermixed and it is a very weak trace anyway. I'll pull it all out," stated the healer getting back her job as she shifted into her healing form. "But what about the traces of the three angels? Should I leave them in there to help Tone and make him stronger?"

Ezekiel considered that possibility. They needed all the help they could get. "Leave the wisps in him. He needs more angelness in him anyway."

With great effort they saw Tone come back to them. "No!" he gasped. "All of it out!" He faded back into his stupor as his aura showed rapidly changing colors even for Tone. It was almost like there was a battle within him and there was no clear winner yet.

"He knows something we don't. Do it now! And fast!" demanded the hunter as the skimmer came to rest near them with what looked like remnants of Bubba splattered all over hull. Nazilaq was by their sides, far too close for safety but not close enough for the help he really wanted to give. He saw the situation and he also knew there was nothing he could do but guard his three friends. The ship seemed to melt around them taking them into the very core of the skimmer as the blades reestablished themselves and the ship glowed with the power of the sailing angel. The few fragments of Bubba that had come in with the trio were quickly and quietly expelled back into the ether.

After making certain there was no parts of Bubba within the room, Arino began drawing the power off as quickly as she could without hurting the human or the warrior who was the conduit for her power. She reached out to Naz who received the demonic power and sent it into ether through the skimmer to be absorbed and dispersed by the natural flow. Tone began to regain his usual shine as the last of the power was drained away.

"Mental note: Do not kick Bubba in the balls. It hurts both of us," jested the still stunned human. "Does anyone have an aspirin?"

"Are you all right?" asked three angels at the same time.

Tone looked at each of them, seeing the concern on their faces and spirits. "How bad do I look? I must look like shit to get Zeke to look that worried. Let me comb my hair." Moving partially out of Zeke's embarrassing embrace, he reached for his head, miming fixing his hair. "What the hell happened to my hair?" he asked trying to lighten the mood. "Oh yeah. Spirit form. No hair." Looking at the angels, he continued. "I must really look bad because that was funny."

Arino changed her look from one of concern to one of relief. "That's the Tone we know and love." She looked at him with the love of the healer. "Thank you, Tone. That was very brave of you. I am in your debt."

Tone could not resist. "A lesser man would suggest mojitos and a sunset in Fiji would be a good place to discuss this debt. I am a lesser man usually but this time I think we're even. It seems like you are always pulling demon shit out of me." He began moving around the room trying to get his bearings. Tone looked around to make certain it was safe for Arino as he felt like he was bumping into things that were not even there. As soon as he regained his equilibrium, he turned to Arino and said, "Besides, I couldn't let Bubba have you when I still haven't gotten a kiss."

Nazilaq chimed in. "It's a good thing you can't kiss her. Zeke would be jealous and that is not a fitting state for an angel." Naz winked at the human.

Zeke finally spoke. "You two had me worried. I'm glad you're both safe and sound." Turning to Tone he said, "What happened? You and Bubba were both sailing in opposite directions by the time we got here. Did that happen when you made contact?"

Tone looked at him and, with sarcasm flowing as freely as the river they had traveled, he replied. "No, Zeke. That happened when we shot ACME coyote rockets at each other. Of course that's what happened when we touched each other! It was a pretty substantial contact. I was trying to drain any power I could out of him and he was trying to eat Arino. He didn't like my taste which is surprising since I have great taste in clothes." He made a show of thinking about his dressing skills and added, "Well maybe not; but I do look good in blue jeans and a t-shirt."

"So if you blast each other back then that gives us another weapon to use against the beast," said Zeke who was planning a strategy now that he knew Tone and Arino were both safe.

"Hey, Zeke, old buddy? You may not have noticed this but that damn near killed me! I don't really see that as a really good first resort attack." Tone was trying to make light of it even though there was real concern in his aura.

Nazilaq spoke up. "He is not suggesting that. Are you, Zeke?"

"Of course not. But it is another piece of the puzzle that Adoneal may be able to use to make us something that can be used to help," explained the warrior. "I think we need to catch up to Irkja and find out what happened to Bubba. Naz?"

They had all expected Nazilaq to begin moving the skimmer with a thought. Instead he explained, "We have an issue with following Irkja. He has been keeping me informed as to where they are. The beast is shifting through the layers of the spirit world. And I mean it is jumping all over the place. We can't follow him without risking some harm to one of us."

"I'm sure Arino can handle it," said Tone, knowing they were talking about him. He looked at all of them. "How much damage has been done by the shift that the Bubbameister did?"

Arino replied, "We don't know. But doing what Bubba is doing I can promise you that it will cause serious damage. We are three-hundred and ninety-two layers above the river and your safe layer. If he pulled you right here without going through the others there should be only minimal damage. You may not even notice."

"And if we skipped along through them all to get here?" asked Tone, nonchalantly examining where his fingernails would be if he had them here.

"You may not be able to go back. It may have caused brain damage," said the healer.

"It's not like I was a poster child for mental health in the first place," said Tone. "Besides the only difference I feel now it that we are being watched. Is paranoia part of the damage deal?"

122

Chapter 25

"Naz, send out a blast," ordered Ezekiel. The pilot sent out a wave of draining power followed by a wave of fire to cover anything that may have been watching them. A shake of his head told all that there was nothing out there watching. Turning back to the human, Zeke chided, "Tone, this is serious! Do you understand what we are saying? You could be a vegetable if you go back to your body!" The angel was truly worried that the human did not comprehend the gravity of the situation. "Doesn't that scare you?"

There was an enigmatic smile on the face of Tone. "Not really. Being paranoid is not a bad thing around here, dude. Arino, baby doll, is there any way you can check me out? I mean other than the way you have been sneaking looks at me ever since we met." There was a certain confidence about Tone now that had been missing previously. His encounter with Bubba had given him hope that he could hold his own in a battle and that had crossed over into other areas.

"Honestly, you don't seem any different than you ever do. Do you know something we don't, Tone?" Arino was beginning to suspect that there was a very real reason Tone was not worried. "Back on earth, are you in a coma already? Many of us suspect that," she said trying to get the information that was such a high priority topic for the angels.

Tone laughed. "No, sweetie. I'm very much awake most of the time. Sleeping is not one of my hobbies." Looking at Zeke he said, "Happy, buddy? Arino says I look fine in every sense of the word!"

Zeke was exasperated at his friend. "You know you are really trying my patience. And it's not like I am known to be the most patient angel in the first place." He could not understand how Tone was as nonchalant about something that could affect him so seriously.

The human had the look that he so often had when tormenting angels: satisfaction. He replied to the worried warrior, "Zeke, if it screwed me up then I'm screwed. But let's be honest. It's not like I'm that normal to begin with. What's a few more damaged brain cells between friends?" Then he looked around the Spiritscape nearby and asked, "Naz, are you sure there isn't something hiding out there? I can't shake the feeling something is watching us."

Nazilaq sent another wave of power out of the skimmer. "Tone, there is nothing out there as far as I can sense. I'm sorry. And as much as I enjoy listening to the debate about Tone's mental illnesses, there is another issue that we need to worry about before we even get the chance to blow his brain up. How are we going to follow the beast?"

Zeke gave Tone one last look of frustration before turning his attention to the skimmer pilot. "Take us on a parallel course. Get us to the same area on this plane and we will find a way to get to it or get it to come to us. Is Irkja still trailing him?"

The pilot paused, making silent contact with his partner, and replied, "Irkja is keeping a safe distance but is staying with Bubba. Setting course now. Hold on. I may have to make sudden changes because Irkja says the beast is not going in one direction for more than one hundredth of a quoll."

"Understood. Do your thing. Tone you get to see it flying outside of the river," said the still concerned Zeke. He was subtly examining Tone but could not see any kind of spiritual degradation either. He considered trying to silently speak to Arino but could tell that Tone was watching the both of them without even trying to be delicate.

"Excellent! Is this where we make it look like a badass crystal Blackbird?" asked the human who was passing through the skins of the skimmer with Arino. The *Hajile-R* went from still to breakneck speed in a thought. They were suddenly traveling away from the river and lake toward what look to Tone like a series of evil looking mountainous spires. "And if you two want to discuss my state feel free. I am reading both of you right now so why don't you just get it out in the open?"

"That is strange. I just felt some power drain off me," said Arino. "Tone?"

"Don't look at me babe. I keep my distance. You are way too cute to blasting into a billion pieces," replied the human. "I swear there is something watching us."

Looking at the other two angels she could see they had nothing to do with it. "Must have been a residual from the encounter with Bubba." Turning to her confusing friend, she got back on topic. "Tone, you do understand what has happened to you, don't you?"

"Yes dear. Bubba took me to a different plane within the Spiritscape here and I may have damaged my ability to get back into my body. Bubba has no plan on going back to his body and he is trying to get me to join him. Messing up my link back to my body gives him more ammo to use to get me to join him. Plus, now I'm getting a funny feeling about things that aren't there." He looked at the shocked looks on the angels. "Oh yeah. I forgot to tell you. Bubba wants me to join him against all of you. Crazy, huh?"

Zeke was the first to comment. "How do you know that? Did you have a real conversation with that thing?" In his mind there was something wrong. He had thought of the beast as something more of a force of nature than something that would have a casual conversation with a human. Was Bubba really something like Tone?

"Sure. We discussed art, literature, whether or not to call him Barbie and the flavor of angels and demons." After a moment Tone added, "Demons are greasy according to Bubba."

Arino asked, "And he wants you to join him? Is that possible?"

Tone looked at her as his aura became very different. He was serious. "We are opposite sides of the same coin, sweetie. When we touched I felt the sensation of the seventeen demons and three angels he has chowed down on. It has driven him totally bonkers. He doesn't care about right or wrong or good or evil. He's a total sociopath who doesn't give a damn about anything but his next meal." He looked at each of his friends. "And I could easily follow the same path. That is why you could not leave any of the traces of the angels in me. It is too tempting and I'm not that strong."

Nazilaq, still following a zigzag course that was moving toward the spires, spoke up. "So you could absorb the power of angels and demons like Bubba? That is more than a little scary, Tone."

Tone looked at his friend and replied. "Naz, I feel guilty eating a chicken sandwich sometimes and don't even get me started on the luau I went to with the whole pig looking at me. It was just too strange seeing the apple in its mouth. I opted for the chili dogs. But devouring an angel is worse than being a baby puncher or giving a puppy a perm. Some things you just don't do because it is not who you are."

The angels all looked at Tone, scanning his entire being, knowing that he was being honest. "Do you think that Bubba is just a sociopath by nature or do you think it is the influence of the demons?" asked Arino. "I could see them causing so much putrefaction of a soul that it would end up like Bubba."

Tone considered that for quite some time. "Honestly, I think there is something else going on. He referred to you as my pets and then said he had one of his own. Something tells me his pet is not as holy as mine are. Hey Zeke. You wouldn't consider wearing one of those shock collars would you? There are times when I really need to get you to behave yourself better."

"Only if I get one for you too," replied the demon hunter. "So he has an ally. Demonic I'm sure. It would not be out of character for one of them to try and use something like Bubba to further their own agendas. But which demon would have that kind of power? Most of them really wouldn't have much use for Bubba. Of the others that would try something like this, all are either healing in Hell or accounted for."

Arino, always the healer, inquired of Tone. "Are you all right with all this? It could not have been easy feeling the spirits within Bubba. Was it like they were trying to take you over or something different?"

Tone was hesitant to answer. He knew exactly how it felt but was reluctant to admit it to his friends. After an intense internal debate he decided they needed to know. "It was different. There was no consciousness to the power of the demons or angels in Bubba. Anything that may have been there once upon a time is long gone. It was just the power of evil or good depending on the thread that I felt. It was very, very intoxicating. I totally understand why Bubba does it. No one could resist that drug. It is like crack, heroin, meth and pot all rolled into one instant addiction."

Zeke could see the conflict in his friend. "It must have taken everything you had to tell Arino to pull it all out."

"You have no idea. And all I got was a brush with what Bubba has. We really have no choice. I'm sure the damage between body and spirit has gotten to the point where he can't go back. But if we let him continue he will keep trying to devour others." Tone waited to make sure they all understood. "Bubba has to be destroyed for your sake as well as mine. Another brush with what he has and I can't promise I'll be able to resist." No one spoke. There were no words needed.

Nazilaq broke the silence. "Did someone call a demon because there is one trying to get our attention?"

Je'relir was in the distance with evil smiles on its faces. There was a not so subtle change in the atmosphere within the *Hajile-R* with the advent of the archdemon. If there had been a temperature in the skimmer Tone would have bet it would have dropped one hundred degrees. The angels were preparing to do any and everything necessary to deal with this thing that had caused each of them more pain than any being other than Bubba.

Nazilaq was ready with everything at his disposal to attack and cause the most devastation possible. There was power flowing through the skimmer as it began to morph into a longer needle shaped form with the blades moving up the body and lengthening to form a spinning series of knives around the outer hull of the skimmer as a defense against any incursions. The tip of the needle had a glow about it that said to all in range that it was ready to send a blast of angel fire at the slightest hint of trouble.

Arino had transformed into her healing form for multiple purposes. She was prepared to heal either of the other two angels or Tone through Zeke if needed. Her healing power was already flowing and had begun working to prepare the angels for wounds that could be healed instantly. A second reason for her change in form was defensive since it would require more effort to hit her since she could move out of the way of most attacks faster than her normal form. The final reason for her metamorphoses centered around an attack that was debilitatingly painful to most demons. She could use the same power that caused healing in angels to create agony that rendered demons unable to defend themselves allowing others to deal the crippling blows.

Those crippling blows would come from the now fully battle ready Ezekiel. Tone was actually frightened by the appearance of his friend. Zeke was glowing so brightly with power that it would have been painful had Tone not backed away in both fear and self-preservation. He knew that much power could be dangerous with his effects on angels and he knew that Zeke may not be thinking clearly in this case. The now familiar tendrils of power were emanating from the warrior ready to lash out and cause pain, suffering, and desolation to his archenemy. It was not the look on his face but the aura of his spirit that caused Tone real concern. There was something about his aura that told Tone there was the demonic version of blood on his mind.

Zeke looked at Tone and nodded. With a smile at the angels Tone said one word, "Poof!" and disappeared. "I'm here if you need me," came his disembodied voice echoing through the ship.

"Tone, you need to stay out of this one. He is too much for you," said Zeke. "We need you to deal with Bubba. Stay safe for once!" It was clear that was not a request to all who heard. Tone was not impressed.

"And what if he's too much for you, buddy?" asked Tone, curious to hear the answer.

"He won't be," he said simply. The discussion was over. "Naz, be ready with everything you have. Arino, you know what to do. Let's see how tough he is now." Zeke ported out of the skimmer and was at the midway point between his friends and his nemesis.

Tone got his first good look at the archdemon and wished he hadn't. This particular demon was not as difficult to define as so many others he had seen since beginning this wandering mission; however, it looked like one of the worst he had ever viewed. It was not as blue as most of them but there was a blue tint to the black of the skin. The body of the devil was what terrified Tone. He had read accounts about moray eels that roamed the oceans. This creature looked like an eel that had grown big enough to eat a bus. The long, thin body was constantly moving and seemed to be able to twist in tighter curves than any earthbound eel or snake. The most terrifying aspect was the heads of this demon. Each end of the demon's body had a head. One end had what looked to be a hairless, black lion with larger than normal fangs. The other end had the face of a horrific infant. Strangely the infant face was scarier than the lion.

"That thing is just wrong in ways even I can find words for," whispered Tone.

"You won't find any arguments from any of us," replied the hyper-focused Nazilaq.

The voice of Zeke was controlled rage as he addressed the demon. "Hello Je'relir. It has been a while. Not long enough."

"Ezekiel, it is always a painful experience dealing with your angelic arrogance." The voices of the demon were the strangest that Tone had heard yet. Each head took a turn saying a word. Back and forth it went with the deafening roar of a lion and the whimpering whisper of the baby. Even the voice was wrong. "If we did not need each other you can be sure I would not be addressing you and your little band of buddies. Where is the human?"

"I'll be right back," said Zeke. He flew down and behind the skimmer to attack three demons who were sneaking up behind them. An imp, something that looked like a gorgon on acid and a blue haze were quickly send on one way trips to heal in Hell with the power of a warrior showing how to end demonic threats. Flying back to his previous position Zeke continued, "I'm sorry. That was rude of me. What were you saying?"

The rage on the infant face of the archdemon twisted it into a horrific, demonic tantrum while the lion head roared its rage. Naz turned the *Hajile-R*'s nose up and to the right and let fly a ball of angel fire that glowed through the ether then split into five separate spheres to connect with five more demons who were blasted back to Hell. The rage of the demon was continued at Zeke through the infant head while the skimmer was cursed through the lion's face.

Zeke looked at the demon and asked, "Is something wrong? It seems that our conversation keeps getting interrupted by those pesky friends of yours. Please don't concern yourself about it. Our skimmer will take care of them so we can discuss the beast." On cue the skimmer sent more angel fire in multiple directions dealing damage to many demons who thought they were well hidden.

Giving Je'relir his most withering look he said, "Now about the beast? Or shall I just feed you to it?"

The twisted voices of the demon jeered, "Like you could." There was a hunger in its spirit as both faces drooled while leering at the warrior. Zeke saw the lust in the eyes and glared back as if challenging his enemy to attack. "I don't need your help with the thing. But you do need mine."

"And you are here to help us? That is very touching," taunted a sarcastic Zeke. "What do you want, Je'relir?" Tone, Arino and Naz could tell that Zeke was hiding his rage behind humor. Zeke was ready to make good on his threat of feeding the archdemon to the arch-beast.

"There is something else here trying to drain my power!" though a concerned Arino. "I feel it again but it doesn't feel like Je'relir!"

"Hang in there Arino. It is just battle feelings. We will take him down and then make sure," thought a focused Ezekiel.

Pure evil dripped from the mouths of the demon as it asked, "How is Adoneal? I hear that archangel is now a retard. That must suck. How did that happen? That wasn't from our last encounter was it?"

"Don't push it, demon. You have no idea what you are dealing with here," came the tense reply from the warrior.

"I really don't like this asshole," whispered Tone to Arino. He did not know how much longer Zeke could refrain from attacking.

"Neither do I, Tone," replied Arino. "But we have to let Zeke deal with it. There is something going on here or one of them would have attacked by now."

"I think that is all of his backup," said Naz as another volley of angelic fire balls flew in several arcs at once. "Tone, do you see any trails I missed?"

Tone looked around, impressed by the power of the skimmer as several trails were heading toward Hell. "I think that's all of them. Nice work. Do you light bonfires with this thing too?"

"Only on special occasions," retorted the angelic sailor. Sending his thoughts out he communicated, *"You are all clear, Zeke."*

The demon looked from the skimmer to the warrior and back again. "I see a sailor and healer but no human. Where is it? Is it hiding in your little toy?" It was clear that it wanted to provoke Zeke into making the first move. All three occupants of the skimmer knew the game that was being played but so did Zeke.

Ignoring the questions about Tone he countered, "You have not answered my questions. What do you want?"

The heads snapped back to looking at Ezekiel. He did not back off or even flinch. "You think I'm going to be bullied into obeying your commands? I'm not an imp. I don't give a shit about you. Do you want to tell me about the human or do I just take everything apart until I dine on its soul? I am ready to have a snack. I haven't gotten to taste a human soul in at least half a quoll. From what I have heard, his will be tasty."

Tone shivered uncontrollably. "Why is he after me? And how does he know about me?" Tone thought about it for a few seconds and came to the logical conclusion. "Dammit! I really hate that little imp!"

"Zadrol?" asked Nazilaq. "So much for him keeping information to himself."

127

"Why would he tell Je'relir? There must have been something in it for him," said Arino. "When we find him I think we need to have a long spirit to spirit talk with that little devil."

"I think I need to give the little prick a little prick with my new knife. Been wanted to see what happens with that whole infection thing." Tone's disembodied voice joked with the angels, "Naz, you bring the beer. Arino, you get the popcorn."

"I'll bring the candy!" shouted Je'relir. "I have excellent hearing, Tone."

"Just once can't you lay low?" came the thoughts from an exasperated Zeke. "You are speaking to me, Je'relir. Leave the others alone."

"I am here to speak to the human. Do you not understand the concept of not giving a shit about you? You are not even worth my time," taunted the demon who was becoming increasingly angry.

Zeke was not letting go. "Why do you want to talk to a human?" He was not going to give any more information than he already had.

"You will never know!" screamed both heads in unison as they sprang at Zeke.

Chapter 26

Many things happened at once. A blast of angel fire burst from the *Hajile-R* speeding toward the archdemon's baby head with the intent of making it stop crying forever. Arino ported out of the skimmer and appeared beside Zeke with a burst of healing energy spreading out toward the lion face of Je'relir hoping to cause the debilitating pain that it caused on other demons. Zeke stood his ground with his angelic touch ready to reach out to the demon and slice it into two as soon as it was in range.

Then everything froze. The blasts of angelic fire and healing power were held in place. The demon looked like it was unable to move forward, caught in mid-lunge. Zeke was not moving but looked ready to overpower Je'relir as soon as everything moved again. As Tone slowly faded into view he was touching a rune on his H'tes and smiling at his fortune. He had touched several runes without any effect before finding one that was useful in this situation.

"Now how am I going to help here?" he asked no one in particular. "And why am I talking to myself?" laughed the human who was the subject of so much debate. He looked around the skimmer and realized that he had never gotten out of it without angelic assistance. Reaching the inner hull he tapped on the crystal and found it as solid as ever. He considered kicking it but remembered his experience with the spirit sphere. That gave him an idea.

"Michael, if you can hear me I have stopped everything with the neato-burrito pocket knife you gave me. But I could use some help here." thought Tone.

There was a long pause making Tone think that Michael was not able to hear him. "Stand by, Tone. It is a localized effect. We are checking to see how far it expands. Very impressive by the way," complimented Michael. "We can't enter the area without the stillness rune affecting us as well. What are you pondering in that devious mind of yours?"

Michael could hear the near manic giggle of Tone reaching across the spirit world as he asked, *"How long would it take to get a spirit sphere here? And could I lift it?"*

"Tone, according to the cherubs the stillness rune made a field that is massive. You don't have control of it do you?" inquired the archangel. Michael understood the plan but saw several flaws.

"Dude, I just randomly pressed runes trying to find a way to help. Don't even know how the hell I did it but I have not taken my finger off this rune just in case." Tone was curious what would happen if he took his finger off the rune.

"Take your finger off the rune," ordered Michael. "But don't touch it again until you want to release everything. Does your H'tes have plenty of power? This will drain it eventually."

Tone released the rune and saw to his relief that nothing changed. "Too cool! There is a butt-load of power in it. Now about that spirit sphere?"

"I'm sorry, Tone but even you can't carry a spirit sphere," replied Michael. "But there may be something else. Adoneal has been working on something that may be helpful. It is a device that you will have to put around a part of the demon. It should temporarily render it powerless and immobile. But it will not last long. It can be brought to you."

Tone was again amazed by the abilities of Adoneal. "Only two problems with that plan. One, I'm stuck in the skimmer. Two, how can you get it here without freezing?"

Michael's words came to Tone's mind. "First, find the rune on the blade that looks like an oval that has fifty lines crossing through it with a smaller oval in the center without lines penetrating it. Press it and let me know how solid the skimmer's walls feel."

"No freaking way!" said Tone aloud. He searched several runes until he found the one Michael described almost all the way to the tip of the blade. He pressed it and felt the wall of the ship. It felt like he was pressing on jelly. He laughed as he considered how Naz would feel if he knew his ship was being made into a topping for toast. He pressed it again and it gave under his touch. He pressed harder and found his arms was beginning to pass though the wall. The sensation of his arm passing through jelly was amusing him until he realized that the wall of the ship was not changing. It was his arm that was the toast topping and the ship was remaining solid. He pulled back and looked at his arm which had elongated but was reforming back into its normal shape. "That is too damn weird!" Tone said to himself.

Michael's voice was in his head. "Is it working? I can't see past the stillness field."

Tone thought back to Michael, "Do you have any idea how freaky this is? You could have warned me. You can be a mean bastard when you want to!"

The archangel's laughter echoed through Tone's mind. "Tell me something I don't know. Just get out of the skimmer so we can capture one of Heaven's most wanted, please."

Tone looked at the still form of Nazilaq. "He can be so bossy! Be glad you work for Donnie." Tone once more pressed against the wall of the *Hajile-R* and found it jellying again. He pressed all the way to his shoulder and still was not through on the other side. Looking at Naz again he said, "If I get stuck I'm gonna be pissed at Mike." With a long look at his jellied hand he put the other arm through the wall and began working his head through it as well. Tone was in the wall of the skimmer up to his legs when his hands finally broke free of the outer hull. Instinctively he tried to use the outer hull to pull himself out and ended up pulling his arms back into the wall of the ship.

"Shit!" muttered Tone, unaware that his words were muted being inside the wall of the skimmer. He once again moved his hands out of the wall of the skimmer and continued his slow but steady movement out of the ship and into the dangerous spirit world. With his last leg free of the wall he moved around the massive blades of the ship, grateful they were still. As soon as he was a safe distance away from it he pressed the same rune again and felt his spirit as solid as it ever got.

"OK. I'm out. That is like swimming in pudding. And not the cheap ass instant stuff. I'm talking about boiling the good stuff that you let sit and get that nice crust on top of it," explained Tone.

"I'll make sure Zeke makes you some when he sees you," teased Michael. "Now the belt is easy to use. Just wrap it around the demon three times and use the hook to hold it in place. Are you ready for it?"

"Sure but how are you..." Tone stopped thinking to the archangel as Michael appeared nearby with his arms out in front of him and a strange leather-looking band hanging from his hands. Michael had ported in knowing that he would be stilled until Tone had done his task.

"You stupid asshole! What the hell are you thinking?" asked Tone to the immobile Michael. "Oh. I get it." He understood the risk being taken by Michael. If Tone touched him there was the very real risk of damage even in the stilled state. This angel was not about to send in another angel to do something that he would not be willing to do himself. "It was still stupid," he said to the stoic spirit.

Tone carefully approached the archangel and pulled the leather strap out of his hands, being careful not to even get close to touching. As he held this strange thing in his hands he realized it wasn't leather. The texture was all wrong. Most leather Tone had seen was smooth but this one had jagged barbs on one side and something like waves on the other. Looking at it he saw that there were runes on both sides of it not unlike those on a spirit sphere. These were not moving but for all Tone knew that was from the stillness he had caused. He wasn't certain but he decided to make sure the barbs were on the side that would be cutting into the demon. It made him smile thinking of this little bit of "screw you" he could give to this monster.

He took the belt and moved to where the action would have been happening if he hadn't stilled the whole battle before it began. Je'relir was still in mid-lunge and the fire of the skimmer and the power of the healer would make contact as soon as he unstilled everything. He could just put the belt on the demon and let it get hit with all kinds of Heavenly power. It would serve the son of a bitch right.

But then what about his questions? If he left Je'relir defenseless against that much power there was no telling if there would be much left to talk other than some pha'ards and a fried demon heading back to Hell for a hell of a lot of healing. Touching it was out of the question. This thing was just too disgusting and Tone didn't want another demon fragment messing with his head or body or spirit or whatever the hell else they messed with.

Tone smiled as he looped the belt around the eel-like body of the creature near the baby-faced head. With some effort Tone pulled the face out of direct contact with the angel fire from the skimmer but made sure there was still a glancing blow to get the demon's attention. He then pulled the belt off that head and moved to the other to do the same but with the healing power of Arino. The demon would survive the attack but would definitely know it had been touched by angels. The only unknown was Zeke. Tone took the belt to the center and pulled it out of Zeke's immediate reach so that it would take some effort for the warrior to have an effect on Je'relir.

Moving to the exact midway point on the body of the archdemon, Tone wrapped the belt around it three times and fastened it with the small hooks that were at the end. As he put it on he realized that it would only go on with the barbs eating into the spirit of the demon. He really liked the way Adoneal made his gadgets. He had a sense of function that Tone almost could mistake for humor if that were possible.

Looking at everything one more time he decided that he had done all the damage he could. For just a moment he pondered the possibility of just thrusting his H'tes into this demon who had caused so much suffering. Tone was sure he had only seen the tip of the iceberg of pain it had caused. He looked at the demon. He looked at the knife. He looked back at the demon. He looked back at the knife.

"Dammit!" he said moving away without striking. He looked at the demon and whispered, "Please give me a reason." As he began to fade from view he pressed the stillness rune on his blade.

The action happened as if it had never stopped with some subtle changes. The lion head of Je'relir caught part of the healing power and caused it to roar in agony. The baby-faced head of was singed by the fire of the skimmer. Zeke stopped in mid strike as the mid-section he was preparing to sever was no longer where it was supposed to be. The belt glowed with the runes sapping and containing the power of the archdemon leaving it motionless instead of lashing out at the angels.

Michael's word commanded, "Stop!" All three angels and the demon turned their heads to face the full glory of the archangel Michael in battle form ready to deal any destruction needed. His power was radiating in many directions but with a strange slowness that allowed Tone be certain he was out harm's way. The power of the mightiest archangel surrounded the impotent demon encasing it even further with the power of the spirit belt draining any power that it may have had.

The demon looked at the belt that had mysteriously appeared on it, the angels ready to deal out pain with a trip to heal in Hell and the powerful archangel ready to fracture it into millions of fragments. Je'relir said the only thing that fit the situation. "Shit!"

"I take it we have your complete and undivided attention, Jehim and Relir?" asked a far too cordial Michael. It made the demon shudder hearing those names coming out of the mouth of one who could clearly deal the kind of damage that would lead to Hell healing for more than he had ever experienced.

Zeke, Arino and the rapidly approaching Nazilaq were still waiting for instructions and explanations to what was happening. With a quick thought all were brought into the picture as to the events that had transpired to allow Michael to have total command of the situation. All were left in awe of the power being displayed by the archangel but even more impressed by the actions and abilities of Tone.

"Now before I separate you into two different demons again I'd like to have a little chat. Is that all right with you both?" asked the friendly archangel.

The belt around the demon was glowing with the runic power that had constrained it while leaving it vulnerable to attacks from the angels. In many ways it was far worse than a spirit sphere and Je'relir knew it. In a spirit sphere there was no danger from those around it until the demon or angels was released from it. With a spirit belt in place there was nothing preventing Michael from doing exactly what he had suggested.

"I am one," said the alternating heads. "Separating me would be a level of cruelty that even you are not capable of rationalizing, archangel." The constant shifting between roar and whimper was more unsettling than any demon any of them had ever heard.

There was a glow about Michael that said he had an ace up his sleeve. "Who said an angel would do something like that? But if there were a human like the one that you claim to want to meet, what would happen if such a soul were to deal some kind of damage to a demon that would lead to a splitting of two merged demons through a fragmentation?" The archangel looked at the demon with more power than even Zeke had ever seen. "That might be a bad thing if I could not stop it."

The arrogance of the demon shown in both sets of eyes as it challenged the angel. "You would never let something like that happen. It is not in your nature." The two-toned laughter sent chills through the very core of Tone's spirit. "The worse you will ever do is send me to Hell to heal for longer than I want. Try your bluff on an imp. I am not that easily swayed." The laughter resumed even louder than before.

Michael stared at both of the heads of the demon and sent out a wave of power that abruptly ended the laughter by slapping both faces with a kiss of archangel power. The mirth was replaced by curses in an instant.

"Damn you to Hell! I will find you and make what was done to the other archangel seem like a kindness when I..." The threat of Je'relir was cut off by another display of what could be done by the most powerful of the angels. The faces of the demon whipped around as they were slapped on the other side giving both heads matching glows of golden power that remained on the faces continuing to burn them with the dreaded power.

"Now do I have your attention?" asked a far less friendly Michael.

The faces of the demon glared back at him saying, "What do you want, ass wipe?" It was so strange to Tone to hear an infant say "ass". He almost laughed at the absurdity of the situation.

Another slap from the power of Michael led to two part unharmonious howls from Je'relir. "Please refrain from calling any angels by such unhygienic names in my presence." Michael listened and heard the snicker of Tone nearby. "Now my first question is about the beast. Are you helping it?"

The spirit belt continued to glow as the power of the demon was restrained. It looked to all around that the belt was beginning to show signs of strain. No one knew for certain how long it would last. All the angels were ready in case it failed. Or so they thought.

"And why should I help you, angel?" spat the demon. Even saying "angel" sounded like an insult out of its mouths. Michael considered swatting the demon again but was beaten to it by Zeke. A gash appeared on the lion's face from the eye to the mouth causing a blue oozing substance to bleed out of the unholy hellion. Michael looked at Zeke with well hidden surprise in his spirit. No words were needed. Zeke backed off and allowed Michael to continue.

"Any other questions?" asked Michael. The demon was now glaring at Michael and Ezekiel with equal levels of animosity. Taking silence as a negative Michael asked again, "Are you helping the beast?"

All of the angels waited for the answer. There was tension in the ether as they waited for it to reply. After what seemed to be an eternity to Tone it finally spoke. "No. Why would I help something that is killing demons?"

"I can think of all kinds of reasons," sneered Zeke. "Gain power. Get rid of rivals..."

"Revenge," added Naz.

"A power play," threw in Arino.

The faces of Je'relir went from one angel to the next. "All excellent reasons but I am not in league with that monstrosity."

"Liar!" shouted Zeke, with his righteous anger beginning to make his control somewhat tenuous.

"No," stated Michael. "It cannot lie while wearing the spirit belt. It will punish if it detects lies just like a spirit sphere."

"Another toy from the one I made into a moron?" asked the demon trying to get a rise out of the angels. Michael was concerned that Zeke would need to be restrained; however, it was not the hunter who lashed out. A blast of angel fire flew from the *Hajile-R* enveloping the demon for an instant. The seared spirit that was left after being consumed in flames was actually smiling through its suffering. "I'll take that as a 'yes'," laughed the demon. "And thank you!"

As the newly impotent spirit belt fell off, Je'relir sent out a blast of demonic blizzard from its mouths that stunned the angels. Each of them found themselves in different situations based on how much of the attack they had received.

As Zeke found himself in the epicenter of the force of the blizzard he chastised himself for allowing Je'relir to distract him from his true mission: protecting Tone and stopping Bubba. He was not worried that Michael or the others may not have been prepared. His real concern was for Tone. Had he been in the line of the freezing blast? Would they be able to find him if he was injured? The warrior could not escape the blizzard from the blast as he tried in vain to break free or port or anything. Nothing worked. He would fight for all he was worth to defeat this abomination and save Tone.

Arino was frozen in place and unable to port by the cold of evil that had caught her without any defenses in place. She began using her healing power to break through the layers of demon touched ice that had encased her. She realized that Je'relir had targeted her with this kind of trap to keep her from being able to heal the damage caused. What if he would phase one of the others? She would not get to them in time.

133

The skimmer caught the chilling blast that caused even the spinning blades to grind to a halt. Nazilaq tried sending his angel fire out of the point of the ship only to find it had to begin burning its way through the glacier-like tomb he was in. He knew he had to leave his ship to help in the fight. As he attempted to port and aid his friends, he found himself beside his ship equally encased in the ice. He guided the ship to begin melting toward him to allow him to escape this trap.

Michael had not let his guard down and was prepared but also caught the worse of the demonic power. The blast from the archdemon was continuous, trying to freeze the flames of power from the angel and the angel's fires blasted back at the demon. As he found himself flying back, caught in the force of the gale, Michael called out for reinforcements knowing that they could use extra angels for this hellion. Through the torrent of the blast the words of the devil echoed, "Don't bother calling for help. They can't hear you through the breeze! I have been preparing this attack against you for quolls." Laughter thundered with the escalating fury of the storm from the mouths of the demon as Michael fought to free himself from the demon charged vortex spinning him farther and farther from the battle.

Alone with the archdemon Ezekiel was fighting with everything at his disposal. It seemed as if they were nearly equally matched. Zeke shielded himself from the blast with one of the many wings of power emanating from his spirit. Another wing flew at the lion's head hitting the scorched face with more angel fire causing it to stop the demonic blast only to have it come back with more fury as Je'relir fuel his attack with rage.

The baby face cried out sending something new at the warrior. A blue sphere of demonic ice sped toward Zeke, spinning and growing, ready to envelop him and contain his angelic fire similar to what had happened to Arino but on a scale that was unimaginably more powerful. The warrior knew that dodging and moving was not an option and porting was blocked. He sent a wave of pure power at the ball knocking it once to send it away from him and then a second time to send it back to its creator. The demonic ice sphere hit the demon only to be entwined in the serpentine body of Je'relir and crushed.

Hit after hit and power after power came the attacks. As long as the other angels were otherwise occupied Je'relir and Zeke were holding their own against one another until the demon cheated. "It seems like there is something missing from your battle, ass wipe. What happened to your little hidden human?"

Zeke had to put Tone out of his mind. This demon needed to be taken out now! Then he saw what the demon was talking about. There was the form of something that looked like a frozen spirit near Arino. It had the look of a human soul encased in demonic ice.

"NO!" shouted Zeke, momentarily loosing focus. That one instance of distraction was all that Je'relir needed. All of the fury of the demonic ice storm came at the angel from two directions and two mouths. As one blast was deflected another hit Zeke from behind throwing him into the full power of the deflected ice. His angel fire was being tested to its limits as all the fury of the merged demon came down on him.

"Any last words?" asked the demon laughing hysterically. The two sets of eyes widened with blue power glowing and growing with the mirth of evil knowing they are about to be victorious. But then something changed. The look in the eyes went from victory to horror as the glow changed from blue to white with thin ribbons of black. With a scream of defeat, Je'relir exploded leaving shards of demon all over the place.

H'tes in front of him where it had thrust deep into the demon, Tone stood behind where the demon had been and said, "Am I the only one who thought it would be a good idea not to be right in front of this ugly ass bastard?"

Chapter 27

"And by the way, oops!" laughed Tone. "I didn't mean to blow him up. Just wanted to send him to Hell. Something tells me he did not see that coming. And what's with the frozen statue of me?"

Zeke was once again at a loss for words. Even Tone could not have escaped from the ice of the archdemon. He looked from the statue to Tone to the statue to Tone and had no words.

"Zeke? Are you having a stroke? Talk to me buddy," jested Tone. Tone was as confused as Zeke about the statue but felt the demon fragments all over the place were a bigger issue. "I'm not cleaning up the mess. I know I made it but demon shards and I don't get along well."

"That's not you?" asked the warrior looking at the ice sculpture. "That's not you!" he said again with enthusiasm. "Don't scare me like that!"

Tone was very amused. "Hey, I'm the one with the heart that can have attacks. You don't have to worry about that or needing clean underwear."

Michael ported back to the battle in his full glory ready to continue fighting. Seeing the shards of demon and the H'tes holding Tone he knew what had happened. He looked at the ice around him he said, "Let's help the others and then figure this all out." Michael already suspected what had happened but wanted to help his angels first. He went to work on the skimmer and Nazilaq while Tone and Zeke sent a fury of angel fire at the still frozen Arino. Zeke kept stealing looks at the ice sculpture of a human soul. After freeing a relieved Arino they went and helped Michael finish with Nazilaq and the skimmer.

Even before the skimmer was thawed, everyone was quickly brought up to speed on what had happened. With a noticeable flourish, Tone spun the H'tes back into its hiding place as the last of the demonic blue ice was melted away from the skimmer. "I think this thing will need a recharge before much longer. It took a lot of power to blast the shit out of the bad guy."

"So Tone can blow up demons too. Glad to know it's not just angels who go to pieces around him," joked the freed Nazilaq. "Just a favor, please don't stab me anytime soon. I've had a bad enough few quolls already." Giving Tone his most sincere look he added, "Thank you for that. Adoneal would be grateful."

Tone and Zeke had not taken the time to talk about what had happened. Tone was not entirely sure how his friend was going to react. It had been Zeke who had wanted to feed the archdemon to Bubba. Would he be angry that he would not have the chance to strike the blow?

"Tone?" began Zeke.

"Zeke?" smiled a cautious Tone.

"You did what none of us could do. I couldn't beat him. I am proud to call you my friend. You have my eternal gratitude for taking out Je'relir." Zeke knew that Tone would never let that rest so he continued. "It would have been too hard to stop because of the changes in me lately." He paused. "Changes because of the parts of you that are in me and the parts of me in you. That bond has made me better and worse."

Arino came to his aid. "It's all right, Zeke. You are better. Just not as controlled."

"And that is how I need you right now," stated Michael to the surprised of all gathered there. "I need you to do what you do without the control you have always shown. You will be restored when all this is done. But not until the beast is defeated any way you can."

Tone chimed in. "So I am a bad influence on you! Too cool. I can't believe I'm a bad influence on a badass angel."

Arino sensed it first. She looked at the melting form that had caused distraction to Zeke. Something was wrong. Illusions were part and parcel to what Je'relir always did. Michael had assumed that it was just an illusion of Tone that had been created as a beguilement. There was something really inside of it.

"OK. We are all wondering so I'll say it. What the hell is it?" Tone looked around at the angels waiting for an answer. None seemed to be forthcoming. "Anyone? Make a guess."

Arino approached the ice and began to use her healing power to softly melt it. "There is something in here trying to look human but I don't think it is." The ice continued to melt revealing something that was human but not. It was fading away from the damage that had been caused.

Arino melted the last of ice and tried to fill it with healing warmth. "Relax. I can help you." The creature flinched away from the healer. It was afraid and hurting like a wounded animal ready to bite the Good Samaritan that freed it. "Please let me help you." It growled at her and moved away to run right toward the intimidating form of Zeke. With a screech it scampered off in another direction to have the fearsome Michael in its way. The blades of the skimmer began to spin slowly blocking another escape route. It made a last dash in the hope of getting away only to land in the arms of Tone sending both bouncing back with a spirit shock.

"OK. I'm not touching that damn thing until it's had it shots!" said Tone shaking from the jolt. "Now that it is not to be confused with a Tone-cicle let me ask again. What the hell is it?"

All eyes and spirits looked to Michael for guidance. "It is a fragment of a human soul. It is like a phased angel or a shard of a demon. It had some kind of consciousness but it is elusive. I cannot read it. Tone, can you sense anything. It has some similarities to you."

Tone gave it the once over three times. "Well it looks a lot like a dog I saw on the street the other day. Other than that I can't tell anything." After thinking a moment he added, "But I think this is what had me so paranoid. This thing has been watching us since Bubba and I locked horns."

"Arino?" asked Michael.

Arino's kindness and healing nature had taken over and she was slowly getting closer and closer to the human fragment. Soft, subtle waves of healing power were radiating toward it to try and bring it some comfort. Her senses were trying to probe it but without much luck. "Nothing, Michael."

"Hey Mike. This isn't part of me from some future time is it?" asked Tone. "I can see myself ending up like this after a party at Arino's place. But please tell me it's not."

Zeke broke his long silence. "It's not you, Tone. I can't touch it."

If Zeke had set off a small tactical nuclear warhead it would have caused less shock. Questions were flooding the ether.

"What do you mean?" asked a near manic Michael.

"How can you tell?" queried a nervous Nazilaq.

"Are you safe from it?" inquired an unnerved Arino.

"Anybody else want a chili dog?" asked Tone. All eyes turned toward him. "I'm hungry and you aren't giving my buddy a chance to answer. Besides Rover over there is really scared and you aren't making it any better." The eyes all moved back to the human fragment and then to Zeke.

Zeke spoke. "When it got close to me I could feel the power trying to get out of me and into it. I don't know if it is trying to drain me or my power is trying to destroy it or if it is both. There is something wrong here and all I know is that touching that poor thing would be cataclysmic for one of us." Looking around at his friends he asked, "Anyone else have that sensation?"

Tone raised his hand. "It did shock the shit out of me. Seriously angels. I'm putting on Depends before I ever leave my body again!"

All of the other angels were confused by the reactions between the creature and Zeke and Tone. Arino made a decision. "I'm going to try to touch it." She looked at her friends and Michael but they all agreed with her decision. Michael gave her a nod. Tone looked less convinced.

"Are you sure, babe? We know what will probably happen if you touch me and we all know how much you want to." Taking on a serious tone he said, "Can you tell if it is as hazardous as I am?"

"It is different than you, Tone. But there is something there that I will not be able to sense without touching it." Arino had made up her mind and there was no changing it.

With a thought from Nazilaq the skimmer's blades came to an abrupt stop and were absorbed as the ship formed into a hollow cone. The angels all began moving in ways that essentially herded the fragment of a human into the mouth of the cone. The mouth closed as Arino passed the opening leaving her inside a hollow section within the skimmer. Every time she closed the distance Naz made the hollow section smaller until there was no way Arino and the fragment could avoid one another.

Arino reached out to the terrified creature with a wave of healing and calming power going before her touch. As she made contact, both spirits screamed. There was a power transfer happening between the two. But it was Arino who was sapping the power from the fragment. Instantly it was gone into the ether leaving Arino floating there with a look of horror on her face.

Naz moved the skimmer from around her and Zeke and Michael rushed to her side to hold her up. The horror had not subsided as she was supported by the warriors. Both angels tried to comfort her.

Michael reassured her. "It wasn't your fault, Arino. There is no way you could have known that would happen."

Zeke added, "You know that it was fading from the start."

The look went from horror to shock to disbelief. She finally looked at them all and found the words. "It was dying. I know that. You don't understand. It had been following us since we found Tone after his kidnapping. That was the last fragment of the humanity of the creature that we call Bubba."

"So it was shedding its humanity," stated Michael as if it were obvious. "I was afraid of that."

That revelation left even Tone without words. All looked at Arino and the place where the spirit had vaporized into nothing. This meant many things to each of them. For Zeke it meant there was no more holding back. For Nazilaq it meant the *Hajile-R* could use anything it had without worrying about harming a human. For Arino it meant there was nothing left to salvage. For Michael it was the realization of his worst fears. For Tone it meant he had no idea what all this meant. But now they knew the truth. Bubba was no longer human. Not anymore.

"Does this mean we can nuke him or whatever the hell you angels have that is like a nuke?" asked Tone who was unsurprisingly the first to recover his words.

Zeke actually chuckled. "Our version of a nuclear weapon is Michael. You saw a little bit of that in the gauntlet."

"But I do not think that will necessarily work on the beast. He seems to thrive on angelic energy." Michael had a look that was more than a little enigmatic. "We will have to try

138

something totally different than that." Before any could ask what he meant he changed tack and redirected the conversation to what he wanted to know. "Arino, how do you know that was the last of its humanity?"

All eyes were on the healer. "It touched me. There was so much I could see in it. Even though there was no real personality left I could still feel its pain and loneliness. It had been following me since we found Tone with Bubba."

"And that was blasted off when we blasted each other?" asked Tone with more than a little joy in his voice.

"Well, essentially yes," replied Arino. "The touch of Tone was enough to shred the last of his humanity. It was unclear how that happened but it did." She paused as if thinking through what she was going to say next. "And part of it touched me."

Michael was in front of her without seeming to move through the space in between. "What does that mean, Arino?" demanded the archangel. She hesitated responding to the demand. "Arino?"

There was a strange quietness as all of them waited to hear the answer. Without warning she turned, reached out and wrapped her arms around Tone. No one was more shocked than the human. The only thing that happened was a warm, healing power washed over Tone making him feel perfect.

"Not that I'm complaining because this feels amazing, but how the hell are you touching me? The last time you came close to me I felt like I had fire-breathing termites trying to eat my liver, gall bladder and one testicle that I am very attached to." Even in the midst of mystery Tone could make them all smile.

Michael was furious. "Arino! What were you thinking?! That could have destroyed you, Tone or all of us?!" The archangel was blazing with angelic fire in his righteous indignation.

Arino released Tone and looked defiantly at Michael. "First of all I knew exactly what would happen because I sent out power before I touched him. It had no reaction so I was certain it was safe. Secondly, the touch of the last bit of Bubba's humanity gave me some insight into the human condition and I knew Tone needed a hug." Looking at all of them she concluded, "And lastly, the real issue had nothing to do with Tone and everything to do with Bubba. If I could touch Tone then the impression I received from the fragment about being the last of the humanity would be verified. By my accidentally absorbing part of Bubba I was able to share a bit of humanity since it was the opposition of power that propelled them back."

Tone raised his hand. "Anyone else confused?" Zeke and Naz raised their hands as well. Michael continued to look at Arino with less anger and more curiosity and concern.

Tone moved a fraction away from Arino and opened his mouth to speak but Michael raised the question that he was preparing to ask, "How much of Bubba did you absorb?"

"Nothing of what Bubba is now. It was the last trace of his humanity that touched me. It was the lack of humanity and the power of the absorbed demons that caused Tone and Bubba to repel one another. Tone is as human as you get!" said Arino.

"And damn proud of it, too!" interjected the human.

Ignoring Tone, Michael asked, "So it is the humanity of Tone and the demon infusement of the beast that caused the repelling when they touched?"

"Precisely," stated Arino. "And there was so little humanity left in Bubba that the touch of Tone ripped the last vestiges out. And then the touch of an angel was too much for a fragment of pure humanity to be able to withstand. My touch destroyed it." There was a heartfelt sadness in her voice.

"So now we need to finish the job and destroy the Bubster before he can recharge his angel mojo by killing more angels," stated Tone.

Arino looked at Tone with concern. "Do you really not want to save one of your own? Granted he has given up so much of himself; but we should try to save him and restore his humanity."

Tone frightened them all by doing something he rarely did. He became deadly serious. "I have seen what he's like. There is no coming back from that. You just said that was the last of his humanity. Without my humanity I could easily follow where he has gone because the feeling of absorbing the spirit of angels and demons is like a drug. There is part of me that wants more but because there is also part of Zeke laced within me I can resist. But just barely."

"I agree. We must destroy the beast." asked Arino. "Michael, is there no other way?"

Michael had a different look than any of them had ever seen. It was clear that he had made a difficult decision. "No, Arino. There is no other option. Nasarg, Vret and I have been trying to find a solution that would not include destruction. It is simply too dangerous. Sending the beast to Hell is not an option because it would destroy any spirits it found there. We have a responsibility to all spirits; angel, demon, human and the others. It will keep causing the kind of devastation that is its stock and trade until it is no more. I'm sorry." Michael truly looked like he hated this course of action.

"I understand," said Arino. "I do not like it but I understand."

Without warning they seemed to be surrounded by cherubs. They were everywhere! Tone had to smile at the little angels who quickly began gathering the fragments of the demolished demon into two separate piles. Tone figured out what was happening without the same link that the angels shared but was confirmed in his assessment when Zeke cleared his mind and allowed him to share. The cherubs had been called in by Michael to gather the pieces of the demon into two groups based on the two demons it had originally been. One pile for Jehim and one for Relir.

In the distance there were two spirit spheres being carried into view by more of the diminutive angels. These two spheres would be the new homes for these devils as Vret studied them to discover how they had merged into the archdemon. Eventually they would be pieced together but there was no hurry. They would never be allowed contact with one another to prevent them from reestablishing the bond that had created such a horrendous horror to the angels. The pieces were unceremoniously dumped into the open spheres as all the fragments were found, sorted and placed in the correct containers.

As the cherubs flew here and there, Arino gave Tone a very thorough examination much to his delight. She checked his spirit for any possible contamination from the explosion of Je'relir but found him to be free from any kind of demonic determinants. The cherubs also flew around him creating an angelic tornado of activity that seemed to vacuum any demon dust leaving Tone with the feeling of a well waxed spirit. One of the cherubs passed before Michael, paused while communicating something unspoken, and then joined its fellow cherubs carrying the spirit spheres away. They were gone in an instant.

"OK. That was interesting," said Tone who could not think of any other way to describe it. "Do they always clean up messes like that?"

Naz answered the question, "Not that I have ever seen. But this was a special situation."

Zeke had been strangely quiet since Arino had embraced Tone. He had a question that had to be asked. "Arino, since I couldn't touch the fragment of Bubba, what happens if I touch you or you have to touch me? I can tell that something has changed between us. I don't know if it's good."

Chapter 28

"If she can touch Tone surely she can touch you," said Nazilaq. Then he looked at Ezekiel cautiously. "Unless you are sensing something."

"No, Naz. Just worried about what this will do to this team." Zeke was staring at Arino. "It's not like you're the only healer. But you are one of the best."

"She is hotter than Raph," added Tone. "And I don't get stoned listening to her talk. But she does have another effect on me that..."

"That we don't really need to hear about," interrupted Michael. "I need to know if you two are dangerous to each other. Find out." There was an urgency in the archangel that caught the attention of all.

"First, Mikey, I was going to say 'that is like making me fall in love with her'. So get your mind out of the gutter. That is where my mind is and there is not enough room for both of us." Tone once again lightened a tense mood with his unusual humor. "And second, what's with the rush to find out? I know it is great that Arino can touch me. Believe me it! It is really great in ways that... But I digress. What's the hurry, Mike? Do you know something we don't?"

Michael turned to look at the human with a glow that was a combination of annoyed and impressed. "Yes I do." He looked at the healer and warrior without elaborating and said, "Arino, please find out without getting either of you hurt." Even though he was polite it was clear that was not a request.

"Hold on, babe. I don't play by your rules, Mike. I want some..." began Tone.

"Anthony, I will explain after we have an answer! Right now I will not explain anything until I know what has happened." Michael had interrupted Tone before but this was the first time the archangel had used a frighteningly soft sound to his speech. It caused all to pay attention and even shut Tone up. The human knew this was not a battle he would win.

Arino and Zeke both nodded to Michael. Zeke looked at Tone, winked and said, "Relax. It's all right." That made Tone even more concerned. Zeke was not that kind to him unless there was some real danger.

"You kids be careful. Use protection!" said Tone trying again to relieve the tension with his humor. It didn't help.

Arino approached Zeke far too casually from Tone's point of view. She transformed into her amorphous healing form to allow her the most flexibility in the event of disaster. Zeke stood still, calmly waiting for the healer's power to touch him. One small finger of healing power began edging toward the warrior while a wing of angelic power moved from the hunter to the healer. It reminded Tone of the first time Arino had tried to heal him. He shuddered. It was almost painful to watch how slowly the energy moved toward his friends.

Nazilaq was watching the human more than the angels. He wished he could help Tone during this experience. He had a suspicion what Michael was planning but he knew better than to try to second guess the archangel. His role was to be a support to Tone in case something went very wrong and to stay in touch with Irkja to keep tabs on Bubba.

Michael was paying close attention to the two he had ordered into harm's way. Even though none of the others could see it he had put up a shield to drain off any power that would cause harm. He had also moved the two farther away than they appeared. He knew that Tone would want to be near the two angels he could touch in case something went wrong; but he was not going to risk Tone as well. The illusion of proximity would be enough to keep the human happy and safe.

Zeke and Arino had felt Michael moving them and understood the precaution. Both were confused by the order but both knew that Michael would not risk this without a very good reason. The power of the two paused before reaching each other as they shared a thought before touching. Arino's power brushed the warrior as his wave of his angelic fire reached the healer. Both angels were drawn together in a pull that instantly made full contact impossible to avoid. As Arino's healing form wrapped around Ezekiel, power blazed as healing energy and battle power combined blinding all of them as it strained against the shield of the archangel. Michael looked to actually be straining to contain the power of the two angels as it continued to create a fountain of fire, spraying and pressing against the shield until it seemed that both shield and archangel were at their limits.

Tone would have been impressed by the display of power if he were not so worried about his friends. As they were in the center of the explosion he could not see them due to the glare. Were they being consumed? Was one of them dying as the other drained them? What the hell was going on?

It stopped abruptly to the great relief of Michael. Arino, in her normal angelic anthropomorphic form stood next to Ezekiel in a very normal looking glow. Neither seemed to be any worse for the wear.

"That was unexpected," stated Naz. "Can you do that again? But not right this second. I don't think Tone is up for it." The human looked ready to pass out.

"That was one of the coolest light shows I have ever seen!" declared Tone. "And I have seen this really cool fireworks display on a lake to music. But that was cooler than seeing red, white and blue explosions to 'Born in the USA'. Please don't do it again."

"Tone, your H'tes please?" asked a tense Michael. As the blade came swinging out of Tone's arm Michael quickly grabbed it and infused it with the power he had just absorbed to protect them all. He held it for longer than any of them were comfortable watching as it looked like he was in pain releasing that much power. When he finally opened his hand, freeing the blade he said, "Thank you. That was more power than even I could hold for much longer. Now you don't need a recharge."

Zeke and Arino had been floating there without saying anything. If angels were vulnerable to being in shock they would have felt it. Even without shock there was obviously something going on. Naz looked at them and asked, "So what was that like?"

Zeke was the first to speak. "It felt like I was supercharged and had to get rid of the power. It flowed out of the top part of me." The warrior instincts kicked in. "If we can harness that power then think of the battles that can be won. Je'relir would not have stood a chance against that."

Arino added, "The power did the same with me but I was thinking about the massive healing we could perform with that kind of angelic fountain. Imagine if we could rain that down on a group of angels in the middle of a battle."

"Are any of you thinking what I'm thinking?" asked Tone smiling.

"That this may be something we can use against the beast?" asked Michael hoping this would be a big reveal.

"Well I was thinking we could have roasted a butt load of hot dogs and still had power for a chili cooker for a great lunch; but we can go with the whole Bubba thing if you think that's a better idea." said Tone, who seemed to genuinely want to try his cooking idea.

Naz turned to the human. "Do you ever eat anything else?"

"Only when I have to," replied Anthony.

"Back to the beast," said an exasperated archangel, looking at Tone. "This may be what we have been hoping for. Vret foresaw something like this happening. That is why Arino has been with you all this time. Vret knew that something, she was not sure what, was going to happen. This is all very new in a few quolls of extraordinary new experiences. Never have a warrior and healer been found to have comparable and compatible powers."

"What does this mean, Michael?" asked Zeke. "I have never even considered something like this working. We have opposite goals most times. No offense, Arino."

"None taken," replied the healer. "I agree totally. So what are you seeing Michael? How can we use this with Bubba? Will it heal or harm?"

Michael smiled at them. "Both. It will destroy the demonic influences but will not affect any angelic energy in the beast. The *Hajile-R* can removed the angelic power and then we will see what we have left once all the Spiritscape powers are gone. If there is anything left to save we may just be able to save a spirit from destruction."

"So everyone wins? Sounds good to me. Now what's the catch? There is always a catch with an archangel!" stated Tone.

Michael looked at Tone with the same look of frustration while being impressed. "We do not know if it will work on the beast. It may just give him something to devour and if that happens Zeke and Arino will be taken by the beast and their combined power will make things worse than before."

"Is that all?" asked a sarcastic Tone. "Here I thought it was something bad."

Zeke spoke up. "I like that plan. It is worth the risk unless you have a better idea, Tone."

Arino added, "And it gives Bubba a slim chance at recovery."

Defiantly Tone declared, "Well, I do have this idea to mess with Bubba but it requires three land mines, a goose, five ounces of key lime yogurt and a kazoo band playing 'Flight of the Bumblebee' but we can try Mike's plan too. Mine would be more fun and interesting though."

"I am glad I can't see into your mind sometimes," stated Michael. "Now all we need to do is find the beast and we can..."

"NO!" screamed Nazilaq. "Irkja!"

Michael was linked to Nazilaq without missing a beat. He looked nearly panicked. "I can't sense him either. Where was he?"

The effervescent skimmer captain's demeanor had changed radically. Gone was the jester and joker to be replaced with a very efficient pilot ready for battle. "He was nearing the Dovhavhads Spires when I lost my link. I suspected the beast was heading there based on the course it was taking. Irkja had moved ahead to try to get a pre-image of the place looking for where it may have been going."

"Call me crazy but those Dove Spires do not sound like a friendly place. You may want to rename them," quipped Tone.

Zeke intervened with Tone so Michael could continue his search for Irkja. "You are crazy, Tone. But you are also dead right. That is a place we suspect is a secret exit from Hell. At least I can keep my promise to take you right to the edge of Hell."

"That is a promise you don't have to keep. Those critters can get out of Hell by pulling on a stalactite and sliding down a secret slide under a stalagmite? Not a very effective prison in my not so humble opinion." Under his humor there was a genuine concern in Tone's question.

"You can insult Hell later. Right now we have a layer issue," stated the archangel. "We need to get all of you to that layer to find Irkja if he still exists." Naz had a glow that showed his concern over that problem and the fear that they were already too late. "I can get you all there without damaging Tone any more but doing this takes me out of the picture. That kind of portal rips through layers and I have to repair them or the whole Spiritscape will fall apart."

Zeke glared at his friend. "How long have you known we could do that? We have been worried about getting Tone home and you could do it the whole time?"

Michael did not back down. He actually grew in power as he began creating a huge portal. "It will take a tenth of a quoll to create this portal," he stated. "I have all the cherubs scouring the layer below us that will be destroyed when I do this. I have to sacrifice an entire layer of the Spiritscape to keep Tone safe but it has to be empty before I can do it." Looking at Zeke he chastised, "That is why I would not consider this option until we had no other choice."

"I apologize, Michael." Zeke looked sincerely apologetic. "That was stupid of me. I should have known that you would not have held back without a good reason."

Michael touched his friend with the power of the warrior. "No apologies needed. It is understandable. But I cannot allow you to go without Tone. I know you want to go now Nazilaq; but if the beast is there I know that Tone has a role to play and you will not survive without him. We have sped up this and the next lower layer to council speed. We are almost ready."

Tone raised his hand. "Let's say for argument that I am not a nearly omniscient angel who understands all this Spiritscape layer shit. Oh wait. That IS me, isn't it? We are moving faster on this layer? Why couldn't you do that this whole time? Would it kill the archangels to help us just a little instead of sitting back on your fluffy, white asses while we do all the work and take all the risks?"

Arino began, "Because it is not supposed to be possible to do that without the kind of power that is nearly unimaginable. It takes almost all the power of all the archangels to do this. And with Michael creating the rip-portal I can sense that it is taking all of them to move these two layers. Right, Michael?"

Michael nodded and added, "And what we are doing will make this layer unsafe for a thousand quolls. We are forcing everything out of these two layers." It looked to Tone that Michael was listening to something. "All clear. Stand by. You four are going to be on your own. I am sending angels to surround the area and will lock the layer once you get there. No one will be shifting out until this is over one way or another.

"Tone, hide and use the H'tes as you can. Use the Stillness sparingly. It will drain the power faster than it can recharge from the ether around it. Nazilaq, you know what to do. Take the *Hajile-R* to the limits. Drain the beast and remind any demons what a skimmer can do. Zeke and Arino, save the new power until you have no other choice. You will know when."

Zeke knew there was something else Michael wasn't telling them. "What is it? I know you better than you think Michael. How bad is this going to be for you?"

Michael smiled at all of them. "Very bad," he said as he dropped the rip-portal on top of them. It was not like any portal they had ever used. The angels, the skimmer and the human all felt like they were being ripped apart, reassembled, and ripped apart again. It seemed to Tone to keep happening over and over until he was sure there was nothing left to put back together. All his pieces felt like they were in the wrong places. Then it was over.

Tone looked at the angels and the skimmer and asked, "Is my nose still on my face? Because if it is on my ass I'm going to be pissed!"

Naz ignored the human. "The skimmer is transforming for battle. Please get in and we will be in stealth mode." The ship had been made into the smallest version Tone had yet seen but still large enough to hold them all. It was a small, elongated pyramid with blades beginning to grow out of every surface. Naz had a spot in the center of the ship separated from the others that would protect him from anything that would try to break through.

"But what about my nose?" asked Tone feeling his face. "I think it is still there."

Arino grabbed Tone and helped him through the wall of the skimmer. "You are fine, Tone. I made sure to put your nose back on your chin where it belongs."

Grabbing his chin, unsure if she was joking for an instant, Tone gave her a look. "Beauty, powerful, and funny. You are perfect!"

"Yes, she is," agreed Zeke with a strange look in his spirit as he gazed at her.

As soon as they were inside the skimmer it moved faster than it had ever moved before. They were making a straight line to the Dovhavhads Spires. All three angels opened their minds to allow Tone unrestricted access. Naz had hidden the *Hajile-R* from casual looks by a strange spinning mode but was forced to concentrate to keep the wake in the ether to a minimum. The speed of the skimmer and the spinning were difficult for Tone to fathom as it created a sensory overload in an area that would overload most humans while floating motionless.

The section containing Tone, Zeke and Arino was the only section without blades on it. This was a section that would open and allow them to get out quickly. Tone had his H'tes in hand ready for action. No words were needed as he faded from view ready to do whatever it took. Zeke had the glow of the warrior in his full angelic glory. His glow had changed over the quolls they had been tracking the beast. It was less golden with more hues making subtle strings throughout. Arino was still in her angel form to keep her power in check until they were in the heat of battle to keep everyone safe from the new found power of the two. The two angels felt the presence and then the touch of their human friend as the skimmer neared the last place Irkja had been seen.

The refraction of the spinning skimmer was making the area ahead of them even more magnified than usual. The skill of Nazilaq allowed them to avoid detection by three boar shaped demons that seemed to be running away from the spires as if they had just escaped from Hell. Two of the demons never even gazed in their direction. When a third turned toward the hidden ship as if it was noticing something out of place, all three were sent to Hell by a series of three angel fire balls consuming them. They never knew what had hit them. Tone was impressed by the damage that the focused Naz could deal on demons.

The Dovhavhads Spires were truly evil looking. They created an image of teeth in the mind of Tone. It was almost like something evil was pressing them up in countless sharpened points. The spires themselves were something different than the Spiritscape around them. They had the bluish tint of demonic activity but also had a mixture of several colors creating a brown undertone with blue lowlights. It also seemed like the spires were moving and growing and shrinking all at the same time.

All of them sensed Nazilaq's excitement as he aimed the *Hajile-R at* one of the highest spires that looked like the tip had been broken off. That broken tip seemed to be covered with demons of the impish variety. It seemed like hundreds of clones were climbing all over everything like ants on a dropped piece of picnic chicken. For a moment the swarm of diminutive demons parted revealing a barely glowing Irkja pinned to a raised dais by broken pieces of the spire. There were more than forty different projections going through the watcher in places where his eyes or spiritual eyes had been.

Standing at the head of the platform with a satisfied look was Zadrol. He smiled at the stealthy skimmer and joyfully waved them over.

Chapter 29

"Tone, would you mind expressing yourself creatively for us all?" asked an enraged but controlled Ezekiel.

"That piece of shit played us! Let's feed that bastard, son of a bitch's ass to Bubba!" screamed the hostile human.

"Thank you," said all three angels.

"My pleasure. Really!" replied Tone.

"Nazilaq, captain of the *Hajile-R*, would you mind clearing a path and sending those demons to Hell?" asked the warrior.

"My pleasure. Really!" replied Naz. Tone looked back at the pilot to see a gleam in his spirit as he prepared for attack.

A burst of fire erupted from the tip of the pyramid that was the skimmer. The flames coalesced into five balls of angel fire, each traveling insanely fast toward the demons. The first exploded into a ring some distance from the ground zero that was Zadrol sending countless smaller fireballs at the demons on the periphery of the gathering. Each of the smaller angelic orbs rolled over imp after imp leaving a trail of demons shooting towards the icy confines of Hell down through the cracks of the spire.

As the fires of the first barrage faded, a second blazing sphere blasted into precision missiles of heat, each finding a separate target that appeared to vaporize on impact. After the fires began to die it was clear that there were charred imps glowing with the golden hues of angelic burns. The pieces of the demons remaining drifted off down into one of the crevasses that the angels knew led to the cool passages leading to a healing in Hell.

With the hordes of imps significantly reduced it was time to send the last three balls of angel fire at the real target. Tone and Zeke were both concerned that Zadrol had not even flinched at the devastation happening all around. It almost looked like the imp was enjoying the show. The threat of impending doom barreling toward the demon actually seemed to make the evil smile grow even wider as row after row of blue tinted teeth seemed to be laughing at the fire.

It appeared that this was about to be a very short battle when suddenly the three remaining angelic fireballs were snuffed out. It looked to Tone like they had landed in a pool of water that had easily extinguished the flames without even leaving the steam an earthly fire would produce. The angels looked at one another understanding the confidence of the imp. There was a barrier that protected Zadrol and those nearby from the attacks of the skimmer.

"How the hell did that little shit do that?" asked a stunned Tone. "Can he do that? Is that even playing by the rules?"

Zeke looked at Arino and then to Naz. "Why can it never be easy?" asked the warrior. "Tone, there is something protecting the imp. The flames stopped like a spirit sphere but it would be visible. Naz, take us in but be careful. Arino, stay back and port in once we are through it."

"I'm backup. Got it." Arino ported behind the skimmer and sent a blast of angel power at a demon that had been trying to hide behind them sending it also into the depths of the spires.

The *Hajile-R* moved toward the barrier faster than Tone would have preferred. "Any chance we can take it easy until we get through whatever angel fire absorbing pudding is out there?"

There was a chuckle from the pilot as he said, "I'd prefer to pound our way through it. Trust me, Tone. I want to save our friend. He is looking bad."

Tone could see that Irkja's glow had dimmed since they had arrived. With hardly any experience with these matters, he had no idea how long the angel could hold on. Tone looked more closely through a particularly magnified section of the hull and saw that the places where Irkja had been pierced were dripping with a golden glowing ooze that was falling into the cracks in the spire. None of them could read anything from the stoic watcher; but all could tell he was in danger of being phased apart without an intervention soon.

The skimmer approached the place where the fires had been extinguished. Tone and Zeke both braced for impact as they sailed smoothly through the non-existent barrier. As Arino ported back beside Zeke, Tone asked, "Are all angel-fire-putting-out demonic barriers that easy to get through? I was kind of expecting something more."

Naz spoke up. "Don't ask us. We've never seen anything like that."

Tone was so shocked that he almost reappeared. "Now you tell me?! Would it kill one of you to tell me more than the bare minimum once in a while? It's not that hard to say, 'Tone, we are winging this one cause we don't know what that shit is.' Seriously. I can handle the truth."

"I think it is Bubba hiding and absorbing angel fire to use against us," said Zeke.

Silence filled the skimmer until the disembodied voice of Tone said, "I take it back. Lie to me please."

"We shall soon find out what this is all about," said Arino. "Naz, would you please open the door?" The section of the skimmer containing the two angels and invisible Tone opened allowing them to face two score of imps with Zadrol ruling over them like a diminutive dictator. The demon was glowing more brightly blue than any of them had ever seen. It was obvious that Zadrol felt the power of the imps around him and had been feeding off that evil energy.

"So, how are my favorite angels today? I heard a rumor that you actually captured that idiot, Je'relir. How did you manage taking that asshole down? I really thought he was too much for you to handle," taunted the imp. "Did your toy ship managed to fireball him to pieces? Or was it you, Ezekiel? Did he finally piss you off enough to let go and kick ass?"

While Arino surreptitiously examined the injured Irkja, Zeke spoke to the imp in charge. "If you only knew, Zadrol. So how did you manage to capture a watcher? That is an impressive bit of work for someone as unaccustomed to actual work as you."

Arino thought to the angels and allowed Tone to hear as well. "There is nothing we can do while Zadrol is standing right there. He has some kind of device under Irkja that will split him into thirteen parts before we can do anything. I can see lines of power to thirteen demons ready to head off in different directions. The imps are faster than I am. We need to move quickly to take out the head imp or Irkja will be in serious trouble."

Zadrol recognized that Zeke was trying to distract from the Je'relir questions but was not to be deterred. "Thank you, Demonbane. But I still want to know if you took out the archdemon. Arino, honey, you know what I can do to Irk whenever I want and I'm sure you told Zekey, too. So just answer the damn question, Zeke. Which angel do I thank for taking out Je'relir? How often do you get thanked by a demon?"

There was a smile that radiated through the whole essence of Ezekiel as he said, "It wasn't the skimmer or me that took out Je'relir." The imp actually looked both shocked and impressed at it turned its gaze to the healer. Zadrol smiled at Arino and gave a courtly bow to the angel he thought had defeated an archdemon. Zeke continued, "She didn't do it either. I know that you and Je'relir have very little in common. Je'relir was large and powerful. That demon caused fear and hatred just by being in the vicinity. You aren't any of those things. But you do have one thing in common."

147

Zadrol looked up from the bow that had been mockingly made to Arino with icy blue blazing eyes. "What do you think I have in common with that moron?"

"There are some things that neither of you saw coming," Zeke said to the head of Zadrol that had fallen off filled with the angelic fire of a H'tes. Zeke attacked with the wings of angel fire swatting and burning the remaining imps. He first eliminated the thirteen who were prepared to take the pieces of Irkja to wherever they had planned. After that the slaughter was planned and devastating. A few tried to get away from the angelic power only to be caught in the blades of the skimmer or the fires from the tip of the pyramid.

Knowing that the others would watch over her, Arino quickly went to Irkja and began removing the spikes of the spires that had pierces him in many small and hideous ways. One imp sprang at her only to be blasted back by the invisible fury of a H'tes wielding Tone. "I've got your back, babe," whispered the human, sending another demon into the fissures of the spires. By the time all the spikes had been removed, Zeke had finished off the last of the demons.

Tone faded into view and asked what all were wondering, "How is he?"

"He will live," said the weak voice of Irkja. The healing power of Arino was hard at work as she had shifted into the amoeba-like form of the healer. Power was pouring out of her and into the watcher as his glow began to grow brighter.

"Hey there, old buddy. Missed you!" greeted Tone. "Well, Naz missed you really. I didn't really even notice you were gone until we all had a Moon Pie break and there was an extra one."

Irkja actually smiled and said, "Thank you all. I don't know how much longer I could have..." A gray tubal arm came out of the crevasse and pulled the watcher down in a flash.

"No!" screamed Arino as her power trailed off behind Irkja.

The gray, black form of Bubba rose all around them from the cracks and creases in the spire. The evil, maniacal laughter filled the ether as the voice thundered, "Those demons really hit the spot with angel for dessert. Now for seconds and thirds and fourths!"

All that could be seen was the gray-black of the beast. Bubba had surrounded them in an instant. There was nowhere to go without porting away leaving Tone in the hands of his rival. They all looked at one another and made the decision. This was it. No more cat and mouse with the beast. It was going to be them or Bubba.

"Hello there, Bubba. How are you today? You have gained weight again," taunted Tone.

"Hello, my friend," said the beast with a warmth that Tone did not share. "If you will give me a moment I will be right with you. I need to do some pest control and right now you have bigger problems to worry about than me."

Tone looked around and saw nothing. "The way I see it you have the problems, Bubster. One touch from me and you are blasted out of here." Tone moved toward the beast only to encounter a barrier. He turned and moved in every direction to find he could hardly move any directions at all. "That's cheating! What the hell is this?"

Zeke rushed to his aid only to be slammed to the ground by one of the many tendrils of the beast. The amorphous arm of Bubba quickly withdrew from the warrior as if it had been stung. "That was unexpected," thundered Bubba. "So, Ezekiel. You seem to have a defense against me. How did you manage to make yourself so unappetizing?"

"You will find I'm full of bad tasting power!" said Ezekiel as he thrust out with several wings of power cutting deep into the beast as Naz sent out a draining pulse in every direction to pull the angelic power from Bubba. Arino had moved to be near Tone to discover what had captured the human. As she looked through her many senses she discovered a spirit sphere that was slightly out of phase with them. It seemed to be hidden between layers of the Spiritscape but was enough on the current layer to hold Tone in place.

Tone began cutting and stabbing at the invisible walls around him but could not tell if he was having any effect. This was the last battle and his friends needed him but he was sidelined. Angel fire burst at the barrier only to bound back and be reabsorbed by the blade. Arino was trying from the other side to find an opening or a crack that could be used to access the device.

The burst from the *Hajile-R* had a dramatic effect on the beast. It pulled out all the newly acquired angel power leaving the beast a shade of black that only existed in nightmares. Bubba struck back at the skimmer shattering many of the new blades that also cut into the beast leaving a black, oozing wound. Nazilaq aimed the skimmer right at the wound and charged into the gap with new blades replacing the broken that ripped and tore at the spirit of the behemoth. The link between the angels gave Zeke access to the weakness in the beast as he sent a wing of angelic power right into the wound causing a screech of pain from the beast.

Tone began hitting runes on the H'tes trying desperately to find something that would allow him to free himself from his cage. He paused before touching the one rune he knew could buy him the time needed knowing that it could stop everything happening but may not leave him any power to help if he freed himself. He touched the rune. Everything stopped within his prison but the effect did not extend to beyond the walls of the spirit sphere. "Damn!" shouted Tone looking at the battle around him and he pressed the rune again saving power for another use. "Arino!" shouted Tone in warning. It was too late. A black arm grabbed the healer causing her to scream. She shifted into her healing form and escaped the grasp of Bubba. "I'm safe. Just get away! Go to Zeke!" shouted Tone. He could see her hesitation as she ducked and dodged arm after arm of the beast that was trying to consume her power. "I found a way to port away. Go to Zeke!" lied Tone, as he disappeared from view.

"Tone!" shouted Arino, not sure if he were telling her the truth or what she needed to hear. She moved to be near the warrior knowing in her spirit that Tone was still in the spirit sphere but also knowing her place was in the battle.

Zeke and Naz coordinated their attacks but they were evenly matched by the beast. Zeke had been caught by a piece of spire that Bubba had thrown at him, spinning him around and leaving a gash across his torso that was bleeding golden power. The skimmer and, by the link shared, Naz were not faring any better with many pieces of both being ripped off by the constant onslaught of the blackened beast. If it were not for the new design by Adoneal the beast would have already broken through the layers of crystal and gotten to the skimmer's captain at the heart of the ship. The outer hull had several breaches and the medial hull was beginning to fail.

Arino went to work on the warrior, continually moving away from the constantly gasping tendrils of Bubba healing his wound. There was little she could do to help Nazilaq while he was still in the heart of the skimmer but she knew that he would need her help if they survived this battle.

Tone, although invisible, was still trying to find a way out of his prison. He knew that they needed his help and that his touch could change the course of the battle. With the power of the H'tes contained within the sphere all he could do was try again and again to breach the barrier with simple, straightforward attacks. Over and over he slashed and stabbed. It was frustrating not knowing if his efforts were making a difference until one stab stuck into the invisible wall. Everything that Tone had at his disposal, his strength, his will, his love, his hate all went into driving his blade further into the wall.

Naz knew that his ship would not last much longer but was not about to give up the fight. He was constantly creating new blades to replace the ones that were severed but there were limits to how much damage could be taken. He was missing several parts from his spirit as the shared link took its toll. If he was going to fall prey to this abomination he was going to make sure there was not much left for the beast to feast upon.

Arino and Zeke were working in tandem as Zeke lashed out at Bubba while Arino healed him over and over. Arino knew there was a limit to how much healing power she could give Zeke before they merged into the supernova of angels. It was getting closer and closer but they both knew it was not yet the right moment. There was still too much of the beast for even their power to defeat. They needed something more but did not know what. That something more was almost freed from his prison.

One last twist of the H'tes and the hole was large enough for Tone to wiggle through. He thought if he lived through this that even a spirit sphere was not going to be able to hold him. He made a mental note to not tell Michael about that. As soon as he had extricated himself from the sphere he looked at the battle and tried to decide how he could help. Just touching Bubba could cause the critter to fly back and buy them time to heal but it would also allow Bubba time to consume more spirits. That was not an option. But holding onto to Bubba and not allowing the throwback to happen could be just what was needed to turn the battle in their favor. The only problem was that Tone did not know what that would do to him.

"Here goes nothing," said the human as he became visible. He reached out and wrapped his arms around the nearest bit of Bubba. The shock was excruciating to both Tone and Bubba. No longer was the beast focused on the angels but all Bubba could do was try to shake off the one being who was an equal. Tone could feel the power of the beast and all the evil that had been absorbed. It felt to Tone as if he were drowning in crude oil that was permeating his very soul. There was no way he could last doing this. There was only one thing left to do. "Zeke, NOW!" screamed an agonized Tone.

Zeke saw Tone holding onto the beast that was shaking him like a rag doll. His essence was beginning to take on darker hues as he was taking in part of the beast. If he and Arino did what he asked he did not know what would happen to the human. If they didn't do what he asked he knew what would happen to him would be far worse. He looked to the healer who nodded in agreement. All heaven broke loose with their power.

The blackness surrounding them was instantly lit up with the power of the linked angels. Zeke and Arino poured everything they had into this last attack, knowing if they failed there would be nothing to stop the beast from destroying them. The beast began to smoke and sizzle with the power of the warrior and healer ripping it to shreds. All the parts of the beast were touched by the power of the two and all the parts were being vaporized by the unusual power of two angels who had been touched by very unangelic powers. Between the power of the Tone-touched Ezekiel and the Bubba-touched Arino the combination was too devastating for the beast.

Tone had reached the end of his strength as he finally let go of the burning Bubba. He was thrown free and landed right where Naz had planned as he had moved the skimmer to be ready for the human. The mouth of the *Hajile-R* closed with its precious cargo safely caught as the burning all around them reached a crescendo.

The last burst from the two angels left no doubt as to the victor of this battle. There was nothing left of Bubba except one tiny fragment of a spirit splayed out on the dais where Irkja had been tortured. An exhausted pair of angels collapsed nearby as the skimmer opened a door for the human to exit. A shaky and trembling Tone moved to be near what was left of the beast that had caused so much suffering.

"Well, Bubba. I don't think you will be coming back from this," said Tone. "But there is one question I have for you. Who the hell are you?"

The dying spirit looked at the human. "You will figure it out, Tone. You made me after all."

Tone looked confused. "I didn't make you, asshole. You tried to make me like you. I think you have had too much angel fire."

"Please just end this. I hurt," begged the remains of the beast.

"Who or what are you?!" demanded Tone. All three of his angel friends were now behind him watching the interaction.

"If I give you a hint will you please just kill me? This hurts so much," asked the former beast.

"Deal," said Tone, holding his H'tes over the beast.

"Remember the dance?" said the beast as its glow faded.

Tone drove his blade into the core of the spirit being careful to contain the angel fire to prevent any charging. The last remnants of Bubba faded away leaving four confused friends pondering the final words.

Chapter 30

"Anyone else wonder what the hell that meant?" asked Tone.

"Any idea what dance that was, Tone?" asked Zeke. "Surely you have some idea." Zeke suspected that Tone was not telling them something.

"No clue," said Tone a little too innocently. "But there is something that I will check out when I get back to Earth if I can remember after all this."

Arino approached Tone. "You still have traces of the evil of Bubba on you. May I help?" Tone smiled and nodded as the healer began to drain off the traces of evil that the touch of Bubba had left. It took a lot of her abilities but she pulled the venom of Bubba from Tone.

"Thanks. I hate the feeling that demon essences leaves in me. Still it is better than the addiction of angel essence. That shit is too good," stated Tone. "Now what do we do from here? Do we have to go back and check in with Michael or the Council or something? And who do I bill for my services?"

Arino continued with her healing powers filling in the gaps on Nazilaq. Adoneal appeared and looked at the situation. "It seems that the skimmer needs to be repaired again," said the archangel and with that preamble went straight to work repairing the skimmer while the pilot was healed.

Tone turned to Zeke and said, "He is kind of creepy the way he just shows up."

"I'll let that comment slide," smiled Zeke. "He does what he does and we don't ask why. All right?"

"I didn't say it wasn't cool," defended Tone. "It's awesome. Creepy, but awesome. Now about my bill?"

"Let's get out of here first and find someplace safe," said Arino who had finished healing Naz as the skimmer was repaired. Adoneal nodded to all of them and ported away. With help from the angels, Tone passed through the walls of the restored skimmer and they moved away from the site of the battle.

As the crystal ring of the skimmer sped out of sight, a hand that had traces of black, blue and gold reached up from the crevasse trying to pull itself out of the darkness. As it closed around the ledge the hand glowed with a green haze as the colors that were interlaced began to merge into one color growing brighter as something unidentifiable began to emerge from the darkness.

The skimmer moved along as the angels and human discussed what would happen next. There was a sadness in the pilot as he thought of his lost friend. There would never be another Irkja. The intuitive Arino sensed his loss.

"Are you all right, Naz?" asked the healer. "I know that you and Irkja were close."

"I really thought we had saved him," sighed Nazilaq. "At least his death was not unavenged." Naz looked at the strange human and gave Tone a nod. "Thank you for taking care of that thing."

Tone was obviously uneasy with the gesture. "Glad I could do my small part. Now, I guess it's time for me to head home," sighed Tone trying to change the subject. "But what do I do about this thing?" The H'tes was in his hand, refracting the light of the Spiritscape.

Zeke looked at his friend. "Well you have three options. First, your job is done. You can give it up forever and go back to your normal life. Second, you can keep it and have it with you at all time so you can battle demons here or on earth. Third, I'll hold on to it for you until you need it again."

"I think I like option three. I'm not real big into fighting demons on Earth but I'll be glad to kick ass and take names here if you need me again," smiled Tone. "So how do I unattach it?"

Zeke created a crystal case ready for the H'tes. "There are six runes you need to touch in sequence to release it. One on each end, one on each side of the blade, and one on each end of the guard. Then just lay it in here and it will be ready when you need it." Tone found the runes that Zeke described and touched each of them in sequence. The blade became something that he was holding in his hand and not something that was glued to his body. He carefully laid the blade in the case and Zeke closed the lid.

"Now it is time for you to keep your end of the deal. I get to meet you on earth, my friend. Where shall we meet?" asked the warrior.

Tone looked nervous. "You're really going to hold me to that aren't you?"

"Yes, Tone. I'm holding you to that." Zeke actually enjoyed watching Tone squirm for a change.

"OK, but let me remind you of a couple of things. Do not be offended if I don't remember much about you. I can't keep all this Spiritscape shit in my head when I go back," said the human. "I would ask two favors. First, don't try to read anything until you get to my house and then do what you do to read the place. Second, give me a little bit of time to get myself together before you show up. If you don't mind just travel like a normal human. I'm really not that far from where you were when we first met."

"Agreed. Now where are you?" asked Zeke, who was truly excited about meeting his friend.

"I'm just down the road from you in Knoxville. You can find me at 2202 Scheel Road. I will be home when you come. It should only take you about an hour or two to get there." Tone paused and added, "I hope you are not disappointed. See you soon." With those words Tone returned to his body on earth.

"What do you think that means?" asked Naz.

"With Tone who knows?" replied Arino.

"Well, I'm off to meet a human. See you soon," said Zeke.

Zeke returned to Earth and was on the same bus finishing the same joke he had started earlier. No time had passed for those around him even though it had been a monumental bit of time for the angel. Everyone laughed at his joke and he continued his travels while engaging with others who needed his special brand of caring.

The bus traveled through the heart of Smoky Mountain National Park with its breathtaking beauty and many pullouts for numerous photo opportunities. Zeke patiently waited for each stop and took many photos of those who would have memories to last a lifetime. The bus driver took them all into the shopping district of Gatlinburg where they all got out and looked in the many shops that offered everything from jewelry to moonshine. Zeke bid farewell to his new found friends and walked down the road to a shop that he knew all too well.

As he left the store there was a roar as the motorcycle he had rented for the day cruised down the road. He drove along Interstate forty with the breeze blowing past him and to the home town of Tone. He naturally knew where Scheel Road was thanks to his vast knowledge; but did not access any information about Tone's home until he was getting off the Suzuki and taking off his helmet. Zeke opened his mind to the truth of this home and laughed out loud as he realized where he was.

The doorbell rang and was answered by a small, plump woman. "Can I help you?" asked the lady.

"Yes. I am Ezekiel Engel. You are expecting me," said the human looking angel.

153

"Yes. Mr. Engel from the state. Glad you made it. I'm Rachel. How was traffic?" asked the suddenly gracious and nervous young woman inviting him in. The house was decorated simply with the only out of the ordinary items being numerous bookcases filled with books of all types.

"Traffic was fine. Please relax, Rachel. This is not an official inspection. I'm just here to check on Anthony. How is he doing?" asked Zeke, smiling to himself. No wonder they couldn't find him.

"He is having a good day today. Do you have his file?" asked Rachel.

"I prefer to find things out from those closest to him. What do you want to tell me?" asked Zeke.

"Well I think you're better off meeting him yourself before I offer my thoughts. He is in his room." Rachel led Zeke down a hallway. "I'll make sure his roommate doesn't disturb you." Knocking on the door, she called out, "Tone, you have a visitor. Mr. Engel is here." She opened the door to a room filled with even more books than the living room. In the middle of the room, in an overstuffed chair, was a small, black man reading a book. "I leave you two to get acquainted. If he starts to rock back and forth just wait a few seconds and he will come back to you."

Zeke could read much in the young man in front of him. Tone was not large. He may have been five feet four. He looked to be about one hundred and twenty five pounds. His mocha colored skin had a glow that showed good health and a happy nature to the angel's senses. It was his mind that was fascinating to the angel. This man, who had defeated demons, stood before the most powerful archangels, and been part of defeating the greatest threat the Spiritscape had ever seen had virtually no memory of any of the evens.

Tone was autistic. There was a level of genius about him even though many of his thoughts even the angel could not understand. Looking through his mind, Zeke could see that Tone had total recall of every scrap of paper he had ever read. Even with this knowledge he still had only fragments of the events that they had shared.

"Hello, Tone. How are you doing?" asked Zeke not sure if the ordered chaos of Tone's mind would recognize him.

Tone looked up at the disguised angel. He looked at him long and hard as if trying to remember some long forgotten memory. "Engel means angel is German. Yes. Engel is angel. No wings. No halo. Engel means angel." Tone looked at him even longer as Zeke could see the strain on his face and the chaos of his mind trying to sort through his memories. "Yes. Engel and angel. Angel and Engel. No halo. No wings." He gave him one last look and said, "Zeke Angel." Tone went back to reading his book on the life of John Kennedy as Zeke sat and smiled at his friend.

Epilogue

"How did the state thing go today? Was he an asshole?" asked Tonya.

"No. He was really cool. He didn't even inspect the cupboards. He just went in and sat with Tone for about an hour. Tone hardly talked to him but the dude was really patient. When he left he thanked me and road off on a bike." Rachel had a quizzical look. "How many state inspectors ride a bike?"

"It takes all kinds, honey," stated the caregiver. "Did it mess up Tone having a stranger in the house?"

Rachel looked back at Tone's closed door. "Not at all. I think he actually liked the guy right off."

"Really? That is unusual. It took him a month to get used to me coming around even with Bobbi in tow," said Tonya. There was a sadness when she mentioned Bobbi's name.

"What is the latest? How bad is she?" asked a suddenly solemn Rachel.

There was a tear in her eye as Tonya said, "No brain activity at all. The stroke killed her but her body just doesn't know to stop. Her family is going to remove the feeding tube tomorrow." She looked at Tone's door. "Does he understand what happened? They have been close since he kissed her at the Prom of the Stars. Did you know she even started rocking back and forth like he does?"

"I really don't think he understands. They danced and kissed but now he won't even say her name. Today he stopped calling her Bobbi and argued with me for ten minutes that her name is Bubba." Rachel had an exasperated look. "What do you think that is all about?"

"With Tone, who knows?" stated Tonya with a sad smile.